**The unease nipped at her heels
all the way up to the house.**

It was too quiet. Rachel shivered in her light dress. Clutching
her jacket around her, she fought the unease that tried to turn
into out-and-out fright.

The front door stood open.

The fright won out, and she almost turned and ran. Then,
from inside, came a whisper of sound. It might have been a
moan. Heart pounding, Rachel tiptoed across the porch and
reached through the open door, holding her breath as she
groped for the switch just inside. The porch lamp came on,
blinding her briefly, driving back the dark. Now she could see
the red splashes on the door.

Her heart contracted to a hurting knot in her chest . . .

Praise for
DEVIL'S TRUMPET:

"Interesting characters, a sharp puzzle, gardening details,
and not one, but two romances make *Devil's Trumpet* a
scintillating mystery debut. Rachel O'Connor is an en-
gaging character, definitely worthy of a series. The pace
is lively and the story intriguing. What more could anyone ask for in a mystery?"

—*Romantic Times*

"Intertwined with all [the] activity surrounding Rachel
and these wonderfully wacky, yet endearing characters is
the opportunity to learn more about the worlds of jazz
and gardening."

For Nate and Jake, always

Acknowledgements

Once again, I'd like to thank Debbie Cross of Wrigley-Cross Books in Portland for her thorough and valuable input. I also owe thanks to Dulcy Mahar, whose well-written and informative articles on home landscaping in the *Oregonian* newspaper's Home and Garden section have given me much inspiration. Andi Schecter also provided me with an insightful critique.

CHAPTER
1

The dirt was winning.

Rachel O'Connor tossed her trowel onto the rock-hard soil and leaned her elbows on the thick rim of the big sidewalk planter. Wiping sweat from her face, she wondered if someone had mistaken a sack of concrete for potting soil at one time— and wondered if dynamite would help. Maybe. Maybe not. Down the block, Julio Peron, her young Guatemalan assistant, was busy hacking away at his planter, instructing their new part-time employee in the art of digging with a mature confidence that made Rachel smile.

Julio had come a long way from the timid and uncertain kid she had hired two years ago. Spider, the new kid, did seem to be learning how to actually work. Finally. For the first couple of days, she had despaired that the skinny, dark-haired city kid, with his Asian eyes and wary reserve, would ever work hard enough to break into a sweat.

Stifling a groan, she picked up her trowel again. Well, they were making progress, at least.

Julio looked her way and grinned. "We finish first, Senorita Boss Lady," he said in his careful English. "You will owe us the milk shakes." He pumped a fist in the air, grinning.

"You're not done yet." She made a face at him and attacked the compacted soil again. The energy of youth, she decided. Or maybe it was testosterone. Probably the latter. Julio seemed to be changing from boy to man even as she watched.

The sun kissed the back of her neck, unexpectedly warm for this early March day, and Rachel was glad of her short-cropped curls. Long hair would be hot. And when it looked like a poodle's coat, why bother? A clod of earth flew up from her prying trowel.

"Ouch! I think that's called assaulting an officer."

Rachel turned to find Jeff Price, Blossom's newly appointed chief of police, laughing down at her from the granite steps of City Hall. "You can arrest me." She tossed her trowel into the planter and offered her wrists. "Please." She made a face. "Maybe I can talk our good mayor into letting me call in a track hoe to take these out. We could plant some nice trees instead," she said plaintively.

Jeff peered into the planter and clucked his tongue at the brick-hard soil. "Tear out these historic fixtures?" He arched his eyebrows. "The populace would rise."

"Historic?" Rachel blew an exasperated breath that lifted her dark bangs from her sweaty forehead. "They're concrete, ugly, and not a whole lot older than I am. Which is *far* from historic, thank you." Fists on her hips, she scowled down the length of Blossom's short Main Street. "And whoever put them in put three on this side of the street, but only two on the other side. That's asymmetrical. Throws off the entire landscape. Yep." She nodded. "They really need to come out."

"Our mayor has faith in you," Jeff drawled. "He believes you can make Main Street bloom with color. I heard him talking about hanging baskets on the downtown lampposts, and planters along the front of all the main buildings."

Rachel groaned. "More automatic watering. More plumbing. I hate plumbing. Why did I get into this business? Why did I say yes to the City Council?"

"Good question." Jeff perched himself on the rim of the half-excavated planter and contemplated the spring sky. "You could go run the family orchard."

"Yeah, right. You mean I could go work for my uncle."
She made a face at him, then boosted herself up onto the
planter rim beside him. "Who will run that orchard until the
day he dies—and probably beyond that. Since we've long ago
reached the mutual understanding that we will never agree on
orchard management, that ends that." She dusted her palms
together briskly. "So, how's the chief business? To blatantly
change the subject. No crime wave in the offing?"

"In Blossom?" Jeff snorted. "This town could almost make
me miss Los Angeles." He grimaced. "Although we did have
a nasty little shoplifting incident this afternoon. At the hardware store." He jerked his head toward the red-and-white
striped awning of the small Ace Hardware store down the
block. "Roth caught the Dougan girl with a CD player. I don't
think he usually would have called us, but I guess it's not the
first time for her. And the player was tagged at nearly one-
fifty. He was ticked."

"Bob Dougan's daughter, Melanie?" Rachel arched her
eyebrows. Dougan was a member of Blossom's City Council—
one of the staunch conservatives who gave the new progressive young mayor a hard time. "I thought she was just a kid—
like in grade school."

"She's sixteen," Jeff said grimly. "And I am now on Dougan's shit list, let me tell you." He shook his head. "I told
Roth when he started carrying that line of cameras and other
small electronics that he needed to lock them up—that they
were a shoplifting risk." He sighed. "He told me I wasn't
living in the city anymore—that we didn't have that kind of
problem out here."

"I guess we do." Rachel touched Jeff's arm lightly, knowing that the confrontation had been uglier than he was letting
on. Roth and Dougan both had explosive tempers, and Bob
Dougan would not be pleased at a confrontation with a police
chief who wasn't yet thirty. Jeff's appointment hadn't set well
with more than a few residents of Blossom. "I don't know
why Dougan was surprised," Rachel said hotly. "Melanie has
been in trouble ever since her mom died."

"Well, he sure did a good job of acting surprised. So how's

your new kid working out—not to change the subject or anything. No problems so far?''

"None at all." Rachel glanced down the block to where Spider and Julio were shoveling soil-compost mix into their now empty planter. They were out to win those shakes. She smiled. "Spider's not a big kid, but he's sure learning how to work hard. Courtesy of Julio. Actually I'm a little surprised at how well he's working out," she admitted. "I have to confess I gave him the job because Willis Bard asked me to, and I got the city contract. I've been sort of wondering if I'd been stupid—but he's doing just fine." She smiled. "Male competition, I think. You know."

"Do I?" Jeff raised his eyebrows, his expression innocent. Then he looked again at the two youths. "What is he? Part Chinese?"

"Willis told me his father was half Vietnamese. His last name is Tran, although his mother is Muir or Moore or something like that." She shrugged. "Spider doesn't talk about himself."

"I'm glad he's working out." Jeff levered himself off the planter. "I have to admit I had my doubts when you agreed to hire a kid from the Youth Farm. There are some tough characters out there—even if they are teenagers."

"You sound like Andy Ferrel." She made a face at him.

"Not nearly that extreme." He rolled his eyes at her. "Our former mayor is not mellowing with age, that's for sure. He and the mayor had quite a yelling match outside City Hall yesterday. It came close to a brawl this time." He glanced at his watch. "I'd better get back to work. It's going to be a long day." He grimaced. "We have that town meeting tonight—about the proposed annexation. That's what Ferrel and Ventura were yelling about. It's going to be a free-for-all," he said grimly. "I just hope I don't have to break up any fist-fights."

"You might have to. Uncle Jack has been ranting about this proposed annexation for weeks now. He's taken to calling our mayor 'The Commie.'" Rachel hopped down from the planter and leaned over to brush crumbs of clay soil from Jeff's uniform trousers. "I think I'd better keep my mouth shut if I go."

"Uh-oh. You're for the takeover, huh?" His eyes twinkled. "Better not let your uncle find out you're a commie, too."

"Heaven forbid." She rolled her eyes, then sobered. "I am for the annexation," she said slowly. "I don't want to see Blossom swallowed up by a ring of cheap condos, discount chains, and fast-food restaurants. We voted in a solid set of restrictions on development inside city limits. They're good for us all, in the long run."

"Whooey, don't let your uncle hear you say that." Jeff shook his head, but some of his levity had evaporated. "I'm not sure any of us can stop progress." He sighed. "And progress is sometimes ugly. Dinner tomorrow night?" He raised an eyebrow. "We can make city politics a taboo subject."

"Dinner sounds great. And I don't see why we can't argue politics. I get lots of practice out at the orchard." She returned his smile, thinking that his eyes were exactly the color of a June sky. They contrasted dramatically with his tawny skin and dark hair—heritage of a dollop of Paiute blood from previous generations. "We could cook fancy instead of going out if you want. I've been eating frozen dinners all week."

"Let's see what we feel like doing." He kissed her hand lightly. "You better go deal with your crew." He nodded toward Julio and Spider. "They look like they're ready for another job."

She looked over at the pair, found them grinning in front of the freshly filled planter, and gave them a mock scowl. "Okay, you two. Since you're so hot, get to work on this one."

"What about our milk shakes?" Spider demanded. "We sure beat your—" He caught himself. "We sure beat you."

Spider was trying to watch his language. It was obviously a major effort. Rachel suppressed a smile. "You get your shakes at quitting time," she said with mock severity. "That's in an hour. Meanwhile, we have one more planter to finish." She nodded at the concrete round she had been hacking at. "You guys get busy while I get the plants in."

Grumbling, they tossed their tools onto the plastic tarp

they'd used for the soil and hauled it over to the final planter. Groans and muttered complaints in Spanish made her think that she had been right about the soil in that planter being particularly bad. Unloading flats of annuals, she began to set the young plants into the rich, new soil. She had chosen marigolds and low-growing snapdragons.

The mayor had originally asked for a red, white, and blue color scheme—but she had talked him into a more subtle and varied assortment of plants: mahogany and orange marigolds, mound-form white snapdragons, with scarlet zonal geraniums for a spot of bright color. Variegated needlepoint ivy would give the planters a nice trailing skirt of greenery that should stand up well to the rigors of urban life—if you could call Blossom's main street an urban setting. She stepped back finally, stretching her shoulders, admiring the newly planted starts. In a couple of months they would indeed look good.

People were exiting City Hall, and Rachel glanced at her watch with a start. Five o'clock. Quitting time, if she wanted to make the town meeting at seven. As she began to set the flats in her truck and put her tools away, the rumble of a big diesel engine made her look up.

"Hey, Rachel." Harvey Glisan leaned from the cab of his big dump truck, a grin on his weathered face. "I brought your bark dust over early. Katy's gonna have the kid tonight, looks like. Carl's already over at the hospital, and I figure I oughta head over there myself. I didn't want to hold you up."

"Oh." Rachel blinked at the load—which had been due to arrive in the morning. She hadn't really thought about Harvey's daughter-in-law's pregnancy as a complication.

"Congratulations," she said. "I was going to have you dump it in the driveway around back of City Hall. Why don't you—"

She broke off as a commotion caught her ear. Looking around, she caught her breath. Spider Tran stood at the bottom of the stairs, fists clenched, confronting City Councilman Bob Dougan.

"Filthy cheat!" the boy yelled. "You stole my mom's money. You—"

Julio grabbed his arm, his face taut with horrified concern.

He muttered something harsh in Spanish, attempting to drag the Youth Farm boy away from the shirtsleeved councilman.

"What are you talking about, kid?" Dougan recoiled, nearly dropping the suit jacket he had slung over his shoulder. "I don't know you."

"You better know me, you slimy asshole." Spider jerked free of Julio's grip. "Go on—pretend you don't know what I'm talkin' about, Mr. Big Shot. You stole my mom's money—all she had, you . . ." He lunged at the councilman. Julio immediately yanked him backward, hissing angrily under his breath as he wrestled with the skinny teenager.

"Spider, stop!" Rachel raced across the sidewalk and flung herself in front of Dougan. "Stop it right now!"

"What the hell's going on here?" Jeff appeared behind the boys, caught Spider by the shoulder, and turned him sharply around. "Knock it off, kid." He shook Spider with casual strength. "Now!"

For an instant, Rachel thought Spider was going to throw a punch at Jeff. Then his face tightened, and he slumped in Jeff's grasp. "Okay, okay already. It's over." He gave Julio a brief glare. "Let go of me, man."

"What's going on here?" Jeff ignored him, glancing from Dougan to Rachel to Julio—who instantly assumed an expression of total innocence.

"This . . . boy got excited." Dougan brushed invisible dust from his jacket. "He started yelling at me. I have no idea what it's all about. I've never seen him before."

"That's shit . . ." Spider bit off the words as Rachel glared at him. "Well, it is," he muttered, staring defiantly at her.

"Are you responsible for him?" Dougan raised his eyebrows at Rachel. "Isn't he one of those kids from that detention farm?"

"Yes, he is, and yes, he's working for me." Rachel lifted her chin, straightening her shoulders in the face of Dougan's steely glare. Her uncle's age, he made her feel as if she'd been called into the principal's office. "He's been a model employee."

"I wonder if you haven't bitten off a bit more than you want to chew, young lady." Dougan frowned. "I'm sure your

intentions are good. I just hope you don't regret your gener-
osity. No harm was really done here.'' Dougan turned to Jeff.
''If being yelled at bothered me, I wouldn't be on the City
Council.''

A couple of the spectators tittered, and Dougan gave them
a wink and a smile. ''If you need me, Jeff, leave a message
on my office machine. I'm late for an appointment.'' He
glanced at his watch. ''Or you can catch me at the meeting
tonight.''

''I don't need to keep you.'' Jeff nodded, and the councilman strode away. Spider stirred, then winced and stilled as
Jeff tightened his grip. ''How old are you?'' he demanded.

''Sixteen.'' Spider stared at the sidewalk, his thin face hidden by the black fringe of his bangs. ''Go ahead and do a
damn drug test. I'm clean. I'm not doin' anything.''

For a moment Jeff frowned at him, then looked at Rachel,
raising one eyebrow.

She shook her head and shrugged.

''What happened here, Peron?'' Jeff turned to Julio.

''No sais.'' Julio shrugged eloquently, his eyes twin pools
of innocence. ''I think *el senor,* he say something.'' His accent
had become extreme. ''Bad, you know?''

''Julio, you speak better English than some folk who were
born here.'' Jeff gave the sheepish Julio a stern glare. ''What
did Dougan say?''

''I . . . did not hear.'' Julio glanced uneasily at Spider.

''He didn't say nothin','' Spider spoke up. ''I did. I should
have hit him.''

''You'd have been on your way back to the farm right
now,'' Jeff said dryly. ''Or in jail, if Dougan decided to press
charges.'' He sighed and turned to Rachel, his eyebrows rising. ''You're going to call Bard about this, aren't you?''

''I guess I'd better,'' Rachel said unhappily. She had
thought Spider was working out. ''I'm sure he'll hear about
this.''

''You behave yourself, kid.'' Jeff stared down at the still-
defiant Spider. ''Not too many people are willing to hire kids
from the farm. If you don't care, don't blow it for everybody
else.''

Spider stared at his feet and didn't reply.

"Let's go." Rachel suppressed a sigh. "You get the tools loaded. Julio, sweep up the dirt you two left on the sidewalk. It's late. Let's get out of here."

She stalked back to her truck, aware of a few murmured conversations and surreptitious glances as the last onlookers scattered. She knew what they were saying. So far, she was the only Blossom resident who had been willing to participate in the Youth Farm's work skills program, although a few kids worked in Hood River. Willis Bard had reminded her at least ten times that she was the model that would hopefully sway the town.

Which way she was going to sway them was suddenly in doubt.

In the barbershop across the street, three elderly men stood like a row of statues in the window, their weathered faces carved into identical expressions of disapproval.

Harvey waited beside his truck, which he had backed into the City Hall driveway. The small, wiry man with a boxer's shoulders raised one thick, iron-gray eyebrow. "Got a wildcat cub workin' for you, gal." He spat brown tobacco juice into the gutter. "You got more guts than me."

"More guts than brains maybe," she muttered. "Go ahead and dump. I didn't mean to hold you up."

"Can't." He nodded at the new blue Toyota Camry parked behind the big truck. "Anyplace else, and I block the driveway."

Rachel glowered at the car. "Locked?"

"Got one of those alarm things. You can see those blinking lights."

"I wonder whose it is." She sighed, forcing herself not to glance at her watch again. Out on the sidewalk, Julio and Spider were cleaning up with exemplary energy.

"It's Dougan's car." Jeff walked up beside her. "He's probably over at the Homestyle. Or Fong's. He eats there sometimes. I'll go look."

"Tell you what." Harvey was shaking his head. "I'm kind o' antsy to get over to Hood River and see how Katy's doin'. What say I lock old Bessie up, give you the key," he said to

Rachel. "You know how to dump the bed, right?"

"Yes." Rachel nodded, feeling honored. Very few people were invited to operate Harvey's beloved equipment. "I'll be working here all day tomorrow." She grinned. "You can tell me all about the new grandkid when you pick up the truck."

"Katy's in labor? Congratulations, Grandpa!" Jeff slapped the older man on the shoulder.

"We're not home free yet," Glisan said, but he was grinning. "You turn around twice and your kids are grown. You remember that, you two." He winked at them, handed the truck keys to Rachel, and gave them a jaunty wave. "See you in the mornin'," he said, and marched whistling up the driveway, his gleaming, hand-tooled boots and slightly bowed legs making him look more like a cowboy from Burns than a heavy equipment operator from Blossom.

"I'll drop by the restaurants and get Dougan to move his car." Jeff touched her shoulder. "You're okay with your farm kid? You want me to stick around?"

"I'm fine." She smiled for him. "Spider's looking pretty chastised. I think Julio really chewed him out."

"You know what you're doing." Jeff brushed her hair lightly with his fingertips. "I hope."

"Me, too." Rachel made a face. "See you at the meeting." She hurried back out to the sidewalk, slammed the tailgate of her truck, and backed it up to her dirt-filled trailer. In spite of her assurance, she was uneasy as she made the hitch. Spider had worked for her for less than a week. If this kind of outburst was going to happen often . . . The two youths climbed into the extended cab without saying a word. Julio looked disgusted and worried, and Spider still wouldn't look at her at all.

The sidewalk was spotless.

Rachel swallowed a sigh. "Let's go get those milk shakes," she said, and slapped her truck into gear.

CHAPTER

2

Rachel let the silence last while she paid for three milk shakes at the Bread Box Cafe and Bakery. Joylinn Markham, the owner, had recently added ice cream to her menu of coffee drinks, sandwiches, and salads, prompted by the rank of riverside condominiums that had gone in near the dock. Slowly filling with retirees and weekend couples, they offered another choice for a new and hungry clientele.

Rachel led the two youths through the sparse scatter of after-work patrons and out onto the patio, glad for once that her friend Joylinn was busy in the kitchen. The feeble breeze made her shiver—the weather report promised frost tonight, and she couldn't help checking the cherry trees ranked on the hills above Blossom. They were still a week away from bloom, she noted with relief. The O'Connor orchard derived much of its income from its Bing and Royal Anne cherry crop. Uncle Jack flatly refused to hear her suggestions that they switch to something with less overhead and more market reliability.

The scatter of afternoon tourists and residents stayed inside with their coffee and snacks, out of the wind. Rachel chose one of the metal-mesh tables near the edge of the empty wood-plank dock where barges had once tied up. Now Blossom's fruit crop went to market on trucks. Beyond an attractively designed cedar railing, the Columbia River churned along, muddy with spring runoff from the recent rains. In the distance, a string of three barges toiled upriver, pushed against the brisk spring current by a sturdy tugboat. On their way to The Dalles, she thought as she sucked thick creamy chocolate through her straw. So much for calorie counting today.

"Okay, Spider, time to talk." She pushed her shake cup aside and stared at her new young employee.

"Why?" He kept his eyes fixed on his untouched shake. "You're just gonna fire me. So do it."

"How about you don't try to read my mind, okay?" Rachel sipped more of her shake. "You tell me what was going on. If it makes sense to me, that's the end of it. If it doesn't, then, yeah, I fire you."

"Just call Willis." He hunched his shoulders, his profile surly. "Tell him I blew it."

"That's what you want?" Rachel asked gently, trying to hide a twinge of anger. Maybe Jeff was right, and these kids weren't reachable after all.

"Stupid." Julio glared at Spider from across the table. "You are stupid." He sucked noisily at his own shake, his expression disgusted.

Spider blinked, his expression briefly uncertain. Then he hunched his shoulders even higher, head ducking between his thin shoulders, like a turtle pulling its head into its shell.

"What did Mr. Dougan do to your mother?" She made one last try.

Spider finally looked up, his muddy brown eyes smoldering. Angry, his eyes narrowed, skin drawn tight across his face, he looked very Asian. "You really want to know?" He picked up his straw and slowly began to strip away the paper. "This neighbor of ours—Mrs. Ramsey—she told my mom about this club she was in. Everybody put money in, and the guy who ran it put it in the stock market, I guess. You got money back. Lots of money, Mrs. Ramsey said." He looked up quickly, his expression wary, as if he expected her to contradict him.

"Sounds like some sort of investment club." Rachel nodded.

"That's it. Only it had a name, like a business." Spider

shrugged. "She was always talking about how she was gonna make a lot of money—enough to send me to college, buy a house, all of that." He lifted one shoulder in an awkward shrug. "She was always talkin' about it. They got together every week—it was like bingo night, you know? Everybody brought cookies and stuff. Then she got this letter from the guy. The one who invested the money. It said how the market had taken this dive all over the world, and too bad, her stock wasn't making any money right now. But to hang on and it would make her a bunch of bucks later on. Sure." He opened his fist, stared down at the crumpled wad of paper on his palm. "Maybe she believes it, but I know better. It was a scam."

"Did she go to a lawyer?" Rachel asked quietly. Across the table, Julio's face was eloquent with anger and sympathy. "Did she get help?"

"She talked to some freebie guy, and he told her the dude might be a sleaze, but he'd given her this paper to sign, you know? And right there it says how she understood that the money could all get lost anytime. Only the way it's written, you'd have to be some kind of geek lawyer to read it." He flung the wad of paper away. "She thinks she'll get more someday, but it's gone. I know it. And it was everything she'd saved, man. She called the number on his fancy letters, but it's disconnected. And his mail is a PO box. So you tell me he isn't running a scam."

"You think it was Dougan?" Rachel shook her head. He was a CPA with an office above the bookstore, next to City Hall. "Did you ever see this guy before?"

"Oh, yeah, I saw him." Spider stabbed his straw through the plastic lid of his shake cup. "He was Mr. Friendly to the women in the club. They were all women, you know? Single moms mostly. Working shit jobs with about enough left for a pizza after you pay all the bills." He looked up at her with an adult wisdom. "Real ready to believe some sucker in a fancy suit who told 'em they could cash in," he said bitterly. "Oh, he was a talker, man. Came out to one of their meetings once—all Mr. Goodwill, doin' this because he cared, you know? That kind of phony bullshit." He flicked his straw with one grimy finger, his eyes hooded. "That's where I saw him—

when I went to walk Mom home. It was him. Mr. City Hall Big Shot. The slime.''

Rachel shook her head. It was hard to credit—Bob Dougan sneaking off to Portland to sucker working-class women out of their minimal savings. ''You might be wrong—about it being him.'' She lifted a hand as his head snapped up. ''You only met him once, right? And I bet you weren't really paying attention.''

''Well . . .'' He ducked his head, looked away. ''I was a little stoned.'' He shot her a defiant glance. ''Not enough to matter, and I don't do that shit anymore. I wouldn't, even if I could, okay?''

Rachel glanced at Julio, who was nodding and sucking at his shake. He believed Spider, she thought. And approved of Spider's attempt to avenge his mother's loss. Rachel sighed.

''All right, Spider.'' She leaned forward, arms crossed on the table. ''I'll make you a deal. I'll keep you on and I'll keep this afternoon's episode between us. But you have to promise to keep away from Dougan—and to behave yourself if he's around—as long as you work for me. Okay?''

He gave her a startled sideways glance, looking uncertain again. ''Yeah . . . okay, I guess.'' He frowned. ''Long as I work for you, okay?'' He offered her a thin, long-fingered hand. ''After that, I don't promise nothin'.''

''After that, it's your business.'' She took his hand and returned his firm handshake. ''I won't say anything to Willis, but Chief Price may. Or Dougan might call the farm. I'll do my best to back you up—keep you on.''

''Thanks.'' That uncertain expression softened his features again, making him look very young.

''Let's go.'' Rachel finished the last of her shake, tossed the cup in the nearby trash can. ''I'm running late. Bring your shake along, okay?''

She dropped Julio off at his sister's mobile home on one of the narrow graveled streets above Blossom, then drove Spider out to the Youth Farm east of town. The guard at the gate activated the automated chain-link and barbed-wire gate and waved her through. The gate depressed her, although she suspected it was more to reassure the local populace than for security. The Youth Farm was a working model farm, raising Suffolk sheep and maintaining a small apple and pear orchard. Most of the property was separated from neighboring farms by standard woven-wire sheep fence—a fact that had bolstered Blossom's generally hostile attitude toward the two-year-old project.

She signed Spider in at the lobby desk and told him she'd see him in the morning. As he disappeared down the hall, she hesitated, glancing toward Willis Bard's office with its neat black lettering—ADMINISTRATOR—on the door. She had met Willis the year before, when he was merely an instructor here, and one of his kids became tragically involved in a local murder. She had had a lot of respect for Bard's commitment and common sense back then. He deserved to hear Spider's allegations against Dougan, she thought with a twinge of guilt. If nothing else, he should know that trouble might be brewing in the future.

But she had promised Spider that she would keep it between them. As she walked past the office door and headed for the electronically locked main doors, she caught a glimpse of movement as someone ducked around a corner, down the hall. Spider? Checking to see if she'd rat on him? Wondering if she had just made a mistake, she waited for the electronic lock to click open.

Spider had given his word, she told herself. He deserved a chance to keep it. But it bothered her all the way home— Spider's certainty about Dougan's identity. He couldn't be right. Dougan was a solid, conservative pillar of the community, who did a lot to support the town's Little League team. She hoped Spider could control himself.

Her cat, Peter, was waiting on the small outside porch that led to her second-floor apartment in old Mrs. Frey's comfortable, white frame house on one of Blossom's quiet residential streets. He arched his back and rubbed against her ankles, complaining loudly that she was late, and he was starving.

"I know, I know, you're dying." She leaned down to rub his chewed, stray-cat ears. "I'm really not that late, you know."

He glowered his disagreement, then ran ahead of her as she

laughed and opened the door. The sinking sun streamed through the kitchen windows, flooding gold light across the white formica counters and wooden floor of her airy living room. Peter leaped onto the back of her secondhand sofa and began to wash himself impatiently.

"Dinner is coming." Rachel got a can of cat food down from the cupboard and opened it, one eye on the clock. She was going to have to hurry if she wanted to make the town meeting. Dumping the cat food onto a plate, she set it on the floor, avoided the furry streak that dashed past her, and headed straight for the bathroom, unbuttoning her chambray work shirt as she went.

The phone rang just as she reached the door, and she sighed and detoured into the bedroom, dropping clothes onto the bed as she grabbed the receiver from the nightstand. "Hello?" She plopped down onto the bed and began to pull off her socks.

"So are you going to the brawl tonight?" Her mother's cheerful voice came over the line.

"I thought you and Josh were in Portland." Rachel wrinkled her nose as she dropped one sock onto the floor. "Weren't you going to the opera or something?" Deborah O'Connor, widowed years ago, had recently married Joshua Meier, a retired surgeon. Now the two of them divided their time between a loft apartment in Portland and Meier's spacious home outside of Blossom—when they weren't camping or traveling. "Don't tell me you passed on *Aida* just to come watch our mayor in a shouting match with Uncle Jack?"

"Is he still so terribly upset about this?" Her mother sounded uncharacteristically worried. "I was hoping he'd have cooled down a little by now."

"Not a chance. Be glad you weren't at the orchard for dinner last Sunday." Rachel stripped off her other sock and wiggled her toes on the braided rug that her aunt had made for her. "Nobody got to squeeze a word into the tirade. He had himself worked into a real frenzy. Hey!" She grabbed for her sock as Peter snatched it. "Darn cat." She glowered as he bounded from the room, the sock dangling like a trophy from his mouth, his crooked tail high in the air. "Actually, I'm glad you're back," she told her mother. "I think you're the only person who can make Uncle Jack listen when he's like this."

"That's only because I don't raise my voice," Deborah said dryly. "So he has to shut up if he wants to hear what I'm saying. Try it sometime."

"I don't think he really cares if he hears what I'm saying," Rachel said grimly.

Her mother sighed. "I hope Jack doesn't get too worked up tonight. This kind of thing is really hard on Catherine."

"Really?" Rachel blinked. "She is the one person who seems able to take Uncle Jack's temper in stride."

"She loves him, dear, so she learned to live with the temper. She doesn't like it any better than the rest of us. Well, maybe between the four of us we can sort of keep him under control." Her cheerful tone sounded forced. "Josh and I are meeting them in a few minutes. We'll work on him."

"I'll be at the meeting, too. I'll help." Rachel glanced at her bedside clock and yelped. "But I'd better get going or I'll have to come without a shower. Believe me, you don't want that."

"Go get in the shower, dear. I just wanted to make sure you were coming along tonight. I'll let you go—see you there. Bye."

Rachel replaced the receiver and went into the bathroom to run a hot, hard shower. Her mother sounded worried. She could count on the fingers of one hand the occasions when Deborah O'Connor had sounded worried. Dressing quickly in a pair of leggings and a tunic that flattered her stocky figure, Rachel decided that she would have to make do with a quick sandwich—which made fitting penance for her milk shake indulgence, she told herself.

As she layered turkey breast, lettuce, and Monterey Jack cheese on rye bread, the phone rang again. Rachel glared at it in exasperation, then ignored it and grabbed for the jar of Aunt Catherine's bread and butter pickles—one of the many home-canned delicacies her aunt supplied her with. Arranging the slices neatly on the sandwich, she listened to her answering machine beep.

"Rachel?" A worried male voice sounded from the speaker. "This is Willis Bard. I got a call today that Spider Tran caused some kind of trouble in town this afternoon. He won't say much about it. Could you give—"

"I'm here." Rachel picked up the phone, eyeing her sandwich ruefully. "Who called you? Councilman Dougan?"

"Oh, God, is *he* involved?" The administrator of the Youth Farm groaned. "He's circulating a petition to shut us down as it is. It was an anonymous call," he said bitterly. "We get a lot of those."

"It wasn't too serious. Just a shouting match between Spider and Dougan. Spider thought he recognized Dougan as the man who had cheated his mother. Mistaken identity, I guess." She shrugged. "He promised me it wouldn't happen again, and I believe him, so I didn't say anything to you."

"You're still willing to keep him on? You're sure?" Willis sounded less than enthusiastic. "That's good of you. I believed that boy had promise when I first spoke to you."

And he no longer did? "Don't worry." Rachel's stomach growled loudly. "I'll keep an eye on him. I'll let you know if anything more happens."

She ended the call, wondering if Willis Bard regretted taking on the role as administrator he had wanted so badly. He had sounded stressed and uncharacteristically irritable. Snatching up her sandwich, she wrapped it in a couple of paper towels and bolted for the door. No way she was going to make the meeting before it started, but at least she wouldn't be too late. Peter regarded her with feline disdain as she dashed out the door. *Those primates,* he seemed to be saying. *Always rushing about . . .*

"Mind your attitude, or no tuna for you," she warned as she closed the door behind her.

Peter ignored her.

CHAPTER

3

Town meetings took place in the high school gym in Blossom. Rachel arrived to find the gravel parking lot filled with pickups and cars. She drove around behind the long, narrow, brick building, finishing the last of her sandwich as she did so. Finding a parking space at last, she pulled in next to a gleaming brown and white Chevy pickup with *Blossom Feed and Seed* lettered on the side. Andy Ferrel was here, of course. Blossom's former mayor never lost an opportunity to voice his opposition to anything proposed by the new mayor.

It promised to be an interesting night, Rachel thought as she hurried toward the gym. No wonder Jeff had sounded anxious this afternoon. The doors stood ajar, and yellow light spilled into the gathering dusk. Someone was shouting inside, and Rachel winced as she recognized her uncle's voice. She glanced at the caged clock on the wall next to the scoreboard as she slipped through the doorway. Seven-fifteen. Uncle Jack hadn't wasted any time losing his temper.

Inside, what seemed to be the entire population of Blossom packed the rickety wood-and-metal bleachers. Rachel glanced around for her petite, dark-haired mother, found her close to the end of the bleachers, waving and patting a space on the bench. In spite of her smile, she looked worried. Aunt Cath-

erine, her graying hair pinned up into a chu.. n-Sunday roll on
her head, glanced up with a brief nod and a preoccupied smile
as Rachel made her way across booted feet to the vacant spot
on the bench.

"You made it in time for the best part of the show." Joshua
Meier, her mother's new husband, leaned across his wife's
slim, jeans-clad legs to wink at Rachel. "Your uncle is quite
an orator when he's angry."

"Don't applaud him." Rachel's mother shook her head at
Joshua. "Yes, he's being surprisingly rational, but who knows
how long that will last? I haven't seen Jack in a rage like this
for years."

Rachel sat down on the wooden bench, its grain polished
to a satiny finish by generations of student backsides. Down
on the varnished planks of the floor, his feet planted on the
scuffed and faded free-throw line, her uncle shook a finger at
Blossom's young mayor. Face impassive, his famous ponytail
showing its first streaks of gray, Phil Ventura sat behind a
cloth-covered trestle table from the cafeteria, set up beneath
the basketball hoop.

"You tell me why we should sit on our thumbs and let you
folks at City Hall tell us what we can do with our land." Her
uncle's voice filled the gym without benefit of the microphone.
Which was to his advantage, considering the behavior of the
elderly sound system. "I work those acres!" he boomed. "Our
family has worked those acres since my granddaddy came out
from Massachusetts and planted the first damn tree. Now you
tell me I can't sell my own land? You're just gonna take it
for the town? What is this? Russia?" He thrust a thick finger
at Ventura's chest. "Last I heard, this was a democracy, not
some damn commie country."

Applause rose like a wave in the bleachers, drowning out
any further speech. But there were some frowns, too, and some
head shaking. Rachel spotted her friend Joylinn Markham
down on the floor, sitting with the four other members of the
Blossom City Council in rickety folding chairs behind the
podium-table. Joylinn had surprised Rachel, and perhaps herself, by running for City Council in the last election, and even

more so by winning the seat. The young owner of the Bread Box caught sight of Rachel and waved gaily.

"Jack is like so many of the orchard folk around here." Her mother leaned close as the applause began to fade. "They don't know what to do with change, so they pretend it's not happening—that they can keep it from happening."

"I'm not telling you you can't sell your land, Jack." Ventura leaned easily on the unsteady table. "You're a smart man. You know that. But if we annex those acres for the city, then anyone who wants to build on them has to file for a city building permit. Costs fifty dollars. Think you could handle that?"

"Yeah, and you got a list of rules and regulations means just about nobody can build nothin' that ain't a darned historical mon-u-ment round here. Hell, your own council won't vote for this kind of crap. You already tried twice."

"And we keep amending the proposal so that it works for orchardists, environmentalists, and the rest of us plain folks who want a nice town to live in. All we're doing is keeping some cheap developer from tacking together a bunch of flimsy condos and junky mini-malls that will look like a slum in ten years." Ventura winced and fell silent as an electronic squeal drowned his words. An acne-spotted teenager darted over to fiddle with the control box on the floor in front of the table.

"Not even the e-lec-tron-ics like what you're sayin'," Uncle Jack drawled. A scatter of laughter answered him, and Phil Ventura joined in, his manner still easy and friendly.

"A lot of you have the wrong idea about what's going on here." Ventura looked around, his hands lifted as he scanned the crowd. "That's why we called this meeting. What the Council is voting on—annexing this land into the city—it's to protect you, me, all of us. And our land. Some of you have maybe seen what's been happening in some towns around this state—Cannon Beach and Seaside on the coast, Bend in Central Oregon. And Hood River. Look at what's going on there. A place becomes popular, folks start wanting to vacation or retire there, and next thing you know, you got cheap motels, video parlors, junky time-share developments . . . How many of you want to live in the middle of that, huh?"

Quite a few people were nodding. "You been to Bend

lately?'' Daren Rhinehoffer, owner of the Riverside Nursery, got to his feet farther down the bench. ''My folks ranched cattle there years ago. They got forced out. Couldn't pay the property taxes once the developments started goin' in. Hey, I want more folks to move out here. It's gonna help my business. It's gonna help a lot of us. But I don't want to live in the middle of a neon strip either, or have to move, because a bunch of developers drive the property values up to where I can't pay my taxes. I say let's have some rules here.''

''Rules, huh? So you're gonna tell me what I can or can't do with my land?'' Jack O'Connor spun to face him, head thrust forward, eyes snapping beneath his thick sandy brows. ''How 'bout I tell you what plants you can sell on that place of yours, huh?''

''Come off it, Jack,'' Joylinn spoke up. ''It's not like that, and you know it.''

''All right, hold it.'' Mayor Ventura waved the mike, and the ensuing squeal silenced everybody. ''Before this gets out of hand, let's define the situation here. What the Council is voting on is the annexation of just shy of two hundred acres of land along the east edge of town. It's got good access to the freeway, and it's where the developers are going to look first. And, yes, Jack, before you tell us, it includes your twenty acres of cherries.''

''That don't produce nothing anymore and cost me tax money,'' O'Connor growled.

''If we annex the land,'' Ventura went on, his eyes on the crowd, ''what we do is we require anyone who wants to develop the land to apply to City Hall for building permits—at fifty bucks each, which just about covers our paperwork costs. We put through some pretty strict regulations this year—and it'll keep a lot of things you folks might not like much out of here. But it won't keep your land from increasing in value as more people want to move out here. It'll just keep up the quality of our town.''

''Way I hear it, your council ain't gonna pass this version any more than your last try. So I don't know why I'm yellin'.'' Jack turned his back on the mayor, his eyes sweeping the crowd. "But I hear that our good mayor is really leanin' on our elected officials. Ain't that right, Pete?"

"Well, the man wants to get his ideas in place, Jack." Pete Suttle, who owned cherries and Asian pears, shrugged from his seat with the other council members. "He's talking 'em up, sure, but he's not blackmailing any of us, if that's what you mean by leanin'. At least, he's not blackmailing me." Suttle waited for the titters to die down. "You all elected us. We're up here to do what you want."

"Some of you, maybe." Jack still faced the bleachers. "What I want is the right to decide what to do with my own land. I say we put it on the ballot—that any annexations got to be voted on by all of us. It's our land they're decidin' on." He spread his arms wide. "What do you say, huh? You willin' to put your John Hancock on a petition? Get this on the ballot in the fall?"

Applause swept the bleachers again. Booted feet stomped, and some people yelled agreement. Down on the gym floor, the five council members looked generally grim. Bob Dougan rose to his feet and replaced the mayor at the podium. "Settle down for a minute now, folks." He tilted his head, waiting for the noise to subside. "What the hell did you elect us for if you want to do our job for us? These kinds of decisions take a lot of thought, and it's pretty darned easy to see one or two examples—like Jack wanting to sell his land here—and miss the real issues underneath it all. This isn't a county is-sue—it's an issue that concerns us, right here in Blossom."

"Bob's right." Ventura took the mike again. "Hey, the Council has opposed me more often than not. I'm no dictator, believe me. I wish." He made a face and grinned with the scattered laughter. "You got to look at a lot of issues when you're talking about annexation—water, access, what a par-ticular type of development will do to our quality of life."

Roberta Guarnieri levered herself to her feet. She wore a pair of faded men's jeans and a plaid shirt, and towered over both Dougan and the mayor. She and her sister owned Blos-som's downtown gas station and ran the town's only taxi and towing service—on a strictly cash basis. Now she ran a per-manently grease-stained hand through her cropped-short gray

hair and stepped forward. "You guys—you elected us." Her
gravelly voice carried easily, even without the microphone.
"You want us to vote for this or against that—you know
where to find us. We publish the schedule for Council meetings in the *Blossom Bee*. They're open to you all. So show
up. Say what you got to say. If you don't show, then don't
whine if we do somethin' you don't like." She nodded once,
marched back to her chair, and folded herself into it.

More than a few people nodded their heads, and for a moment the gym was quiet.

"Well, I'm tellin' you what I want." Uncle Jack took the
floor again. "I'll be comin' around with a petition to make
annexation a voting issue. Any of you want to help me, I could
sure use it." He looked around the gym, his expression grim.
"Nobody tells me what I can or can't do with my land. Not
the Feds and sure as hell not this wet-behind-the-ears mayor."

As Jack stomped off to his seat, Joshua Meier stirred beside
Deborah. "I guess he forgot you own part of that land," he
murmured to his wife.

"Well, he does most of the work." Deborah shook her
head. "He doesn't mean anything by it."

Joshua grunted and gave Rachel a sideways look. "I think
your Rain Country Landscaping was a good idea," he said
with the merest trace of irony in his tone.

"Me, too." Rachel nodded, but her smile was superficial.
Uncle Jack was indeed worse than she'd ever seen.

He kept quiet for the rest of the meeting, though, as a suc-
cession of Blossom residents marched to the podium to give
their views—some more coherently than others—on the proposed annexation, and the operation of the town government
in general. The annexation issue was eventually replaced by
arguments over loose dogs, a proposed stoplight on Main
Street, and various other town concerns. Mayor Ventura did a
good job of fielding most complaints, managing to maintain
his easy manner in the face of the most rambling and irate
speaker.

Rachel was impressed with his manner. The young mayor
represented the change that was happening all along this part
of the Columbia River—agriculture and timber giving way to

the tourist industry. The election had been bitterly fought, and his victory was a message, since he was seen as an outsider, despite his childhood summers spent in Blossom. Rachel felt a brief pang for the lifestyle of family orchard and farm that was fading away in front of her eyes. Some—like her uncle—would fade with it, she realized with sudden clarity. He couldn't make the change. She took her mother's hand, understanding her worry suddenly. Deborah looked over to meet her daughter's eyes and smiled sadly.

When the meeting finally broke up, most people shuffled down the hall and into the cafeteria where women from the Blossom Grange served fruit punch and cookies. Aunt Catherine made her way to one of the long formica-topped trestle tables to take up her station at one of the punch bowls. "If Jack thinks I'm going to go door-to-door with his petition, then he better think again." She smoothed the thick roll of her hair with one hand. "I got enough to do this time of year, what with the spring spraying and getting the garden in. That's Jack for you." She sighed with good-natured exasperation. "Jump into something first, and figure out how to make it work later." Shaking her head, she picked up a big steel ladle and began to fill paper cups with the bright red punch.

"Well, at least he's willing to do something. That's more than a lot of folks are willing to do. Hi, Rachel." Brian Ferrel picked up a cup of punch and grabbed two sugar cookies from the big platter next to the punch bowl. "How's the landscaping business?"

"Not bad. Hi, Andy," she greeted his father, owner of Blossom Feed and Seed, and the former mayor of Blossom.

He gave her a brief stare, his eyes glittering, fever-bright. "Ventura's a dangerous man." His voice grated. "He fooled the lot of you. He's gonna kill this town." He glared down at the cup of punch in his hand, then tossed it back like a shot of whiskey. "He'll kill it," he said softly, "unless somebody stops him right now." His lips thinned as his eyes fixed on the mayor surrounded by a knot of residents. Crumpling his empty cup, he dropped it into a nearby trash can and stalked toward the main door.

"What's with him?" Rachel looked at Brian with surprise. "I know he took his loss hard . . ."

"Understatement of the decade." Brian lifted one palm, his smile tight. "We don't see eye to eye on the store anymore, either." He gulped his own punch, tossed the cup into the trash can, and hurried after his father. Rachel felt briefly sorry for him. He'd been a high school friend; his wit and easy humor had brightened the classroom. Running the feed store under Andy's critical eye had dimmed some of his youthful humor. She wondered if he had really wanted to stay in Blossom.

"Rachel, hi." Joylinn Markham wove gracefully through the crowd, a cup of black coffee in her hand. "So when is your uncle going to run for mayor?"

"I could believe anything." Rachel laughed and took a cup of punch from the table. "Aunt Catherine says he's going to have to do his own signature gathering, though."

"I don't know why he's even worried." Joshua Meier joined the conversation, hand in hand with Rachel's mother. "You folks vote down nearly everything Ventura asks for. Except Rachel's city landscaping contract." His eyes twinkled. "Was that your doing?"

"I bribed the other four with brownies," Joylinn said with a straight face. "Seriously, though, I doubt it will pass. Suttle and Dougan are lined up against him."

"As usual," Joshua said dryly.

"Well, yes." Joylinn wrinkled her nose. "I'm for it—I don't want that Seaside clutter growing up around us. This time, though, Hank West is voting with me. Roberta's against it."

"Roberta?" Rachel's mother raised her eyebrows.

"She's kind of a stubborn free spirit at times." Joylinn wrinkled her nose again. "She's not much in favor of governments doing this kind of thing. But Hank West, over at the bank—he's for it. Which kind of surprised me," she admitted. "Usually we're on opposite sides."

"Well, it sounds as if it won't pass—not with a three-two vote. We know Dougan and Suttle won't budge." Rachel's mother sounded relieved. "Although I have to say that I'm not going to enjoy looking out over those young Fuji apples that just started to bear and find myself staring at a bunch of condominiums.''

"Condos?'' Rachel blinked. "You mean that developer really is going to buy it? I thought it was just talk.''

"Oh, no. It's gone well beyond the talk stage,'' her mother said grimly. "Although the developer is holding off on signing anything until this annexation vote has come and gone.''

Sudden shouting from the hallway brought all their heads around. With a sinking heart, Rachel recognized her uncle's loud, angry tones. "What the hell do you mean—you're in favor of this thing? You turned into a commie overnight? Huh?''

Jack O'Connor burst into the cafeteria on the heels of a stone-faced Bob Dougan.

"I'm talkin' to you, Bob. You turn yourself around and hear what I got to say.'' He grabbed Dougan's shoulder, jerked the councilman sharply around to face him. Dougan's eyes blazed, and he yanked his arm free.

Behind the refreshment table, Catherine stood indecisively, her eyes full of alarm, the ladle dripping crimson spots onto the flowered apron she had donned. Rachel's mother muttered something under her breath and started for the two men. But it was Jeff Price who got there first. He emerged from the hallway and shoved between them, just as Uncle Jack's fist rose.

"You gonna punch an officer, Jack?'' Jeff drawled.

Jack O'Connor's lips drew back from his teeth. "You used to sneak cookies in my kitchen. Don't you give me any lip, boy.''

"I'm not giving you lip.'' Jeff spread his hands, casually blocking the older man's path. Dougan had turned away, straightening his sports jacket, and was now making his way toward the punch table. "This isn't the place,'' Jeff said quietly, holding Jack's gaze. "Somebody might get hurt—beside you and Dougan.''

"I wasn't plannin' on punching him out.'' Jack looked away, a tic pulsing at the corner of his mouth. "We're not through here, Bob.'' He raised his voice. "You hear me? I want to hear how come you're turnin' on folks—how come you sold out. What was the price, huh? How much, Bob?''

At the table near Rachel, Dougan's shoulders stiffened, and his hand trembled just slightly as he reached for a sugar cookie.

"Come on, Jack." Jeff took his arm. "Lots of family here tonight. Let's keep it friendly."

"I heard you the first time, kid." Jack shook his arm off, but the gesture lacked force. "I said what I wanted to say. I'm through. For now." He shot Dougan another murderous glare. By now, Catherine was on her way across the room, her round face troubled, her hands bunching the punch-spotted fabric of her apron.

Jack turned on his heel and pushed his way out into the hallway. Rachel's mother met up with Catherine at the door, and the two women hurried after the vanished Jack.

"I'd better join the family parade." Rachel tossed her empty punch cup into a wastebasket. "I'll catch you later, Joylinn."

"Good luck." Joylinn frowned thoughtfully at Dougan. "Sounds like I was wrong about the lineup."

Rachel nodded but didn't answer. Worried, because her mother was worried, she threaded her way through the thinning crowd, returning greetings absently, craning her neck to catch sight of her mother and aunt. As she passed the refreshment table, she heard Dougan speaking, using his council-meeting voice.

"We got a good town here—a good life. We don't want to bring big-city problems in here. And if we don't work at holding on to that lifestyle we got—we're going to have all of Portland's troubles—gangs, drugs, the works." She didn't stop to hear folks' reaction to his speech, but Rachel wondered, as she worked her way toward the door, how much his daughter's escapade today had changed his mind about protecting Blossom.

"They went out to the parking lot." Jeff fell in beside her. "I haven't seen Jack that worked up since the night he caught us joyriding on the new tractor."

"Mom's worried." Rachel halted in the high school doorway, searching the parking lot anxiously. People were leaving. Headlights slashed across chrome and paint like searchlights, but she didn't see any of her relatives. "I guess he had a solid buyer for that land." She squinted as a pair of headlights flooded them with bright glare. "Mom said the developer was waiting on the annexation vote to close the deal. Where did Jack *go?*"

"There's your mom." Jeff took her arm as Deborah hurried up with Aunt Catherine.

"He jumped in the truck and took off." Her mother's voice crackled with anger. "Acting like a pouting teenaged boy. What did he think Catherine was going to do? Walk home?"

"Oh, he knew I could get a ride." Catherine patted her arm. "He's just in one of his moods, Deborah. He'll go have a beer or two, yell a lot, and be fine when he gets home. You know how he is."

"You're a whole lot more tolerant about that than I'd ever be," Rachel's mother said grimly. "We brought Josh's MG, and we don't have a whole lot of room. Jeff, are you through here?" She looked up at him. "Would you run Catherine home? It's on your way."

"I'll take her home, Mom." Rachel touched her mother's hand. "Don't you go looking for him now. Catherine's right. He's just going to go blow off steam at the Dew Drop and then he'll be home."

"He can get there in Roberta's cab." Deborah tossed her head. "I'm going after his keys."

"You go on home with Joshua." Jeff patted her shoulder. "I'll run Catherine home and then I'll hit the Dew Drop. Herb knows Jack. He'll probably call Roberta himself if Jack's getting too loaded. I might just run him home myself."

"I'll go with you. Yes, I will." Rachel met his eyes as he opened his mouth to say no. "He'll be less likely to pick a fight if I'm along."

"She's right," Deborah said slowly. "Don't let him push you into a fight, Jeff. He's in that kind of mood." She searched his face anxiously. "He can say some pretty nasty things when he's like this."

"I've probably heard worse." Jeff smiled gravely down at her. "It's all right."

"Thanks for doing this, Jeff." Deborah tossed her head. "Honestly—that man. If you want to let him sleep in the jail, it's fine by me."

"Well, it's not fine by me." Catherine looked at her sister-in-law in horror. "An O'Connor in jail? Deborah!"

"I was kidding, dear." Rachel's mother put her arm around her sister-in-law's shoulders. "You go on home. Jeff will get Jack there safely."

"All right." Catherine bit her lip. "I worry," she said apologetically, as if Jack's temper was her fault. She was the one who picked up the pieces after one of his outbursts. Rachel had long ago lost count of how many workers quit or were fired in the heat of a shouting match, only to be rehired after Catherine had intervened, soothing workers' injured pride with gifts of food and money.

"Thanks, Jeff." She took his hand as Deborah went off to find Joshua, and Catherine went in to collect the jacket and purse she'd left inside. "You really don't have to do this."

"But then I'd either have to arrest Jack for a DUI, or live with myself if he hit a tree on the way home." A hint of a smile touched his eyes. "You sure you want to spend the next couple of hours chasing around the midnight countryside with me?"

"Hey, he's my uncle, after all." She tucked her arm through his and smiled, telling herself that they'd find Jack, and it would go just as her mother had predicted.

CHAPTER

4

Aunt Catherine treated them to a gentle defense of her husband's temper all the way out to the orchard. "He really has mellowed," she told them as Jeff turned his new Jeep Cherokee onto the gravel driveway that led north from the county road, down a lane of thick-trunked and gnarled old apple trees. They had been planted by Rachel's great-grandfather decades before, when he had built a house from rough-sawn planks and planted the first orchard trees.

The original house had burned, but the square, white farmhouse that had replaced it was nearly as old. Tall and austerely functional with narrow sash windows, it stood firm against the winds that thundered down the Gorge during the winter. Rachel's eyes went automatically to the upstairs corner room she had had to herself, as the only girl child in the family. Her two cousins had shared the big bedroom across the hall, and they had had plenty of pillow fights up and down the wide hallway as kids. On the coldest winter nights, water would freeze in the glass on her bedside table.

"He'll be fine, Aunt Catherine." Rachel shook off crowding memories as she leaned over the front seat. "We'll make sure he gets home all right."

"He wasn't like this." Her aunt turned faded hazel eyes on

her niece. "I don't know what's getting into the man. He's been so . . . touchy lately." She bit her lip suddenly, her eyes glittering with tears.

"Aunt Catherine, don't worry." Feeling awkward because she couldn't ever remember seeing her aunt cry, Rachel touched her shoulder. "Do you want me to stay?"

"Oh, no, dear, that's not necessary." She managed a smile. "You're right. He'll be fine. I just worry. More than I used to, I think." She opened the door. "Happens as you get old, I suppose."

"Of course, he's touchy." Jeff helped her out of the Jeep with gentle courtesy. "Everything's changing. Makes a lot of people touchy around here."

"You're right, Jeff." Aunt Catherine brightened. She paused on the porch steps, marked by rusty rings left by the clay pots of geraniums that were still stored in the root cellar for the winter. "You turned out to be a good man." She touched his arm, gave him a wan smile. "Your mother must be proud."

"Thank you." Jeff bent his head.

Rachel looked away. She had never told Jeff that her aunt had intercepted his letters to her after he and his mother had moved to Los Angeles. She had been quietly opposed to their friendship all through high school. Rachel had never asked her why. She pushed gently on the freshly painted porch swing. Her father had built it for her mother's birthday, when Rachel was eight. He had sawed and nailed and sanded the smooth white wood out in the shed behind the barn and had sworn Rachel to secrecy. She had helped him finish it with coats of glossy paint. When it was done, Rachel had tied a big pink bow on it. Her father had sneaked out of bed before dawn to hang it and had waked Rachel to help, as he had promised.

Her mother had come out onto the porch in her bathrobe just as they had finished. She had made a small gasping noise, then had laughed and thrown her arms around her husband's neck, and her eyes had glittered with tears. When Rachel had hugged them both, a little jealous, proclaiming her part in the building, her mother had pulled them both onto the new swing to rock and watch the horizon pale with dawn. Then they had trooped into the kitchen to make scrambled eggs and biscuits and cocoa and coffee all together, before anyone else was up.

Her parents' love for each other still amazed her. She took her eyes away from the swing as Catherine opened the front door. It wasn't locked. Not too long ago, nobody locked their doors out here—but that was changing, too. She locked her apartment when she left. "Call me on my cell phone if he shows up here, okay?" She kissed her aunt tenderly on the cheek, then hurried down the steps and climbed into the front seat beside Jeff. "He'll be there," she said. "At the Dew Drop."

"Probably." Jeff sighed. "Your aunt is a solid woman." He looked at Rachel for a moment, as if he wanted to say more, then put the Jeep abruptly into gear.

Uncle Jack wasn't at the roadside bar and grill called the Dew Drop Inn. He wasn't in Fong's red vinyl and candlelit lounge either, or at the Main Street Tavern at one of the pool tables. "Hood River?" Jeff asked, as they left Fong's.

He looked exhausted. Rachel shook her head. "Let's quit," she said. "He's a big boy and he's not stupid. He'll call Roberta or sleep in his truck."

"Meaning you'll wait until I leave you at your place, then take off for Hood River?" He raised an eyebrow as she winced and looked away.

"There aren't that many places he could be in Hood River at this hour." He put the Jeep into gear.

"Why would he go there?" Rachel threw herself back against the fabric upholstery with an exasperated sigh. "Why not the Dew Drop? He could rant all he wanted there and have an applauding audience."

Her cell phone rang.

"Thank God." She snatched it up from the seat. "Aunt Catherine?"

"Sweetheart, he's home." Her aunt's voice came over the instrument, blurred by faint static. "He's fine, dear, and I'm so sorry if you and Jeff have been out looking for him all this time . . ."

"It's fine, it is." She rolled her eyes at Jeff, who shook his head and made a face. "Talk to you later. Did you call Mom?"

She had called Rachel's mother first. "I'm sorry, Jeff." Rachel leaned her head back against the seat and closed her eyes. "I don't know why we were all so worried."

"Well, I'm glad to know he's home in one piece." Jeff did a neat U-turn on the narrow county road. "I'll take you home."

Rachel tried vainly to stifle a yawn. "Hey, that wasn't personal!"

"We're both beat." He leaned across the seat to kiss her lightly and quickly on the side of the mouth.

When they reached Mrs. Frey's house, he climbed the outside stairs to the door with her, kissed her gently and fully, but didn't ask to come in.

"Forget it, cat," she told the purring Peter, who rubbed against her ankles as he followed her inside. "I remember quite well that I fed you. There's dry food in your bowl, and breakfast is happening way too soon." He pouted, and she ignored him as she stripped out of her clothes. Late. She winced as she looked at the clock. Nearly two A.M.

She tumbled into bed and was asleep before Peter could get himself settled on the foot of her bed.

She yawned all the way out to City Hall in the morning—much to Julio's amusement, after she had picked him up. A white layer of glittering frost coated every tree branch and blade of grass, glittering like diamond dust in the morning light. Overhead, the cloudless sky promised a beautiful spring day. Not a breath of wind ruffled the broad expanse of the Columbia. Mist drifted in wisps above the water, and the sloping hills on the Washington side reflected in the blue-gray water, green with spring grass. Upriver, the wooded walls of the Oregon side drew together toward The Dalles, softened by trailing rags of fog. No hardy sailboarders bothered with the windless river today.

Spider was waiting for them, leaning against the door of the battered van that belonged to the Youth Farm. He straightened as soon as he caught sight of her, spoke to the driver, then hurried over as the van pulled away.

"Hey—somebody dumped that truckload of bark dust last night." Spider's brown eyes glittered with excitement. "All over this car. Whoever owns it is gonna be pissed!"

"What?" Rachel slammed the truck door and raced down the cracked concrete of the City Hall driveway. It was early—the parking lot was empty, except for a battered blue Datsun that belonged to old Jesse, the janitor, and one of Blossom's two black and white police cars. Rachel halted, her stomach contracting. Harvey's big dump truck sat where he had parked it—but the box had been lifted to dump position, and a brown mountain of bark dust mounded beneath the gate. It covered the hood of Dougan's parked car. Brown dust frosted the unburied portions of the car and the weed-riven concrete around it. Julio whistled a low note of appreciation.

"How?" Rachel asked faintly. She groped in her pocket for her key ring, remembering belatedly that she had simply stuck the key in her pocket. These were clean jeans. She checked her pockets carefully, knowing that she hadn't picked up the key from her dresser this morning. Wallet, pocketknife, comb, truck keys. No small silver ignition key. She had no memory of taking it out of her pocket last night. "I can't believe this." She glanced around, half expecting Dougan to come striding down the sidewalk. "I *can't* have just dropped it here. It has to be at home. Let's get going," she snapped at her two rapt assistants. "We either get this car cleaned off fast, or Dougan lands on all of us." Although he had to have seen this mess. Surely he hadn't left the car here on purpose overnight. He lived two miles out of town. "You get the wheelbarrow, Julio. Shovels, Spider! And the brooms." She couldn't wait to hear what Bob would have to say about *this*.

Feeling her too-short night in every muscle of her body, Rachel took one of the shovels that Spider brought. "We might as well start spreading it," she said as she and Julio rapidly filled the barrow. "We're going to cover all the beds around the building. The rest is for the War Memorial Park, down the street. Just dump the barrow into the beds—make sure the loads touch each other but don't cover any plants.

We'll rake it out later. We'll pile the rest—'' She broke off abruptly as her shovel struck something buried in the brown bark dust. "Now what?" She pushed bark dust aside, sneezing as fine brown dust drifted into the still morning air.

"Senorita O'Connor, stop." Julio's voice was hushed.

She looked down, wiping dust from her face. Her shovel blade had exposed a scrap of gray cloth and something brown—a man's shoe, she realized with dull shock.

There was a foot in it. And the gray cloth was the cuff of a pair of pants.

Rachel took a single step backward, the shovel clattering on the concrete as it slipped from her grasp. "Julio—Spider, stay right here. Don't touch *anything*. Don't let anybody else touch anything either." She broke into a run across the parking lot, around the side of City Hall to the small brick wing out back that housed the Blossom Police Department and the two-cell jail. Spring grass had sprouted vigorously in the cracks that zigzagged across the gray concrete. Part of her mind noticed, and noticed the first yellow dandelions nodding in the weedy clumps that grew in the cracks along the foundation.

She reached the door, beneath the floods that still glowed with wan light in the bright morning. Rang the tan plastic doorbell, wanting to press her face against the mesh-reinforced glass in the door, wanting to pound and yell. A shape moved inside, and the door opened.

"What's up?" Lyle Waters faced her, his expression cool. Older than Jeff, he had not forgiven the relative newcomer for obtaining a position he felt belonged to him. "You got a problem?"

"A body." Her voice sounded hoarse in her ears. "There's a body. Under the bark dust."

Lyle's gray eyes narrowed in his long face, and his expression hardened. Pushing past her, he strode across the parking lot, one hand brushing the leather holster on his blue-clad hip. The two youths stood shoulder to shoulder like stone statues, Julio slightly taller than the wiry Spider, their expressions identically wary, their eyes identically alight with excited curiosity. He gave them a pointed stare, then knelt quickly beside the exposed foot, brushing away more bark dust as he put his hand on the sock-clad ankle. Shaking his head, he got to his feet again, brushing bark dust from his uniform, his eyes scanning the dust-covered ground, following the tracks the three of them had made through the powdery stuff as they had begun to work on the pile. Shaking his head again, he turned to Rachel.

"You dumped this?"

"No, of course not!" She pressed her lips together. "I . . . it was still on the truck when I left last night . . . after five-thirty more or less. I don't know how . . ." She licked her lips, her mouth bone-dry. "I remember putting the key in my pocket. I *couldn't* have dropped it here. It must be at home . . ." She faltered and fell silent. "I think so," she said in a small voice.

"We'll go look." Lyle gave her a brief cold glance. "As soon as I get things secured here. Who else had a key?"

"Harvey Glisan." She swallowed. "He said he was going over to Hood River. To the hospital. His daughter-in-law is having a baby."

Lyle grunted.

Rachel picked up the shovel she had dropped, struggling to remember. Light-headed. She had taken the change out of her pocket . . . she remembered that. Remembered taking off her watch. Pulling out her wallet and tossing it onto the dresser.

What if she had dropped it? And some kids got to playing. Or somebody. And the bed got lifted . . . and somebody was standing behind it . . . There wasn't that much on top of the . . . the body. She straightened, knuckles white on the shovel. It couldn't *kill* someone. They could just sit up, brush it off. They wouldn't *die* . . .

"Hey, you!" Lyle's shout jolted her from her nightmare imaginings. "Knock it off."

Rachel turned to find Spider clutching the other shovel, scooping frantically at the bark dust.

"You gotta dig him out!" Spider's voice was shrill. "He might be alive."

"He's dead, kid." Lyle grabbed Spider by the shoulder, wrenched the shovel from his grip. "You screwed up evidence, punk. Give me that."

"You can't. He might—"

"He's dead." Lyle shoved him forcefully away from the body. "Sit down, kid, or I'll damn well put cuffs on you. I've got to check this for prints," he told Rachel, handling the shovel gingerly.

"I brought it with me. It wasn't here." Rachel turned to Spider. "Are you okay?"

Shivering like a nervous dog, Spider flinched as she touched him. White ringed his muddy irises, and he looked up at her with a numb surprise, as if she had materialized from thin air. "Sit down," she said urgently. "We're in the way." She pulled his stiff, unyielding body over to the concrete-block wall that edged the parking lot. "You, too," she told Julio, and they all sat together, still as statues. Lyle was talking on his cell phone, his back turned, his words brisk and angry.

Calling Jeff, she guessed. He should be on his way in by now. Sure enough, within a handful of minutes, the Jeep swung into the driveway, scattering bits of gravel as it took the turn too fast.

"What happened here?" He unfolded his lanky height from the car, his face without expression. His official look, she thought. It had frightened her once—that icy look. As if the man she knew had departed and a cold stranger had possessed his body. She knew now that he was still in there. Some shadow in his past made that cold distance important. She wondered sometimes if he'd ever tell her about it. She waited while he spoke briefly to Lyle.

"Tell me the whole story." He came over to where she sat with her two assistants.

Spider had drawn into himself, shoulders hunched, face pale, his eyes fixed on the scuffed knees of his jeans. Crumbs of bark dust clung to the fabric. Lyle had gone inside and returned with a roll of yellow tape, which he was stretching across the driveway. The janitor—old Jesse—watched from a ground-floor window, his vein-webbed, weathered face creased with excitement.

"From the beginning," Jeff said, and his eyes flickered in her direction. "Are you okay?" he asked gently. "You're white."

"I guess . . ." She swallowed. "Do you ever get used to this?"

"I hope not." He made a move as if to put his arm around her but stopped himself. Lyle had begun to photograph the scene, the camera snapping, making Rachel want to giggle because it reminded her of the tourists on Main Street, snapping away at the old brick buildings with the bright flyers in the windows announcing an equipment auction at the county fairgrounds, a 4-H barbecue, and a Fruit Growers' Association meeting at the Grange. She swallowed the urge to laugh as Jeff squeezed her arm.

"Hang in there," he murmured. "So the bark dust had been dumped when you got here?"

She nodded, miserable again. "Spider saw it first." Speaking through a tightness in her throat, she went over the events of the morning as he listened gravely and took notes." I . . . I'm sure I put the key in my pocket, but I don't remember." She cleared her throat, fighting tears. "Jeff, I might . . . I might have dropped it. Someone might have found it and . . ."

"Easy. It's all right." Jeff closed his notebook and put a gentle hand on her arm. "Let's go see if it's at your apartment. If you have it, then that sure limits the number of people who could have dumped that bed." He glanced over at Lyle. "I'll be right back. And you two stay put." He gave Spider and Julio a stern look.

"We will be here." Julio straightened his shoulders and gave the slumping Spider a narrow glare. "I will make sure," he announced.

"Good." Jeff nodded, then touched Rachel's arm.

They took his Jeep, to Rachel's relief. For once Mrs. Frey's elderly Galaxy wasn't in its place. She must have been out doing errands. Rachel led Jeff upstairs, brushing past the offended Peter without a greeting.

Hurrying into the bedroom, she went right to the dresser where she deposited her wallet, watch, and keys each night.

No key lay on the polished birchwood.

"I know I put it in my pocket. I *remember*." Frantically Rachel peered beneath the dresser. "How could it have fallen out?"

"I've done that—dropped something onto the ground that I thought went into my pocket. Easy with a small key. Or maybe your cat knocked it off." Jeff got down on his knees to help her search. They spent a half hour scouring the apartment, but in the end, had to give up.

"I guess I did drop it," Rachel said in a small voice.

"Stop it." Jeff took her by the arms. "We don't even know that the bark dust killed him. It's not your fault, in any case."

"But . . ."

"No." He shook her very gently, then kissed her on the forehead. "It's not. Listen to me!"

"Okay, okay." Rachel smiled for him, although the tears lurked just behind it. "Maybe I'll find it later." She looked around the apartment, feeling like a stranger suddenly. "I'll call you right away if I do."

Jeff held her hand on the way down the steps, but when they reached City Hall again, he had resumed the cold distance of his job.

Lyle was carefully clearing the body, scooping the bark dust into Rachel's wheelbarrow, which Julio then emptied onto a tarp spread out on the pavement. A dozen people had gathered to watch and murmur from behind the yellow tape, including Roth Glover from the Ace Hardware, Carol Edwaller who owned the drugstore, and most of the staff from City Hall. As they approached, Lyle suddenly stood up. "I'll be damned," he said.

Bob Dougan lay dead on the concrete, his face pale and waxy, coated with brown dust. The bark dust covered him to his shoulders, as if someone had tucked him into bed beneath a thick brown quilt. His face looked oddly . . . peaceful.

"I dream this," Spider whispered. He stood close to Rachel, his eyes fixed on the supine figure. "It pours down—dirt— out of the sky. And he stands there, just looking at me. And I'm yelling at him, telling him to move, just move, but he doesn't, he just stands there looking at me, and the dirt covers him up, over his head, and I realize he's standing in a grave, and I yell and yell, and he just stands there. Until . . ."

"Who?" Rachel asked softly. "Who do you dream about?"

"My dad." Spider turned eyes like empty windows to her. "At the end there's just dirt. No stone."

"Looks like he was stabbed." Lyle pointed at the black plastic handle of a clasp knife emerging from the dust like an excavated tool at some archaeological dig.

"That looks like one of the buck knives I carry." Roth Glover spoke up. "That kid was hangin' over 'em when he come in to buy screws yesterday." He pointed an accusing finger at Spider.

Spider Tran lifted his head sharply, as if someone had called his name. Without a sound, he crumpled, folding into a limp heap on the bark dust–covered concrete.

"Spider!" Rachel dropped to her knees beside him.

"Good timing on my part, I see." Dr. Miller, Blossom's elderly resident physician, knelt beside her. "Bob'll wait." He lifted Spider's eyelid, checked his pulse as the boy stirred. "Just fainted, I think, but I'll check him over." He shook his gray head, his face lined and sad. "Bad doings today," he said as he got to his feet. "Bad enough to make anyone pass out." Shoulders bowed, he turned to the body waiting for him.

CHAPTER
5

"Thank God Spider is in the clear." Willis Bard, administrator of the Youth Farm, sank into the padded chair behind his cluttered desk. "That's all we'd need. A homicide." He ran a hand through rapidly thinning hair and stared at his palm, as if he expected to find something there. "Although this may sink us anyway. The publicity is just what we don't need right now." He moved an untidy stack of papers out of his way and sighed. "Not with that petition going around to shut us down."

"I think there's been some petition or other circulating since you opened," Rachel said dryly. "My mother always said that Blossom signs more petitions per capita than any other town its size."

"Really?" Willis blinked at her and ran his hand through his hair again. Rachel felt a brief moment of pity for him, guessing that his idealism was taking a beating behind that desk.

"So Spider has an alibi?" she asked.

"Oh, yes." Willis nodded. "After that altercation with Dougan, we got more than one call. I gather it was quite a show." He sighed again. "I put him in the secure dorm. Not that I think he'd run away," he added hastily. "But if anyone made any accusations, I wanted to be able to document his presence here, you see.''

Yes, he had changed a bit since he'd assumed his new role. The new dorm assignment must have felt like punishment to Spider, Rachel thought. She'd seen the secure wing, with its mesh-covered windows and locked doors. Troublemakers got locked in there at night. Losers, Spider had once called them. "What about the knife?" she asked. "Did they find any prints?"

"They found one." Willis shrugged. "Not Spider's. And I believe him when he says he didn't take the knife. It didn't kill Dougan anyway. They found that out at the autopsy. He was killed by a blow to the head, and then stabbed. Don't ask me why." He shrugged and tapped his fingers on the desktop. "So why did you want to see me?"

"Spider didn't show up for work this morning. I need him. I just wanted to make sure he'd be there tomorrow."

"You're kidding." He stared at her. "You're *asking* to take him back?"

"Yes." Rachel met his stare. "I wouldn't have hired him if I didn't need the help. I don't have time to go look for somebody else in the middle of a job. It'll put me behind schedule. If he's not a runaway risk, why not let him work?"

"I'll have to think about it." Willis frowned and looked away. "I'm not sure it's a good idea for him to be out on the city streets right now."

"Would you have had to think about it last year?" Rachel said softly.

"That's unfair." Willis swung his chair around sharply. "The situation isn't the same. I have different responsibilities now."

The pain in his eyes stabbed Rachel with quick guilt. "I apologize." She let her breath out in a slow sigh. "You're carrying a lot on your shoulders. I . . . was thoughtless."

"Yes, you were." Willis sat back in his chair. "So what is your interest in this boy? He's only worked for you for a week. Why make all this fuss for him?"

Fuss? Oh, yes, he had indeed changed. "I . . . I just think Spider deserves a chance." Rachel frowned. Inadequate explanation, but she wasn't really sure why it was so important to her to let Spider keep working. "What happened to his father?"

"His father?" Willis narrowed his eyes. Shrugged. "He walked out on the family when Spider was ten. He was half-Vietnamese—the son of a Saigon whore, the mother tells me. I gather he . . . wasn't too stable mentally. At least by her account."

Unstable, Rachel thought. Generic word. Willis's brief, cold description didn't match the anguish in Spider's face when he'd described his dream of watching dirt bury his father. "So, can I keep him?" She smiled down at Willis.

"I should say no." The young administrator rose, frowning. "I should play it safe. Spider has already received a lot of public attention, and our position is pretty shaky right now." He looked away, ran his hand through his hair again. "Okay, fine. He'll be there. I just hope I don't regret this," he said softly.

"You won't." Rachel nodded. "I promise."

As she started for the door, Willis cleared his throat.

"I hope your uncle has a good alibi for that night."

"What?" Rachel turned sharply.

"For the night of the murder." His eyes held hers briefly, unsmiling. "I was at that town meeting. I heard him threatening Dougan. A lot of people did."

"That's silly." Rachel laughed, although a thrill of alarm ran through her. "Uncle Jack is always yelling about something. Nobody took it seriously—not even Dougan, I'm sure."

"I hope you're right." Willis sat back down at his desk and reached for his stack of papers. "I really hope you're right."

Rachel marched out of the office without answering, leaving the door ajar. Striding down the pastel hall, her cheeks burned. She felt . . . rebuked. How could anyone seriously consider . . . But Willis was a newcomer, she thought fiercely. He didn't know Uncle Jack. Movement near the end of the hallway caught her eye, and she turned in time to see a slight figure duck back around a corner.

"Spider?" She looked down the intersecting corridor, half expecting him to have disappeared, but he was there, slouching against the wall, a carefully disinterested expression on his thin face. "You ready to go back to work tomorrow?" she asked lightly. "We're starting on the Memorial garden, and it's going to mean a lot of wheelbarrow and shovel work. You up for it?"

For a moment his hostile expression didn't change. "No way they're gonna let me out of here."

"Go ask." She jerked her head at Willis's door. "See you tomorrow." She went on down the hall, and as she turned the corner, she thought she heard the soft sound of a door opening and closing behind her. When she glanced back, the hallway was empty. As she pushed through the heavy front doors with their electronic locks, she wondered if he'd show tomorrow or not.

To her surprise, her mother was parked in the circular driveway out front, her feet propped on the passenger door of her little bottle-green MG Mini, a book in her hands. She waved as she caught sight of Rachel, and sat up straight. "I stopped in at the Bread Box and Joylinn told me you were out here. Come on—I'll buy you lunch."

"I'll get my truck."

"Oh, ride with me." Her mother grinned and pushed her unruly black curls back from her face. "I'm still looking for any excuse to show off my baby, here." She patted the gleaming new paint on the vintage MG lovingly. "I still can't believe it. What a birthday present!"

"Josh loves you a lot, Mom." Rachel climbed into the car's sleek bucket seat. "You don't mind bringing me back?"

"More driving time." Her mother laughed and put the car into gear, shifting quickly through the gears as they pulled onto the county highway. "I thought we'd go to the little roadside place that opened just outside of Hood River," she said casually. "You know—the one that used to be an old diner?"

"Sure," Rachel said, a little surprised that they weren't going to the Bread Box or Fong's. She squinted at her mother as the wind whipped her hair around her face. In spite of her mother's smile, telltale lines of tension showed at the corners

of her mouth, and her knuckles gleamed as she gripped the
leather-covered steering wheel.

Her mother was not a white-knuckled driver. Rachel leaned
back in the seat, all conversation impossible in the rush of
wind and engine roar. They were on old Highway 30, paral-
leling the asphalt river of the Interstate, flanked by cherry trees
clothed in spring leaves and the first white petals of unfurling
buds. Midweek in this cold spring, the town was still fairly
free of sailboarders and tourists. The parking lot of the newly
remodeled diner—the Mount Hood Diner—was only half full
when her mother swung the MG into an empty space and
parked.

"Whew." Rachel got out, laughing and trying to untangle
her windblown hair. "You ought to be on the racetrack."

"I stayed within the speed limit." Her mother smiled, the
skin crinkling at the corners of her eyes. "Mostly."

A stand of Douglas fir hid the interstate and the river, but
farther up, a tidewater tug churned along, guiding three barges
downstream from The Dalles. Rachel's mother paused for a
moment, her eyes fixed on the distant barge, her expression
suddenly sad.

"Tell me." Rachel touched her arm, worried now.

"You know me too well." Her mother forced a smile and
nodded.

They took a corner booth, away from the other diners—a
fair mix of locals and tourists. The red vinyl and gleaming
formica of the table matched the early fifties photos of the
diner and the surrounding countryside that decorated the walls.
The chrome jukebox on the wall of their booth completed the
atmosphere. Rachel half expected the waitress to appear with
a blond ponytail and saddle shoes, but the young man who
took their order wore khaki-colored slacks, a polo shirt, and
an apron. The menu offered mostly upscale hamburgers and
hotdogs, although it did include some imaginative salads. They
also offered milk shakes made with real ice cream and genuine
fountain sodas.

"I hear this place is great for breakfast," her mother said
absently. She was examining the selection offered by the jukebox, frowning slightly. "Josh has been wanting to try it."

"How's Josh?" Rachel eyed her huge platter of chicken Caesar salad with some apprehension. "I think I'm going to need a doggy bag for this."

"Josh thinks I'm getting too upset over all this." Her mother picked up her salmon burger and took a halfhearted bite. "I probably am, but . . ." She shrugged. "How can I not?"

"Upset over what? The murder?" Rachel finally located one of the elusive chunks of chicken breast buried in her wilderness of lettuce and speared it. It was good, she decided. Grilled, not broiled. Too bad it was in such short supply. "Willis Bard—at the Youth Farm—said something about Uncle Jack being a suspect. I thought he was just throwing a rock at me, you know? I'd just kind of insulted him."

"Half this town thinks Jack got drunk and bashed Bob Dougan's head in." Her mother fiddled with one of the thin wedges of pineapple that decorated her coleslaw. "It could have actually happened that way."

"But it didn't. Right?" Cold trickled down her spine at her mother's long silence.

"No." She shook her head finally, decisively. "Jack may be a hothead, but he can't lie worth beans. No, he didn't do it."

"Since when did talk ever bother Uncle Jack?" Rachel tried to laugh, but it lodged in her throat with one of the large dry croutons, and she coughed.

Her mother pushed her plate away and reached for her glass of iced tea. "You have to understand." Her dark eyes fixed on Rachel's face. "When Herbert Southern came by with an offer from that developer to buy that twenty acres, you thought it was because of Will that I hesitated, right?"

"I know Dad was always against selling any land," Rachel said slowly. Her mother was shaking her head slowly.

"It was an admission of failure, Rachel. That's why I didn't want him to do it. Jack feels the same way about family land as Will did. But it's wearing him down—the rising cost of the chemicals and labor, all the new environmental regulations, the competition from Mexican apples. The latest downturn in the Asian market is the last straw. Lord knows if we can even sell our Golden Delicious crop this year. There are warehouses full of last year's apples all over the globe. Jack has been watching everything he and Will built up trickling away a bit at a time—like a sand castle eroding on the beach. His own sons don't want to stay in this business—too much work for not enough money. That's what they both told him.''

She hadn't wanted to run the orchard, either. Rachel poked at a limp ring of onion with her fork. But it hadn't been the work or the money that had deterred her. It had been the realization that she would always work for Uncle Jack—obey his decisions—as long as he lived. He still wouldn't admit without prodding that her small orchard of horizontally espaliered apples had more than paid for the extra labor of stringing the trellis wires. He hadn't trellised a single tree since.

"It's taking a toll on him," her mother went on. "It's putting an edge on him that wasn't there before. He's getting . . . brittle.''

"Uncle Jack has been yelling and threatening people with mayhem for as long as I can remember." Rachel put her fork down with a tinkle of metal on stoneware. "It's silly to think he really went after Dougan.''

"Yes, it is." Her mother lifted her head, her eyes snapping at last. "I know Jack didn't do it. But it scares me—that a part of me thinks he could have done it, and that a lot of people think he *did*." She gave Rachel a lopsided smile. "Like your friend Jeff, for example.''

Your friend Jeff. Such a chill to those three words. Such distance. "Of course, he knows Uncle Jack didn't do it." Rachel felt her face flaming. "He's known Uncle Jack all his life. We were out *looking* for him when . . ." Rachel broke off, because it hit her suddenly that Uncle Jack had no alibi for a considerable chunk of time that night. "Willis said they did the autopsy," she said hesitantly. "When did . . . ?''

"I don't know." Her mother shook her head, worry lurking like dark shadows in her eyes. "I don't know anything at the moment." She fumbled in her shoulder bag for her wallet, waved Rachel's protest away. "I only know that Jack didn't do it, and that it's going to hurt him if people in town start pointing fingers. A lot more than he's going to let on."

"I have faith in Jeff." Rachel took a last swallow of her tea and got to her feet. "He'll find out who did it."

"I hope so." Her mother dropped a generous tip onto the tabletop. "I really hope so, Rachel. I worry about your uncle." She squeezed her daughter's hand. "And I didn't buy you lunch to bribe you into talking to Jeff. I just needed to talk about it with someone. Thanks for letting me share it with you," she said as they got back into her MG. "I have to be so confident in front of Catherine. And . . . I'm not really."

She pulled out onto the old highway in a flurry of gravel. In spite of her worries, she seemed to relax on the way back to town, swinging the small powerful car through the curves in the old road with casual skill, her head back, dark hair combed by the wind. Rachel admired her mother's petite figure, so different from her own stocky build. At least she had inherited her mother's dark hair—which contained only a few gleaming threads of gray yet.

"I'll call Jeff tonight," Rachel promised as they turned onto the Youth Farm driveway. "He'll fill me in on what's going on."

"Thank you, dear. He must be under a lot of pressure—a chief of police as young as he is."

"Jeff wouldn't . . ."

They both broke off as they caught sight of Catherine's little Ford Ranger pickup, parked next to Rachel's truck. Catherine flung the door open as they pulled into the next space, and stumbled out. Her faded ginger hair had come loose from its knot and haloed her round, slightly sunburned face in uncharacteristic wisps. The top button of her blouse wasn't fastened, and her slacks looked as if they'd been worn for two days at least. It shocked Rachel. No matter how hard they worked at the orchard, her aunt always looked as if she had just finished dressing—not a wrinkle or a hair out of place.

"Deborah! Oh, Deborah." Catherine threw her arms around her sister-in-law. "He did it. That Jeff Price—how could he! I can't believe it!"

"Aunt Catherine? What happened?" Rachel hovered at her aunt's shoulder, her earlier chill returning to grow icicles in the pit of her stomach. "What did Jeff do?"

"That . . . that *boy* actually arrested Jack." Aunt Catherine whirled to stab an accusing finger in Rachel's direction. "He came to the house and *arrested* him!"

"Why?" Rachel felt briefly dizzy, as if the ground had shifted under her feet.

"Are you sure he arrested him, Catherine?" her mother asked gently. "He read him his rights and everything?"

"He took him away." Aunt Catherine crossed her arms, her face stony. "In the police car. Isn't that enough? Right into town, right in the middle of the day, where everyone will see. Everyone will talk. Everyone . . ." She turned her pale eyes on Rachel again, her colorless lashes making her eyes seem to bulge. "He's had it in for your uncle ever since he was a boy. Because we wouldn't let him take you out on dates. I always knew he wasn't to be trusted."

"Catherine, that's enough," her sister-in-law said sharply.

"You know that's not true." Rachel clenched her fists. "You're wrong about this, I know. Jeff doesn't have any reason to arrest Uncle Jack." But everything had suddenly and subtly changed, as if she had stepped across an invisible line and into another universe. In this universe, her uncle could be arrested for murder, and Jeff could get revenge for . . . "No." She shook her head. "Jeff's the most honest person I know. I'll go down there right now." She pushed past her mother and aunt and unlocked her truck door. "I'll find out what's going on. I'll call you." She was babbling, using words to drown the thoughts that clustered in her head like fluttering bats. If he really had been arrested, he'd need bail. A lawyer. Something.

"We'll wait for your call," her mother said, her face full of worry. "Catherine and I will be at the orchard. We'll wait to hear from you. And Rachel," she said and then drew a deep breath. "Don't forget who you are."

"I know who I am, Mom." Rachel gunned the engine and pulled fast out of the Youth Farm driveway.

CHAPTER

6

Jeff wasn't in his office. Lyle Waters was, and he told her he didn't know where Jeff was, and that, yeah, Jeff had brought her uncle down for questioning, but he hadn't been under arrest. He said that they both left. With that, he went back to his labored two-finger typing on the police department's outdated computer with the coffee stains on the keyboard. Rachel let her breath out in a rush and left the office. No help here—getting more than three words at a time out of Lyle took a major effort.

She called the orchard from the pay phone in the hall, just inside the door with its electronic lock. Her aunt answered and thanked her for the meager news. Her tone was uncharacteristically cool. She told Rachel that her mother was outside, and didn't offer to go get her. Wounded, without really being willing to call it that, Rachel hung up. Nothing to do but go back to work.

She and Julio had started working on Blossom's tiny Memorial Park this morning. The size of a small parking lot, a gray granite memorial stone stood in the center of trampled, ancient bark dust, flanked by two wooden benches. The park baked in the summer. A graveled path led from the Main Street sidewalk to the stone. The gravel had nearly vanished into the dust, and when it rained, the path was muddy. A couple of recently planted zonal geraniums—put in by some anonymous mourner, perhaps—drooped in dismay at the cold spring, dropping yellowed leaves on the hard gray soil that surrounded the stone.

Julio was chopping weeds and tough grass from the hardened soil along the sidewalk. He looked up, grinned, and jerked his chin toward the rear of the park as Rachel approached.

Spider chopped fiercely at the soil around the stone. He didn't look up as Rachel cleared her throat.

"Welcome back," she said.

"I went and asked him. I told Mr. Bard that I might as well be working as sitting around playing video games." He looked up finally, gave her a crooked grin, then grimaced at the fractured chunks of hard clay at his feet. "If I'd known you were doin' this, I'd have kept my mouth shut. You got any dynamite?"

"Feet." Julio made stomping motions and nodded, back to his role as mentor here. "No, *no.*" He snatched the grub hoe from Spider's grip. "Like this." He chopped with vigor, digging up huge clumps of packed clay and scattering it across the weedy ground. "See?" He thrust the tool back into Spider's hands.

"Yeah, I see." Spider looked less than thrilled. "Dynamite would work better."

Rachel rolled her eyes. "Well, you beat me back to the job," she said, feeling suddenly better in spite of her worries. "We need to dig this all out and replace it with decent soil, but the mayor says it isn't in the budget," she said briskly. "So we'll just do what we can with amendments and put in plants that can take that kind of condition. Tough, not fancy."

"You can make up for it in the flower bed around the memorial itself." They all turned at the sound of Mayor Ventura's baritone. "I was on my way back from lunch and thought I'd see how you were coming along," he explained as he crossed the small lot. "So what do you want to put in there?"

"How about Oregon grape?" Rachel reached through the

window of her truck for the design she'd drawn up earlier in the week. "It'll take the sun, it's a native, and we can make the soil adequate for it. It makes an attractive hedge, and it'll provide good food for any birds we can lure in here."

"Long as they're not pigeons." Ventura rolled his eyes. "Sure, Oregon grape is fine." He looked over her shoulder as she unrolled the design across the hood of her truck.

"I thought we could put in a couple of trees here, and here. Maybe maple. Between them, they'll shade the benches for most of the day in the summer. In the winter, they'll get full sun. It'll give people a nice place to sit. And this cluster of rhodies and azalea here will screen the walls of the building, and lead the eye to a focal point—the memorial stone. By the way, take a look." She nodded at the windowless west wall of Castle's Dry Cleaning. "That old ad painted on the brick is kind of historic. Maybe you should think about getting someone to restore it."

"You're kidding." Ventura squinted in the bright sun as he eyed the scabby wall. The faded ad was still faintly visible—a sheaf of fat wheat ears against a backdrop of rolling green fields and a distant farm. Ornate black letters trumpeted *Oregon Mills Flour—Best for Bread,* outlined with traces of gilt. "Well, it beats big-city graffiti." He laughed, but his eyes glittered with sudden excitement. "You know, I might bring it up to the Council. It resonates with the theme here—remember our heritage, even as the world changes. Even Bob would approve that one, I bet." A frown shadowed his round face, and he tugged at his ponytail. "Terrible thing—terrible for all of us. You know, I'm going to miss Bob." He shook his head. "He opposed me on just about every major issue that came along. Everybody knew it. So when he came around to my way of thinking—like with this annexation—it really meant something to people."

"So he really did change his mind about voting for the annexation?" Rachel rolled up her design and slipped it into its cardboard tube.

"Yeah, he did. Surprised the heck out of me." The mayor shook his head. "Came into my office a couple of hours before the town meeting. Told me if we all played ostrich, the world

would roll over us like a tide, and too late we'd wake up to
wish we'd kept our heads up and maybe built a few dams.''
Ventura shook his head again. "Pretty eloquent for Bob, I've
got to say. Dunno what got into him, but he had the feel of a
man on a crusade. Damn.'' He looked away. "I hope Jeff finds
the murderer fast.'' His lips tightened. "This is hitting the
town hard—especially right now, when folks are so divided
about our future. We don't need to be suspecting each other.''
He gave her a brief sideways glance.

He meant Uncle Jack. So it really was getting around—that
he might have killed Dougan. "He didn't do it,'' Rachel
snapped.

"I didn't . . . Your uncle, you mean? Of course not.'' But
his eyes looked here and there and not at her. "I see you're
still using the boy from the farm.'' He changed the subject
briskly. "Good for you.'' He hesitated. "Did you by any
chance find my leather jacket lying around when you were
cleaning up yesterday?''

"No.'' Rachel frowned. The mayor wore his buttery-soft
elk-hide jacket everywhere. He joked that it would take a visit
from the President himself to make him don a suit coat instead.
"I didn't see it. Did you lose it?''

"I wore it in the morning, but it turned warm. I remember
reminding myself to take it with me when I left.'' His eyes
flicked back toward Spider again. "I might have hung it on
the side of your truck while we were discussing your plans
for the park. Your . . . uh . . . new employee was admiring it
the other day, when we were discussing the planters. He liked
it a lot.''

Spider again. Rachel stifled a sigh. Even the mayor with his
ponytail and his progressive beliefs . . . "I don't remember
seeing it,'' she said slowly. "I don't see how Spider could
have taken it, if that's what you're suggesting.''

"Of course I'm not suggesting that,'' Ventura said a trifle
too sharply. "I just wanted you to keep an eye out for it,
please. I could have left it somewhere in the building, I suppose.'' He shrugged. "I could have left it on the coatrack. I'm
sure it'll turn up. Who would steal it?''

"I'll keep an eye out for it.'' Rachel replaced her plans in the truck. "But one of us would have noticed it if you'd hung it on the truck." She stressed the "us" just slightly.

The mayor actually blushed faintly. "Just thought I'd ask. I'll bring up that ad at the next Council meeting. By the way—how is your schedule for new clients?" He gave her a tentative smile. "I've been staring out at my backyard and thinking that it's the most boring piece of real estate I ever looked at. My sister had a few things to say about it when she visited. No sense in wasting the talents of a top-notch designer—not when I've got her right here in front of me."

"Well . . . sure." Rachel blinked in surprise. "I could take a look at it. I've got time right now." Actually, the city work was her only project at the moment. Demand for landscaping wasn't too great in the area yet. "When would you like to have me come by?"

"Let's see . . ." Ventura pulled a small personal diary from his pocket and thumbed through it. "I've got a meeting with the Council—about appointing an interim council member—this evening. That's going to be a rough one." He grimaced. "How about tomorrow? If I buy you a take-out lunch from the Homestyle Cafe, could you do it at noon?" He looked anxious. "I'm pretty busy all week."

"Noon is fine." She nodded and grinned. "Make it a lunch from the Bread Box, though. Think about what you want most between now and then, okay?"

"I don't have a clue," he said cheerfully. "Do you know where I live?" He gave her a crooked smile when she nodded. "Yeah, I guess everybody does. See you at noon."

He turned abruptly on his heel and strode briskly down the block toward City Hall.

He had bought a small house on the outskirts of town that had belonged to the Van Orn family—one of Blossom's oldest orchard families. Peter Van Orn had built it for his unmarried sister back in the forties. Mirabella Van Orn had never married, had been fiercely active in town politics. She had ultimately become Blossom's only woman mayor—one of the first women mayors in the country. Her grassroots election sweep had apparently surprised everyone—even Mirabella Van Orn, if the stories were true. She had done a good job.

The small house had been known as the mayor's house ever since. Rachel watched Ventura bound energetically up the steps of City Hall and smiled. She had a feeling his purchase of Mirabella's old residence hadn't been accidental. Acutely aware of the changes confronting the Columbia River Gorge, as tourists, vacation-home owners, and retirees replaced fruit and wheat as the economic mainstay, Phil Ventura had made himself the focal point of both hope and anxiety in the town. He had a good sense of theater, she thought. Tomorrow wasn't going to catch the town by surprise. Not if Phil Ventura had anything to do with it.

The tiller roared to life. Julio began to fight it through the hard soil along the sidewalk. Dust billowed up in tawny clouds, drifting across the sidewalk. Good thing not many people were on the street this time of day, Rachel thought as she put her plans away. Those Oregon grape plants were going to need a lot of help. She looked around to see what Spider was doing. Squatting in front of the granite memorial, he scrubbed vigorously at the base of the stone with a rag, his eyes narrowed with effort. He was cleaning lichen out of the engraved letters of names, she realized as she approached.

"Someone there you know?" She looked over his hunched shoulders.

"Nah. I don't know. Don't you guys ever clean this?" He gouged at a stubborn wad of gray lichen with his thumbnail. "I bet my dad came here. He was crazy, did Mom tell you? He checked 'em all out—all the stones, all the plaques. Everything. That's where he went when he took off." He flicked the bit of lichen away and wiped his hand on his jeans. "He used to take me along, when I was little. We went to San Diego one summer. Mom freaked. It was hot. I went swimming in the ocean. The water was really warm. "

"Was he looking for someone?" Rachel asked softly.

"His father." Spider finished cleaning the last names and looked up. "Back in Saigon, his mother told him that his father was from Oregon. I guess Dad thought maybe he died. 'Cause he never wrote her, or came back for them, like he said he would." He traced the now-clean curves of a J with his fingertip. John Morgan. "He kept looking for his father's name on the stones. He had a picture of him, too. Him and my grandmother, from when they were married, I guess. He said they got married. He'd show the picture all over town— ask people in stores and gas stations and stuff if they knew him. I guess he had a bad time, getting out, getting here.'' Spider picked a last fragment of lichen from beneath his fingernail.

''Mom wouldn't have given that money to that creep if he'd been around. Or maybe she would have. Dad might have believed him, too.'' He shrugged and looked up at her. ''What do you want me to do now?''

He referred to his father's father and his father's mother as if they were not part of his family. Strangers.

The way her aunt had spoken to her.

''You can keep working on these beds.'' Rachel nodded at the neglected flower beds that fronted the slab. The unhappy geraniums struggled with dandelions for space in the narrow strip of dirt. ''Tell me about how your mother lost her money,'' she said, sitting on one corner of the bench.

''She had this friend, like I told you. They played bingo every Thursday. She told Mom that she could double her money in a year. There was this meeting at this lady's house. She invited my mom, so she went.'' He stuck the blade of the shovel into the hard clay, stomped on it hard. The soil crumbled, and he pried up a thick chunk, hard as a brick. ''She sent in five hundred dollars. Everything in the savings account. She got a check for fifty a week later. Then another fifty. Man, she was excited. Fifty a week.'' He pried up another chunk of tan soil. ''Then—no more checks. Her neighbor said just wait. But when my mom called the office number on the letter— the phone was disconnected.''

''Did he have a business name or something?'' Rachel asked thoughtfully. ''Was he representing a company?''

''West Coast Tomorrows.'' Spider leaned on his shovel, glowering at the chunks of clay he'd excavated. ''You got any dynamite?''

''I'll get the wheelbarrow. We're digging it all out. I'll go get the trailer. We're going to start from scratch with this bed—bring in some soil, even if I have to buy it myself.''

Rachel went back to her truck to unload her wheelbarrow, wondering if it was really possible that Dougan had been involved with a fake investment scheme in Portland. It sounded like some sort of pyramid scheme, she thought as she trundled the wheelbarrow over to Spider.

It didn't fit with her impression of Bob Dougan, conservative pillar of the Blossom community.

Julio had reduced the compacted soil along the sidewalk to a finely churned bed. It wasn't as bad as she had feared, Rachel thought with relief. She couldn't afford soil for both the memorial bed and the borders.

"Rachel?" Harvey Glisan waved to her from the sidewalk. "You sure are beautifyin' this city, gal." He nodded at the bright blossoms in the newly refurbished planters along the street. "You think they'll let me have Old Bessie back? I got a job this afternoon and I need her." He nodded at City Hall. "She's still got that crime-scene tape all over. Figured they'd be done with her by now."

"I don't know." Rachel felt herself blushing. "Lyle told me this morning not to touch anything over there. That's why we moved over here. You're right. Seems like they ought to be finished."

"I got to ask somebody." Harvey spat tobacco juice into the street, his expression disgusted. "How's a man gonna do a day's work without a truck, huh?"

"So are you a grandpa?"

"Hey, you bet." A wide grin creased Harvey's weathered face. "Biggest boy you ever saw. Ten pounds one ounce. They had to cut him out, but everything went fine. He's gonna be a linebacker, sure. Already grabs hold of my thumb—not even two days old."

"Ten pounds! Congratulations!" She forced a smile. "That must have been a load to carry."

"You should have seen her." Glisan chuckled. "Tiny as she is, she was as big as a house up front. You got the key, by the way? Or does Jeff have it?"

"Uh . . . I kind of lost it." Rachel swallowed. "I . . . it must have fallen out of my pocket."

"I got a spare. Don't worry 'bout it." He shrugged. Chuckled. "I dropped one into one o' those porta-potties once. Always carry a spare now."

"Harvey, who else has a key?"

"Nobody." He shrugged. "I got two and I gave you one. That's it." Glisan fished his snuff can from his pocket and pinched up a generous wad of brown shreds. "Got too much money tied up in my equipment to pass out a bunch o' keys. Carl needs to use something, he knows where the keys hang, in the house." He placed the snuff behind his lip and nodded as one of Blossom's two black and white patrol cars pulled into the lot behind City Hall. "There's somebody. Got to go get my truck. Talk at you later, gal." He waved one grease-stained hand and strode off across the street.

Rachel closed her eyes. If she hadn't lost the key, it wouldn't matter if Uncle Jack had an alibi or not. But if she hadn't dropped it, the bark dust wouldn't have been dumped. She snapped her eyes open and set her jaw. "Hey, you guys." She jerked her head at her truck as Julio and Spider looked her way. "Come get these sacks of pumice off the truck. You can start working it in, and make sure you mix it thoroughly." She directed this last to Spider, who was still a bit casual when it came to working amendments into soil. "I'll go get the trailer and pick up the mushroom compost." She tossed her work gloves on the truck's seat and started across the street, while the two youths began to unload the truck.

At the foot of the steps, she paused to check on the drippers she had installed in the newly refurbished planters. The tiny valves were working perfectly, metering out water at a steady rate of two gallons per hour, right at the base of the plants where a minimum would be lost to evaporation. If this area continued to grow in population, Rachel thought grimly as she climbed the steps, drip watering would become a lot more important. One local aquifer served Hood River and Blossom, and more wells were beginning to run dry by the end of summer.

Harvey passed her on the way up the steps. He grinned, gave her a thumbs-up, and vanished around the side of the building to where his beloved truck was parked. Rachel crossed the marble tile of the main lobby, her steps echoing from the ornate plaster ceiling. The building had its own scent. She had tried to analyze it—had decided that it was a mix of floor wax, dust, ancient tobacco smoke, and age. Today it made her nervous.

Pushing through the glass-paneled door at the back of the building, she walked down the short hall to doors lettered *Police Department* and pushed through them. Lyle sat at a desk behind the formica counter, facing a lean man in his thirties wearing a suit that flattered his slender build. Both men looked up as Rachel entered, and a brief frown crossed Lyle's face.

"Sorry." Rachel looked around swiftly. "I thought Jeff might be back."

"Not yet." Lyle tapped an impatient finger on his notepad.

"Rachel O'Connor, right?" The man in front of the desk rose to his feet with catlike grace. "I saw your photograph at your aunt and uncle's house, but I don't believe we've actually met. What a shame." He offered her a charming grin and a long-fingered hand. A diamond sparkled in a thick gold band on his right hand. "I'm Ransom Loper, from Seattle. I'm buying that acreage from your uncle. Or I was," he added regretfully. "I guess I won't be, if that annexation plan passes."

"I know you're a busy man, Mr. Loper." Lyle scowled at Rachel. "I really appreciate you taking the time to stop by. I won't keep you long."

She was clearly being dismissed. "Nice to meet you, too, Mr. Loper."

"Let's all hope that we can still do business. I'm looking forward to working with your uncle. It's a prime piece of land from a developer's point of view—good slope, nice view. I've put in some really super condos, over east of Hood River." He smiled again, his eyes on her face. "I'd love to show you the plans. Get your opinion. It's your land, too, right? How about if I buy you lunch sometime? It's going to be a truly innovative development. A gated community. Privacy and security. Exclusive."

He was still holding her hand. Rachel felt her cheeks heating, and extricated her hand, feeling intensely awkward and very aware of Lyle's amusement. "Tell Jeff I dropped by," Rachel said, and fled. "He reminds me of a used-car salesman,'' she said out loud as she trotted down the steps. And she still didn't know what had happened to Uncle Jack.

Her cell phone rang. Stopping in the middle of the bottom step, she pulled the unit from its leather holster on her belt and answered.

"Rachel, he's back home." Her mother's voice sounded thin over the phone. Stressed. "One of the Taxi Sisters brought him. I guess Jeff just wanted to ask him questions. But you know Jack's temper." Her sigh whispered in Rachel's ear. "I don't think it went well."

Great. Rachel closed her eyes briefly. "How about if I come by for dinner?" she suggested. "I could be there by six-thirty. Want me to bring something?"

"I'd love the company." Relief brightened her mother's tone. "I already told Joshua I'd probably spend the night. Both Jack and Catherine are in a state over this. To be honest, it would take a huge load off me if you were here, too. And don't bring anything. Cooking is a good way to distract Catherine."

"I'll be there," Rachel promised, and ended the call. Her uncle's temper could be a serious liability, she thought grimly. This time it might cost him more than a good employee or two.

As she went to get her truck and pick up the compost for the Memorial Park, she wondered again where Jeff was.

They got more accomplished in the Memorial Park that day than Rachel had expected. When she returned with her trailer-load of compost, Spider worked like a demon, hauling the compost to the dug-out beds, then loading the crumbled clay onto the now-empty trailer. Spider worked on the irrigation lines, cursing softly under his breath in Spanish as he hacked trenches through the rocky soil.

Rachel wondered if Spider's energy wasn't his way of saying thanks for keeping him on. She didn't mention the mayor's jacket to them. If they had found it, they would have told her. Julio would have, anyway.

She caught her own mental reservation about Spider as she entered the Blossom Market after work. Smaller than a chain-store supermarket, larger than a mom-and-pop operation, it combined the attributes of both. The walls, wire carts, and aisles mimicked the big chains, but if you really wanted a certain brand of peaches, or a particular type of frozen vege-table, John Carey, the owner and manager, would try to get it for you. A chain store had recently opened on the outskirts of town, but most residents still shopped with John. The day's news came free with the groceries. Joylinn Markham had even started selling her bread at the market.

Rachel picked up one of the battered plastic handbaskets from the stack by the door and headed for the cheese aisle. Cooking might distract Aunt Catherine, but Aunt Catherine's idea of good food ran heavily toward macaroni and cheese, tuna casserole, and green-bean bake. Her mother would silently appreciate a nice selection of appetizers. So would she, Rachel thought as she leaned over the cheese cooler. Havarti was about as exotic a cheese as the Market handled, but she added a round of domestic blue and a round of smoked Edam to her basket, along with some stone-ground wheat crackers and a tin of smoked oysters. These were her passion alone, but, hey, she deserved something for soothing Uncle Jack, she told her nagging conscience. And she hadn't gained a pound in the last month. Green olives completed the decadent assortment. And, of course, she realized that she needed cat food, toilet paper, tomato paste, and flour.

As she headed toward the front, she smiled at the paper decorations strung from the lights. This must be Hawaii Week. John was really into theme weeks—Cinco de Mayo featured bright pinatas and a special on refried beans and chili. Rodeo Week featured cutouts of bull-riders and broncs, along with a sale on barbecue sauce. Columbus Day Week meant spaghetti sauce and crepe streamers. Today, pastel crepe paper streamers draped the overhead fluorescent, dangling honeycomb paper pineapples and colorful cutouts of bananas and orchids with the Dole company logo branded on each. Mollie, John's sister, wore a green raffia grass skirt and a half dozen paper leis as she operated the cash register. Her son Brad, stocking canned veggies on aisle three, wore a single strand of white shells around his neck and a sulky expression.

"Where's your grass skirt?" Rachel couldn't resist asking as she lugged her goodies frontward.

"Karen wanted me to wear a cloth one," he said morosely. "It was brown, with white flowers on it." He slammed two cans of extra-fancy peas into place on the shelf.

"Hawaiian warriors wore skirts," Rachel remarked blandly. "I guess they were pretty fierce."

Her only response was a growl and the metallic thunk of can hitting can. Hard. More dented goods for the half-price bin, if he wasn't careful. Smothering a grin, she hurried on up the aisle, gratefully depositing her now-heavy basket on the checkout conveyor.

"Why didn't you get a cart, honey?" Mollie shoved her mass of permed blond curls back from her weathered face. Gray roots showed beneath the yellow strands. Time for another trip to the Hood River beauty parlor she frequented, Rachel thought. Mollie had quit going to Carol Peters's Blossom Beauty Bar ever since Carol had accused Mollie's ancient one-eyed heeler-cross of fathering a litter of pups on her papered Lhasa apso bitch.

"I heard about your uncle." Mollie tossed her head as she slid the cheeses and grocery items over the scanner. "You know they've got it in for him. You just know it. We ought to go down there with signs. Make 'em back down. Demand a recall and run that big-city man right out of town."

"Who's got it in for whom?" Rachel blinked. "What are you talking about?"

"It's who's got it in for *who*." Another blond head-toss. "I know my grammar, thank you. I used to write for the *Columbia Republic Youth*, back when it was still published. "That . . . *mayor* of ours is who I mean. And his handpicked chief of police, too. Now I know that Price grew up here, but it wasn't like they ever really *belonged*. His mother came from I don't know where—back east or something. She sure kept to herself. Never even joined a church or helped with the Blossom Festival—and I asked her, because I ran it four years running. That was back when you were a kid, of course. But face it"—Mollie snatched a plastic sack from the roll beneath the counter—"they're out to stop anyone who gets in their way. Like your uncle, with his petition to stop all this crazy annexation."

"In . . . in their way?" Rachel said faintly. She couldn't decide whether to laugh or get angry. "What are you talking about?"

"Them tryin' to pin that murder on your uncle." Mollie dumped the cheeses into a plastic sack, tossed the cans on top of them, added the toilet paper. "The mayor and his Portland buddies want to own Blossom, like they own Hood River.

Drive all us honest farming folk out of business, so they can buy our land cheap, put up a bunch of fancy restaurants and condominiums, and sell 'em to rich Portlanders for vacation homes. That's why he appointed a kid to be his police chief. Yuk! Do you really eat these?" She dropped the tin of oysters into the sack with two fingers, as if it was dirty laundry.

Rachel drew a deep breath, then clamped her jaws together and bit her lip until it hurt. "Oh, those oysters are pretty good. That's twenty-seven ninety-five?" she chirped in a strangled falsetto. "I have the exact change." Shoving a wad of bills and coins at Mollie, she fled the store.

"Whoa, girl!" Joylinn Markham grabbed her by the elbow as they nearly collided in the doorway. "What happened to you?" She pulled Rachel around to face her, out of the way of the trickle of after-work shoppers exiting with six packs of beer and gallons of milk. "You look like you're about to burst into tears."

"Or hit someone." Rachel shrugged off Joylinn's hand, marched over to her truck, and dumped the plastic sack into the bed. The cans clanged like off-key bells against the metal. "Do you know what Mollie just said?"

"Let me guess." Joylinn sighed and leaned against the fender beside her. "That Jeff and our mayor are trying to frame your uncle."

"Oh, Lordy." Rachel buried her face in her hands. "Is this all over town?"

"I hope not. But one of my regulars was spouting it in the Bread Box today. And she's thick with Mollie—always buys a cinnamon roll and mocha to take back to her, for her break— so I guessed."

"I mean . . . that's so crazy! How could anyone . . ."

"This is Blossom, honey." Joylinn gave her a crooked smile. "We don't have any more crazy theories than the rest of the country, maybe. But we get to share them in this size town."

"Jeff!" Rachel's eyes widened. "What if he's heard this?"

"Well, he grew up here. He knows how folks talk."

"I'm not sure about that." Rachel remembered Mollie's verdict on how they hadn't really belonged.

There was a grain of truth to that pronouncement. His mother *had* kept to herself, and Jeff had always been reserved—almost an outsider in a town where you had to work at being an outsider. He hadn't been in 4-H, belonged to the Church Youth Club, or even showed up for the dances at the high school. "He brought Uncle Jack in for questioning, but he's not in the office now," she said in a small voice. "Aunt Catherine is pretty upset."

"I'll bet she is. Honey, are you in a rush?" Joylinn touched her arm lightly.

"Not really." Rachel hefted the sack in her hand. "I'm supposed to be out at the orchard for dinner later."

"Why don't you walk back home with me? I've got a nice bottle of chardonnay in the fridge. I think we could both use a glass."

"Sounds good to me." Rachel put her groceries on the front seat of her truck, then turned a questioning glance on Joylinn. "Weren't you on your way into the store?"

"I just stopped by because I saw your truck." Joylinn smiled. "I wanted to open that bottle of wine. You looked like a perfect excuse."

Rachel laughed as they crossed the small lot and headed down the street toward the river. "So I need a glass of wine because Jeff suspects Uncle Jack of murder. Why do you need one? Long day at the restaurant?"

"Oh, today is just rent day." Joylinn made a face. "I'm still not quite making it, and when I write that check, I can't help wondering if I'm not crazy for opening here, and not in Hood River. Not that I could have afforded a decent location there. . . ."

"Oh, Joylinn, you're doing so well!" Rachel stopped short and turned to face her friend. "I mean . . . you are, aren't you? Seems like every time I go in there, there's a ton of people."

"More than there used to be, yes." Joylinn pushed her hair back from her face. "I'm not really complaining. It takes a long time to really establish a restaurant. I knew that when I started. Don't start worrying about me yet, okay?" She shaded her eyes as they reached the end of the sidewalk, her eyes on the matte gray surface of the wide Columbia. "I'll make it.

Sometimes it just seems like a lot of work.'' Beyond them, the street ran on for a half block, flanked by an abandoned warehouse, the sheets of plywood that covered its windows reflected in a huge puddle in the cracked and buckled street. ''I'd rather work hard for myself than work less for someone else,'' Joylinn went on with determination. She skipped across a narrow place in the puddle. ''I found a great shortcut down to the boat. Except when it's really wet. Then you need a small boat.'' She led Rachel around the side of the warehouse. Damaged fruit boxes had been stacked in the muddy lot behind the warehouse, and a couple of cats darted away to disappear between the stacks as they walked past. New green shoots decorated the arching canes of blackberries that had taken over much of the lot. In a matter of weeks, the boxes would vanish beneath a mound of blackberry leaves.

''Last summer, I picked enough berries back here to make a dozen pints of jam.'' Joylinn nodded at the sprawling berries. ''I have to keep pruning them back, though, or they grow over the path.'' She turned into a narrow slot between the berries and a scrubby belt of Scotch broom and young hawthorn. The rocky path led down to the riverbank at an angle. A couple of crows lifted from the bank where they had been devouring the remains of a fish, squawking in annoyance at the intruders.

''There. See?'' Joylinn gestured as a small plank dock came into sight. ''I didn't lose us in the mud after all.''

Two small houseboats were tied to relatively new pilings along the rickety dock. A long flight of wooden stairs led up the bank to a gravel driveway at the top. Joylinn had found the houseboat for rent two years ago and had moved in with delight. She had spent the first year sleeping in the Bread Box's office. There hadn't been enough money for two rents, she had explained to Rachel, but had declined to share Rachel's cramped apartment.

''Peter would never share his sofa,'' she had said.

Joylinn hopped lightly down onto the houseboat's deck. Rachel climbed cautiously after her. The sensation of movement beneath her feet always felt strange for a few minutes. Cedarplank siding covered the small, square structure. It had a new metal roof painted in soft blue, and planters all along the rail.

Joylinn had scrubbed years of gray weather from the planks and had painted the boxes and rail in white and a blue that nearly matched the roof. Blue curtains hung in the window— made out of sheets, Rachel knew, but with the bits of lace trim Joylinn had added, they looked fresh out of the store.

"I really love this place." Rachel followed Joylinn through the door, slipping her shoes off before stepping onto the braided oval rug that covered the painted plank floor. "It's so cozy."

"Fabric and paint." Joylinn took off her sweater and tossed it onto the small love seat that flanked the woodstove on its brick hearth, along with a brightly upholstered chair. "Cheap interior decoration."

"But you can sew." Rachel examined the neatly piped slip-covers with envy. Color filled the large single room, lending the space a cheerful spring feel. Sprays of alstromeria and salal stood on the small table in a cut-glass vase that Joylinn had found at a garage sale. A daybed piled with pillows served as extra seating and became Joylinn's bed at night. "This place was such a dump." Rachel sank onto the sofa with a sigh. "You've done so much with it."

"Tell you what—you do the planters at the bakery for me, and I'll be more than happy to slipcover anything you want." Joylinn returned from the small kitchen area in the corner with a dewy bottle in one hand and two wineglasses in the other. "They looked like refugees from the dust bowl last summer."

"You need to put in drip watering." Rachel leaned forward to take the glass of pale wine that Joylinn handed her. "That's the real secret of gorgeous planters. That and grooming. You have to deadhead and prune just about every day."

"Free cinnamon rolls for life?" Joylinn winked as she curled up in the chair. "In return for keeping them up? You know I have a black thumb. Except for herbs." She nodded at the planters on the houseboat deck. She grew most of the herbs she used at the Bread Box in them.

"You know, that's a tempting offer." Rachel smiled. "I think I'm persuaded."

"It's a deal." Joylinn leaned forward to clink glasses with

Rachel. "Until they run me out of town along with the mayor."

"Are you really catching some of this fallout, too?" Rachel sipped her wine and rolled her eyes in approval. "You've got to be kidding."

"Well, I voted for the annexation." Joylinn slipped off her shoes and stretched her long legs out in front of her, frowning critically at her stockinged feet. "I didn't win too many popularity points doing that, let me tell you." She made a face at her feet and wiggled her toes. "It's only our city building codes that are keeping Blossom from turning into a neon pit stop on the way to Hood River. But you'd think we were asking folks to give away their land! And some of them are the same ones who complain the loudest about development like the complex where I opened the Bread Box. I guess it's ugly if somebody else made money off of it. Go figure."

"I think you've just described Uncle Jack." Rachel twirled her glass, watching the wine swirl.

"Oh, yes. I know your uncle's politics quite well, thank you." Joylinn laughed and reached for the bottle, shaking back unruly ginger curls. "He was a member of the Coffee Club." She tipped more wine into her glass, then raised her eyebrows at Rachel.

"No, thanks. I'd hate to have Jeff pull me over for a DUI. What Coffee Club did Uncle Jack belong to?"

"I just call it that." Joylinn set the bottle back onto the low table. "He and a few other folks used to get together every morning and argue over weather, prices, politics, whatever. It was good theater. Want something to eat?" She bounced to her feet and headed for the kitchen corner. "I've got some cheese crackers. Kind of an experiment."

"Have you ever known me to turn down food?" Rachel frowned and sat up straight. "Didn't Bob Dougan come into the Bread Box a lot? Was he a member of the club?"

"He sure was." Joylinn leaned over the formica counter that divided the tiny kitchen from the rest of the room. "He and Jack were usually on the same side, too. Which makes it even more weird that Jeff—anyone—would suspect your uncle of killing him."

"I can't believe Jeff really suspects him." Rachel looked away. "Did Dougan ever talk about investing? Like in stock?"

"Oh, sure." Joylinn carried in a blue earthenware plate piled with crispy brown rounds of cracker. "He talked about it all the time. You could call it boasting, I guess. He was always telling people about his latest success—how he'd made a bundle by turning over some high-tech stock just before it fell—that sort of thing. He was always urging your uncle and the rest of us to invest—told us there was big money to be made in the stock market, especially now that you could invest on the Internet and not have to pay big broker fees." She set the plate on the table, her expression suddenly thoughtful. "I never thought about it much, but he never gave any real tips. People would ask him to recommend something, and he was always kind of evasive. He'd say everyone had to play the market their own way. I wonder if he was just making up stories to impress us." She eyed Rachel curiously. "Was he? Does it have something to do with his murder? You have that look in your eye. . . ."

"I don't know." Rachel finished the last swallow of wine in her glass. "That kid from the Youth Farm who's working for me—Spider—he thought he recognized Dougan. He thought he was the man who cheated his mother out of some money in a phony stock scheme—some kind of pyramid thing. I didn't believe it at first . . . but now I wonder."

"Bob Dougan?" Joylinn's eyebrows rose. "*Our* Bob Dougan? The man who donated the money for the new Little League uniforms? Mr. Community himself?"

"I know." Rachel helped herself to one of the thin, crisp crackers. Sesame seeds coated the top. "Bob Dougan walked on water. As I said, I didn't believe it either. I still don't, really." She took a bite. "Wow," she said with her mouth full. "These are great. Start selling them, please."

"They take too much time, alas." Joylinn nibbled at one critically.

Rachel helped herself to more of the crisp, cheesy rounds. "Who else is part of this coffee group, do you remember?"

"Oh, it varies a lot." Joylinn frowned. "Let's see . . . Roberta Guarnieri, and sometimes Earlene—"

"The Taxi Sisters?"

"You bet." Joylinn laughed. "They're dyed-in-the-wool libertarians, and they love to argue. They could always get a rise out of somebody. Then there was Hank West, from the bank, Carol Edwaller, Andy Ferrel—he was the one who did most of the arguing with Roberta and Earlene—and sometimes that developer guy. The one who bought your uncle's land—what's his name?"

"Loper." Rachel blinked in surprise. "I just met him today."

"He's the only outsider. If I think of anyone else, or hear anything, I'll let you know." Joylinn shook her head. "I still don't believe it, about Dougan, though."

"There's probably nothing to the story, but you never know." Rachel glanced at her watch. "Thanks for keeping your ears open. And now I'd better run." She grimaced. "I think Mom needs some moral support up at the orchard."

"I wondered if she was staying out there. I saw her husband downtown this afternoon. He looked a little lost."

"Poor Joshua." Rachel carried her glass into the kitchen. "He has to keep his mouth shut around Uncle Jack as it is—they're poles apart politically. I think he's staying away from the family until this all blows over."

"Good luck with Jeff." Joylinn touched Rachel's shoulder as she ushered her out to the dock. "If you need to unload later, call me. Anytime, okay?"

"I will." Rachel gave her friend a grateful smile. "If Uncle Jack is half as upset as Mom made it sound—I may need to."

"After this settles down, let's take some food and a bottle of wine and go have a picnic," Joylinn called after her. "Just the two of us. One of these nice spring days."

"It's a date." Rachel turned to wave. "And thanks for the wine." A little regretfully, she climbed the steps to the gravel drive up on the bank, deciding not to opt for the muddy shortcut. Since she had started her landscaping business and Joylinn had opened the Bread Box, they had spent very little time together outside of the bakery. Once upon a time they had regularly gone into Hood River together or clear into Portland to shop, eat lunch out, and take in a movie. She missed Joylinn's clearheaded pragmatism and easygoing tolerance.

Resolving to take more time for her friends, Rachel walked the three blocks to the market, where she had left her truck. She would be a little late for dinner. They ate early at the orchard.

The interlude had been worth it, she thought as she started the engine. She felt a lot more relaxed than she had after her interchange with Mollie. And she had found out that Bob Dougan boasted about his stock market earnings.

Interesting, that.

She hoped Joylinn was right that Jeff could handle the rumor. Backing out of the lot, Rachel took the small county road that wound along the side of the Gorge between orderly rows of apple and cherry trees. The cherries would bloom soon, but the apple buds were still tightly closed on the leafless branches. It would be cold again tonight. Not frost-cold but chilly. No blossoms or young fruit to worry about yet, at least. In spite of her worries, the neat ranks of trees filled her with a sense of peace and pleasure. Those trees represented thousands of long hours of labor and love, worry and nurturing, repair in the wake of ice storms and windstorms, hope and triumph when an experimental variety did well.

Our lives here are recorded in the trunks and limbs of fruit trees, Rachel thought, and felt unexpectedly full and content.

CHAPTER
8

She slowed as she neared the crest of the slope. The driveway to the orchard was marked by two pillars built by her grandfather of fieldstones, hauled from the newly cleared land on a wooden sledge, drawn by a team of draft horses. *O'Connor Family Orchards* glowed in freshly painted red letters on the wooden signboard next to the right-hand pillar. Her father had made that sign after a windstorm damaged the original. Her mother had refinished it this past summer. Uneasiness banished her earlier sense of peace as she drove slowly up the lane. Nothing was really wrong, she told herself. Jeff didn't really suspect her uncle, and after a while the talk would fade away, as it always did.

She hadn't managed to banish the uneasy knot in her stomach by the time she reached the turnaround in front of the house, though.

The front door opened as she parked in the wide graveled circle. Her mother came out on the porch. Elbows propped on the rail, she watched Rachel climb out of the truck and slam the door. "Sweetheart," she began, but before she could get out another word, the door burst open behind her.

"Hey, she's here. The gardener!" Uncle Jack emerged onto the porch, waving gaily as if she was a featured guest at a family gathering. "Come on in. You're just in time for a quick drink before supper. Bet you need one after planting petunias all day," he said jovially as she climbed the porch steps. "We finished the spraying yesterday. Catherine's fixing a bang-up spread, so you better be hungry."

Up close, the golden flood of evening light couldn't hide the flush on his weathered face or the tight lines at the corners of his mouth. Rachel smelled alcohol on his breath and suppressed a sigh. His temper was bad enough when he was cold sober. "Hi, Uncle Jack." She kissed him on the cheek. "I hear they questioned you about Dougan's murder, too."

"What?" Uncle Jack, arms around her in his usual bear hug, narrowed his eyes and leaned back. "What's this? That snotty kid's after you, too? Why, I'll . . ."

"Jeff's questioning everybody who had anything to do with anything," Rachel said, letting the small lie stand. "I lost the key to Harvey's dump truck, so he talked to me. He even talked to Harvey."

"Stupid young punk. He oughta know you and Harvey got nothing to do with it."

"He's just being thorough, Uncle Jack. How are you doing?" She put her arm around her mother and gave her a cheerful hug. "I was over at Joylinn's houseboat, just before I came here. You know, she's still not quite breaking even. I can't believe it—with all her business."

"I think she mostly sells coffee and rolls." Her mother picked up the cue gratefully. Joylinn was a safe topic of conversation, at least. "She probably needs more regular customers for her lunches," her mother went on. "I've been in there at noontime. She doesn't have nearly the business that the Homestyle Cafe does."

"Not yet, but she will." Rachel strolled on into the living room with her mother and uncle, pretending not to notice his slightly uneven steps.

But Uncle Jack wasn't about to let the conversation get away from him that easily. "Why the hell would that young punk think Harvey might have somethin' to do with the killing? Is he stupid?" Her uncle's voice was rising. "Why would Harvey kill Bob? I tell you, that boy . . ."

"He doesn't think Harvey killed anyone." This tack wasn't working. "He was at the hospital watching his granddaughter be born." Still trying for a casual mood, Rachel strolled across the room to rummage among the bottles spread out on the cherrywood sideboard, next to the front window. Bottles of tonic water flanked a plate that held a quartered lime. A green bottle of Tanquerey gin stood with a plastic ice bucket in a puddle of meltwater on one of Aunt Catherine's plastic serving trays. Someone had drawn initials on the slick orange surface of the tray. D.O.M. Deborah O'Connor Meier. Rachel glanced at her mother, but she was absorbed in rearranging the silk flowers that Aunt Catherine kept on a side table. Rachel reached for a glass and one of the bottles of tonic.

"I'll do that, m'girl." Her uncle appeared at her side. "I'm still bartender in my own home." He took the glass from her hand and scooped ice into it. "You had a hard day working. Me, I just got to sit around and answer questions from a kid cop who used to eat at my table. Good thing the sprayin' was done, or I'd really have been sore."

Rachel took the glass he handed her, tasted it, and managed not to grimace. Drink this down on top of Joylinn's wine and an early lunch and she'd end up on the floor for sure.

"Here's to the first O'Connor to get arrested in the family." Uncle Jack lifted a fresh new drink into the air. "A new milestone in the family history!"

"You didn't get arrested, Jack, and you know it." Rachel's mother abandoned the fake flowers. "And you've had more than your share of gin. I'll just drink this one, thank you." She lifted the glass from his hand and took a pointed sip of it.

For a moment Jack glared down at her, and Rachel held her breath, waiting for her uncle's temper to explode. Then he shrugged, laughed his booming laugh, and put his arm around Rachel's mother. "Will lucked out when he met you, Debbie." He gave her a resounding kiss on the cheek and let her go. "And I've never seen you drink more than one drink in an evening in your life. Don't think you're foolin' me." He grinned at her. "Better watch yourself tonight, Cat?" He turned to the kitchen, cheerful again, his mercurial temper shifting like an unpredictable fall wind. "Since I can't drink, can I eat? How's dinner comin'?"

Rachel looked at her mother, who rolled her eyes and shook her head swiftly. All during her childhood, she'd seen her mother deftly shift Uncle Jack's impending rages into unexpected cheer. It never failed to amaze her—and she still didn't know how her mother did it. She hid a smile as her mother put a finger to her lips, then poured half of the unwanted drink into her aunt's ancient and dusty dracaena plant.

Maybe the evening would go all right after all.

They sat down to one of Catherine's classic dinners—meat loaf, with a casserole of frozen green beans from last summer's garden, baked with canned mushroom soup and topped with crushed potato chips, mashed potatoes, rolls, and squares of lemon Jell-O with canned cherries from the orchard embedded in it and topped with a mayonnaise dressing. A fat and calorie nightmare, Rachel thought wryly, but the aromas rising from the dishes swept her instantly back into childhood, to the endless summer days when she chased after her older cousins, or rambled beneath the whispering canopy of leaves—or spent the long day picking up drop apples for cider, or pitting cherries for canning.

She forked up the overcooked green beans, cut into the thick slab of meat loaf seasoned with catsup and Worcestershire sauce, and found it all unexpectedly wonderful, calories be damned.

Her mother and Catherine began to clear the table. Rachel started to help, but subsided into her chair at her mother's brisk head-shake. Clearly it was her turn to distract Uncle Jack.

"I met Ransom Loper today," she ventured, hoping this was a good topic. "He seems real excited about the development he's putting up on the old orchard. It sounded nice."

"Yeah. He makes everything sound great, doesn't he? But he's stallin' on closing the deal." Her uncle's face clouded, and he picked at a crumb from his roll on the tablecloth. "He figures Ventura's gonna railroad one of these city liberals onto the Council, now that Bob's gone, and they'll pass that bloody annexation bill after all." He brushed the crumbled bit of roll away with such violence that his water glass rocked precariously. "Why the hell do you think Bob got killed, huh? They'll pick us all off, one by one."

"Oh, come on, Uncle Jack." Rachel kept her voice light, kicking herself for her stupidity. "Nobody killed Dougan to get him off the Council. I heard he was going to vote *for* the annexation, not against."

"He might've said so, but he wouldn't do it." Uncle Jack slapped the table with a dismissive palm. "You spend your life taking care of your land—working it, sweating for it— you're not gonna let some city official tell you what you can and can't do with it. No." He slapped the table again, more sulky than angry. "Bob would never have sold us out. Not his neighbors. His friends. You're not still seein' that punk, are you?"

"What?" Rachel blinked at him, feeling that she'd missed a line. "Seeing who? You mean Jeff?"

Uncle Jack nodded once, his eyes on her face.

Trapped by his stare—too late to look away—Rachel stammered. "We . . . Sure, we're still friends." She was blushing, furious at herself for doing so. From the corner of her eye, she caught her mother's resigned expression.

"Dessert!" she announced loudly and with forced cheer. "Chocolate brownies. With walnuts."

"So it doesn't matter to you?" Uncle Jack leaned forward across the table, as if he and Rachel were the sole inhabitants of the planet. "It doesn't matter to you that he's tryin' to put me in prison on a murder charge? You just go on bein' friends?"

"I . . . He's not . . ." Wan words. In an instant, Rachel had been transported back a decade or more, to those terrible moments when Uncle Jack had leaned across the dinner table, his eyes pinning herself or one of her cousins, firing out the accusation, the demand for confession, admission, or repentance. They had all dreaded those moments—all the kids. *It's like he strips you down to your shorts,* her cousin Jerry had once said. *Then he yanks those off you, too.* "He's just doing his job," she said. Lamely.

"You see that sign on the gate, out at the road?" Uncle Jack's face had turned to cold stone. "O'Connor *Family* Orchards. That means it's your business, too. Somebody goes after one, they go after the *family*. And the *family* deals with it. It's your land, too, girl. They're after it.''

''Nobody's after your land.''

''That so?'' Uncle Jack rose slowly from the table, leaning on his palms, breathing hard, as if he'd been running. ''Are you part of this family or not? I'm waiting for your answer.''

Rachel felt the color draining from her face, refused to acknowledge her mother's urgent look. She rose, too, trying to catch her breath. ''Uncle Jack, I know you didn't kill Bob Dougan.'' Her voice wavered, in spite of herself. ''Jeff knows it, too. He's doing his job, that's all. He's got to do a good job, even if it means asking you questions.''

''That's your choice, then?'' Contempt blazed in her uncle's eyes. ''You're takin' his side? Blood doesn't mean nothin' to you?''

''*There is no side!* No one's after you or your land.''

''*My* land? Okay. My land, then.''

''Stop it! Uncle Jack, this is crazy.'' Rachel struggled to speak calmly, but her chest was tight, and tears pressed against her eyelids, scalding hot. Her mother stood frozen in the kitchen doorway, her expression tight and closed. ''You're blowing all this out of proportion,'' Rachel said desperately. ''You're making—''

''You're not part of this family—fine. Get out.''

''Jack!'' Rachel's mother stepped forward. ''Stop this, right now.''

''You're drunk,'' Rachel said. She didn't speak loudly, but the words clapped like thunder. Instant silence gripped the room, so complete that Rachel could hear the tick of the grandfather clock at the end of the hall. With a choked sound, she turned her back on them all and fled, pushed the heavy front door open, leaving it standing wide as she pounded down the steps and across the gravel to her truck.

It seemed to take forever to fumble the key into the ignition, out in the driveway. She sweated, waiting for her uncle to come roaring out onto the porch, waiting for her mother to come out and tell her she had to go back in and apologize. ''Never,'' she whispered through gritted teeth. ''It was the truth." But the front porch remained empty, the wide planks warmed by the yellow glow of the bug light beside the door. The key turned, the engine roared. As Rachel wheeled the truck around on the gravel, the front door closed gently.

She didn't cry. All the way home she didn't cry, although tears stung her throat, and her anger at her uncle surged and waned like stormy waves pounding a beach. He was drunk. She was tired of everyone indulging his temper and his drinking.

He was under a huge amount of stress. Her mother had said that selling that land felt like failure. . . .

Fleeing the seesaw arguments in her head, she parked in the gravel space next to Mrs. Frey's rose garden and took the steps to her apartment two at a time. Peter was waiting for her, but as she charged up the stairs, he darted out of her way, ears flat to his skull. "It's all right," she said with a gasp, trying to catch her breath. "I'm just upset." He streaked past her as she opened the door, leaping onto his perch on the sofa back, where he glared at her briefly before beginning to wash himself vigorously.

Rachel crossed the apartment, feeling like a stranger in the familiar space. No messages on her answering machine. The steady glow of the light stabbed her. She and Jeff talked every day. Usually several times. With a quick glance at the clock— it wasn't *that* late—she picked up the phone and dialed, needing to hear his voice right now.

"Hello?" He answered on the first ring, and his voice sounded brusque. Tense.

"It's me." Rachel waited, the heartbeats of passing silence chilling her. "Rachel," she added.

"Hi." He sounded cool. "What's up?"

The whole awful evening crashed in on her in an instant— her argument with her uncle—the sense that maybe, just maybe, she had fractured something that could never be repaired. . . . "What's up?" Her voice squeaked. "I was . . . I was worried. I haven't heard from you all day."

"I was busy." His inflection didn't change. "Actually, I was just on my way to bed."

Stunned, feeling as if he had just reached through the phone

Mary Freeman

to slap her face, Rachel stared at the ivory-colored instrument in her hand, wondering numbly if she had indeed wandered into another universe. "Fine." She tried to swallow the bitter tide of fury in her throat. "Fine. You're busy. And I wouldn't want to keep you from going to bed. Good night." She slammed down the phone and stomped into the kitchen. "Come on, Peter." She forced a cheerful note into her voice. "I'm done wasting our time. I'll feed you."

Peter sidled into the tiny kitchen alcove, giving her a very feline and very skeptical stare as she opened the can of cat food. But he pounced on it with his usual enthusiasm, devouring every crumb, and then retreated to his sofa to polish his whiskers. Rachel rinsed the plate, put it in the dishwasher, and went into the bathroom to wash her face and brush her teeth. She ran the water loudly, telling herself she wasn't going to answer the phone tonight, no matter what. Let the machine catch it.

But the phone didn't ring.

It wasn't until she had climbed into bed and turned off the light that she burst into tears. Finally.

CHAPTER
9

The phone rang as Rachel was leaving the next morning. She grabbed it, telling herself she didn't want it to be Jeff, that she was merely hoping it was a new client.

It was, sort of. A woman asked her if she did lawn mowing, and spraying for weeds. Rachel told her politely that, no, she didn't, but she knew of someone who did. She gave her Julio's number.

The pang of disappointment as she hung up the phone couldn't quite be dismissed as heartburn. "Hey, *I* never said anything to make him mad, cat." Hands on hips, she regarded Peter, who blinked back from his sprawl on the sofa back. "And it's time for you to go out, boyo."

Peter yawned, stretched languidly, and hopped down. He stalked past her, tail in the air. Laughing at her.

"Remember who feeds you," Rachel threatened as she locked the door behind her.

She picked up Julio and, on the way into town, asked him if he'd noticed whether the mayor had his jacket with him when he had stopped by the truck on the day of Spider's upset with Dougan.

"I do not remember," Julio said with careful precision. "He has lost it?"

"Yes." She nodded. "I don't remember either."

He frowned pensively through the windshield, not saying anything more until they reached the center of town. "Senorita?" he spoke up at last. "You can get a picture for me? Of the jacket?"

"I don't know." Rachel glanced at him. "I could ask him for one. Why?"

Julio glanced away, then looked her squarely in the face. "There are some . . . little markets. For buying clothes. Chickens. Vegetables. Tools, TVs, radios." He shrugged. "Nothing new, you know? All old."

"Flea markets?"

"Some of the things that they sell there . . ." He paused, looked briefly away, then met her eyes again. "I think perhaps . . . one or two, they are . . ." He made a gesture with one hand.

"Stolen?" Rachel prodded gently.

"Perhaps." He looked unhappy. "I think . . . I could go there, here. I look for a jacket to buy, you know? If I see the missing one . . . I could buy it."

And perhaps some of those "flea markets" were run by friends of his, who would get in trouble if the mayor's stolen jacket turned up there. "I'll see if I can find a picture." Rachel nodded as she pulled over to the curb at the tiny park. "And I'll give you some cash. If you see the jacket, buy it. Nobody has to know where it came from."

"*Gracias*, Senorita Boss." Julio grinned and shoved the door open. "I will look."

The van belonging to the Youth Farm pulled up then, and Spider climbed down. Rachel put the two youths to work setting plants. The drip tubing was already in place, but during the night, she had decided that the flow rate she'd planned wasn't enough for the shrubs, considering the reflected heat that the brick wall behind them would generate. She would have to run to the hardware store for more drippers, because of course she was out of the flow rate she wanted. Then she would have to spend a wasted couple of hours replacing the insufficient drippers with the new ones. One step forward, one backward. . . .

Feeling irritable and incompetent, she stalked into Roth Glover's Ace Hardware store. Roth himself was at the register, elbows on the counter in the narrow space between displays of screwdrivers, rat poison, key rings, and breath mints, reading a newspaper. He looked up as she entered, ran a hand over his thinning hair. "Mornin'." He gave her a broad smile. "What can I get for you, lady?"

She gave him her order, hoping that he had them in stock. And he did. He did a good job of keeping the supplies she needed most often in stock. As he rummaged in the back room for her drippers, she leaned on the counter to scan Blossom's weekly newspaper, the *Blossom Bee*. Beneath the paper's logo of a tough-looking honeybee with its stinger showing, black type proclaimed: Police Focus on Local Orchard Owner in Slaying of Blossom Councilman.

Glover emerged with a box of drippers as Rachel groaned. "Hallie never mentions any names," he said, glancing down at the offending article as he set the box on the counter. "Waste of time to go sniffing after Jack. He never killed nobody." He shook his head and peered over his narrow reading glasses. "You're friends with him—you talk to that boy about this?"

Nobody needed to mention names. "No." Rachel pretended to study the label on the box. "Haven't seen Jeff. But I don't think he really suspects Uncle Jack."

"Lot of folks think the mayor's behind it—you know, kind of setting Price after him." Glover nodded, light glinting on the glossy scalp that showed through the carefully brushed strands of graying hair. "Funny, though. You know, Bob acted kind of strange when I saw him that afternoon—that day I caught Melanie with the CD player under her jacket." He shook his head, clucked disapprovingly. "Kid had enough to buy it in her pocket. Why do kids do that—steal? My dad woulda tanned the hide off my butt if I'd ever done that."

"How was Bob strange?" Rachel fished her wallet from her pocket.

"Well, I knew he'd be mad as a scalded hog when I called him. But you know, he wasn't so much mad as . . . well, odd." Glover shrugged and rang up her purchase. "Didn't say nothin' to Melanie except to go get in the car—just kind of sad-like. Then he said something about setting examples, and how we can't ask our kids to be any better than us." Glover shook his head as he handed Rachel her change. "Dunno what he was talkin' about. Bob Dougan's set about as fine an example around here as anyone. Better, maybe."

"Did you tell this to Jeff?" Rachel pocketed her change and picked up her drippers, trying to hide a twinge of excitement.

"Well, you know, he never really asked me much." Glover looked away and cleared his throat. "Except where I was that evenin'. Which was home with the wife, watching TV, like we always do."

"Maybe you should tell him. Maybe it's important."

"Yeah, I suppose I should." Glover folded up the *Bee*. "Guess I will."

"Roth?" Rachel paused in the doorway. "Did Dougan ever talk about investing?"

"Like in stocks?" Glover looked surprised, scratched his head, then took his hand away quickly, as if he was trying to break a habit. "Not that I recall. I don't know nothing about the stock market. Got my savings in an IRA at the bank. Nice and safe. That's as close as I get to the stock market."

"Well, thanks." Rachel waved and hurried back to her truck. She tossed the drippers onto the front seat, then closed the door with determination and marched down the block to the pay phone on the corner.

Of course Lyle Waters answered. "I need to talk to Jeff," she said firmly. "Tell him it's important."

Lyle hesitated, and Rachel wondered irritably just what instructions he might have had about calls from her. So her tone was decidedly cool when Jeff finally came on the line.

"I'm glad you're in," she said with admirably restrained irony. "There's something you might want to know—about Bob Dougan's murder."

"Rachel . . ." His voice sounded harsh and irritable in her ear. "Don't get involved in this. I'm not asking you. I'm telling you."

All her anger from the night before came back in a rush.

"Tell me anything you want," she snapped. "As long as my uncle is a suspect, I'm involved."

Silence.

"Don't hang up." Rachel drew a deep breath and tried again. "There's something you need to know. Joylinn overheard Bob boasting about his investment income at the Bread Box, but says he refused to give anyone any tips or information on how he got it. That goes along with Spider's accusation that Dougan cheated his mother with a phony investment scam. And Roth Glover says that Dougan was acting odd the morning before he was killed. When he went to pick up his daughter, he said something about setting a bad example for her. Maybe it has something to do with why he was killed."

For a long moment, silence hummed on the line. "I'll talk to Glover," Jeff said at last. He sounded thoughtful. "He hasn't been very helpful so far. I'll try again." Another pause. "Thank you," he said. "Rachel . . . you really do need to stay clear of this. Please."

"I . . . I'm sorry, Jeff." She swallowed, her throat tight. "I can't."

"Okay." Those two syllables revealed nothing. "Thanks for the tip," he said and hung up.

Slowly Rachel replaced the phone. When she turned around, Ransom Loper, the developer, was leaning against the wall smiling at her. "You're pretty even in work clothes." He swept her with an up-and-down look of open appreciation. "I'd love to see you dressed up. Can I bribe you with dinner?"

Rachel opened her mouth to give him an emphatic no thanks, then smiled instead. "Well, maybe." She tilted her head. "I'd like to hear exactly how one goes about developing raw property."

Ransom's grin widened. "You got a date, dear. How about tonight? Say, seven?"

"Sure." Rachel nodded.

"Where shall I pick you up?"

"Oh, I'll meet you," she said quickly. "How about Fong's? I love Chinese."

"Let's do Hood River. Or even Portland." His eyes glittered. "I know some really good places there."

"I've got to get up early." She gave him a smile. "I'd better stick close to home."

"Fong's it is." He looked briefly annoyed, then turned up his smile again. "See you at seven."

Rachel waved, then walked thoughtfully back to her truck. She just hoped Jeff didn't choose this night to eat out.

Or maybe that would be a good thing. She reached her truck and stowed the new drippers in her toolbox behind the cab. As she started to get into the cab, she noticed her mother just coming out of the medical and dental clinic down the block.

"Mom!" Rachel cupped her hands around her mouth, then waved. But her mother simply swept the block with an unseeing look, then climbed into her little MG which was parked at the curb.

Mom had seen her. She had looked right at her. She yanked the truck door open and slid behind the wheel as her mother drove past. Rachel honked the horn. Dark hair tossing in the wind, her mother didn't even look around.

After last night, this was too much.

Rachel started the truck and pulled quickly out onto Main Street. Traffic was light, and only a single pickup separated her from the MG. But the pickup's driver was in no hurry. Teeth clenched, Rachel tried to keep the sports car in sight as the driver in front of her meandered through the center of town. When he finally swung into the parking lot of the Blossom Feed and Seed, Rachel let her breath out in an exasperated rush and stepped on the gas.

The MG had already vanished around the curve at the east end of town, where the road bent away from the river and wound up across the slopes of the Gorge. On her way back to the orchard? Rachel wondered. That was the last place she intended to go. She pressed harder on the accelerator, not looking at the speedometer, swinging the pickup around the tight curves in the road as fast as she dared go.

Aha. There, just entering the next curve, was the bright blue rear of the MG. Rachel accelerated down the straight stretch of road, hand poised over the horn, but the MG had vanished around the curve before she got close enough to honk.

Her mother was not obeying the speed limit, either. Rachel

braked for the curve, but even so, her tires hit the shoulder, raising clouds of dust and causing the truck's rear wheels to slither as she corrected. The MG had gained distance. She leaned on the gas pedal, her truck's engine roaring as she shifted down and accelerated hard.

Coming out of the next curve, she almost passed the small side road that led back toward the Columbia, but it was gravel, and a faint dust trail hung in the air. Aha. She hit the brakes, tires squealing briefly as she stopped hard. Backing up, she took the side road, hoping that someone coming west hadn't turned down here. It didn't really go anywhere—just back along a bluff over the river. Mostly it was used by the dirt-bike and four-wheeler crowd, who had long ago churned the passable sections of the bluff into ugly gashes of eroded mud.

She had to slow down some. The winter rains and off-road traffic had rutted the road badly, and the county didn't have the money to keep up every dirt byway and lane. Not a good time to break an axle, she thought, but then, the MG would have to slow down even more. It wasn't built to hop potholes. . . . Sure enough, green glinted through the brush where the road bent northward up ahead. Rachel sped after it, catching up at last. But as she swung—way too fast—into the tight curve, she saw the little wet-weather stream too late. It cut across the track, having long ago washed itself around the rusted and plugged culvert. In the dry summer it would be no problem. This time of year, a deep swamp of mud filled the lane, rutted with the churned track of heavy-treaded tires. A snapshot image of a mud-crusted and abandoned jack imprinted itself on Rachel's retina. Then her front wheels hit the soft mud and sank. She slammed on the brakes, lurching forward against the shoulder harness, heart sinking as she felt her rear wheels slide and skid sideways. Then the engine stalled, and silence filled the cab, broken only by the tick of hot metal and the liquid trill of a finch in the brush.

"Oh, shit," Rachel said with enormous feeling. Then she noticed the MG, nosed head-on into the sere tangle of winter-killed weeds, a hawthorn sapling bent flat beneath the frame. "Mom!" Rachel flung the door open, leaping out into ankle-deep mud that she barely noticed. "Mom, are you all right? Mom?"

"Right here, sweetheart." Her mother straightened up from the far side of her car, one hand pushing at the tangle of dark hair that had fallen across her face. "Oh, child." She shook her head. "What were we doing?"

"Playing catch-me?" Rachel, suddenly aware of her wet feet, looked down at the brown puddles forming around her mired boots. "What a mess."

"Are you all right?" Her mother waded through the weeds to the edge of the swampy ground. "You're not hurt?"

"Bruised, I think." Rachel rubbed at her chest where she had slammed into the shoulder harness. "Glad you taught me to use seat belts." She grimaced. "That's what I get for acting like a teenage boy with his first off-roader."

"Ditto." Her mother sighed and sat down on a relatively dry bit of ground. "Can you get your truck out? I'm not mired, but I'm afraid to try and back off that bush I flattened. I don't know what kind of damage I did."

"Let me try." Rachel looked down at her mud-crusted work boots, made a face, and slopped around the front of the truck to lock in her wheel hubs. Scraping off as much of the sticky black goo as she could, she climbed gingerly into the cab, started the engine, and shifted into four-wheel drive. The truck rocked and slithered, and for an instant the wheels caught. Then they began to slip. Low range wasn't enough to back her out of the mire. The mud was clear to the axle by the time she shut off the engine.

"Lovely." Her mother stood as Rachel lowered herself from the cab once more and waded toward more solid ground. "Now what? I left my cell phone at the house, I'm afraid."

Rachel flourished hers. She had long ago written the Taxi Sisters' number on a piece of tape and stuck it to the back of her phone. Just in case. Roberta answered on the first ring. She grunted once or twice as Rachel described the situation to her.

"Even the kids get their damn Jeeps stuck back in there," she said when Rachel had finished. "Be out as soon as Earlene gets back." She hung up.

"She'll be along," Rachel answered her mother's questioning look. "When she has time." She was not going to make her lunchtime appointment with the mayor. With a sigh, she slopped back to her truck, found his number in her client book, and called his office. He was in a meeting, but she left him a message, apologizing and telling him she'd stop by another time, at his convenience.

"Well, knowing Roberta, we might as well find a nice spot and make a picnic of it," her mother said as Rachel put away her phone. She held up a half-full bottle of sparkling water in one hand and a crumpled bag of pretzels in the other. "There's a path, just beyond the Le Brea Tar Pits there." She gestured toward a narrow trail that threaded away through the scrub toward the river.

"Why not?" Rachel waded back to the bank of the mud hole and scraped the worst of the mess from her boots. She followed her mother along the path, ducking under the thorned arches of dead blackberry canes, her feet squishy and wet inside her soaked boots. "How come you took off like that?" she demanded as she ducked under a particularly thick sprawl of thorns. "You wouldn't even look at me."

"How come you started chasing me?" Her mother didn't look back at her. "We could have both gotten killed."

"You didn't have to keep going. You could have stopped."

"You could have just called me later."

"I didn't want to call you later, I wanted to—" She broke off as they emerged from the tunnel-like end of the path, her mother stopping so suddenly that Rachel nearly ran into her.

The path ended on a barren thrust of land that jutted out over the river. A gull wheeled overhead, skimming away toward the distant curtains of stone that hemmed in the Columbia. Winter-beaten grass covered the small isthmus of land, and stones ringed a blackened circle full of cold ashes and bits of charred wood. The small stream that had mired the truck emerged to their left, winding across the isthmus and spilling over a lip of worn rock in a silvery tail.

"How lovely," her mother said softly. "You know, we are both idiots."

"It occurred to me," Rachel said, starting to smile. The

smile turned into a giggle. "It didn't bother me enough to make me stop, but I did think about it."

Her mother laughed, smile lines crinkling around her eyes. "If I ever had any doubts that someone might have given me the wrong baby at the hospital, they're gone now." Suddenly they were both laughing, hugging each other.

"The convention of idiots is now in session," Rachel said through her own laughter. "Nice to know we're really blood relations." Rachel looked around and nodded at a couple of sawn trunks that flanked the fire pit. "Let's have our picnic. I'll have to come back here when it's dry enough to drive."

They sat side by side on the trunk, then turned to face each other, with the blue distance of the Gorge spread out in front of them. On the Washington side of the river, tiny trucks and cars—seemingly no larger than toys—crawled along the riverside highway, and the deforested hills rose in water-sculpted curves above wide water. Her mother offered her the bottle of water and set the opened bag of pretzels on the log between them. "Not a high-calorie lunch," she said and smiled.

"That's for sure." Rachel drank some water—it was nearly flat—and passed the bottle back to her mother. She picked up one of the stale pretzels and nibbled on it, watching a bevy of small birds harass a small hawk down near the river. "How come you were angry last night?" she said softly.

"You were rude."

"Yeah, I was." Rachel picked at the crystals of salt on the pretzel. "But what I said was the truth."

"Truths don't always need to be spoken out loud."

"Maybe." Rachel glanced up at her mother through the fringe of her bangs, surprised to see a pensive, almost sad expression on her mother's face. She reached out suddenly, impulsively, and touched the back of her mother's hand. "I feel like . . . You want me to side with the family, just like Uncle Jack does. To stop being friends with Jeff."

For a space of time, her mother was silent, her eyes on the birds and harassed hawk. It finally disappeared into the tree canopy below, the sound of the birds' shrill chirping muffled by leaves and twigs. "What does family mean to you?" she finally asked.

"I don't know." Rachel shrugged and frowned. "You and Dad, I guess. Uncle Jack, Aunt Cat, and the boys." She shrugged again. "Then there are all the New York relatives. Is that what you mean?"

"Sort of." Her mother picked a pretzel from the bag and held it, turning it over and over as if she'd never seen one before. "Where I grew up—everyone lived close by—aunts, uncles, cousins. Nothing much really changed after my mother died and we moved in with Aunt Esther and Uncle David. We still did the same things with the same people on holidays, everyone helped everyone else sew costumes for the school play, and the same grown-ups told me to comb my hair and act like a young lady." She smiled, her eyes bright with old memories. "Not that they had much success, but they tried. And then . . . I fell in love with your father." The bright look in her eyes deepened and softened. "I thought my family was going to be furious—he wasn't even Jewish. But they . . . weren't. They were sad, which made me angry." She gave Rachel a sideways smile. "You feel so *guilty* when someone is sad. Anger isn't quite guilt-free, but it's better." She shook her head. "You know, I didn't think much about how things would change, with my living out here and the rest of my family back there. Oh, we talk on the phone all the time. But I'm not *there.* And most of the family still is—even though more of the kids are moving away to jobs in other states. I felt so lost at first." She began to crumble the pretzel slowly between her fingers. "These people were farmers—they didn't think the way I did or share the same holidays. I felt so lonely sometimes. But then you were born, and that changed things. One day I woke up and realized that we had a family again— all of us. And I realized how much I had missed that."

"But you left your family for Dad." Rachel stared at the drying splotches of mud on her boots. "What are you telling me?"

"I think I told you last night—Uncle Jack is getting brittle. A break with you would be his fault, maybe. But it would be a break, and I don't know how easy it would be to mend. He's lost his sons, you know. They're never going to come back here. They don't belong here anymore."

"So you want me to be some kind of rescuer?" Rachel stood, hands thrust into her pockets, staring down at the top of her mother's dark head. "You want me to tell Jeff to get lost so we can preserve this family? What about Joshua? You didn't tell him to get lost so the family would stay intact."

"I know," her mother said, still looking down at the crumbling pretzel in her hand.

"So what's the difference here?"

The wind blew down the Gorge—the wind always blew. It carried the sound of birdsong and rustling fir needles, freighted with the scent of spring earth and the first new leaves. It blew chilly and damp, and Rachel shivered. "It's Jeff, isn't it?" she said softly. "It's not just that you don't want me to break away from the family—you don't want me to get involved with Jeff."

"No." Her mother shifted on the trunk. "That's not quite it." She looked up at Rachel. "Will came with a high price tag for me," she said, her eyes on her daughter's face. "He was worth it. Oh, he was so worth it." Her voice caught, and she looked away, blinking. "I just want it to be worth it for you—the price you pay when you commit your soul."

"You don't think Jeff's worth it."

"I think Jeff is a good and honest man." Her mother faced her again, her expression serene. "I don't know if he is good for you or not. Only you can know that. I just want you . . . to be sure. Before you break something that you can't put back together again."

Sure. Rachel looked down at the scatter of pretzel crumbs on the trampled ground beneath their feet. "I'm not sure," she whispered. "I'm not sure of anything." She turned away, blinking in light that suddenly dazzled her eyes, saved from any more of this conversation by the welcome rumble of Roberta Guarnieri's big tow rig.

"And I don't think you have anything to worry about, anyway," she said, and hurried back along the trail, prodded by a double blast of Roberta's horn.

"I'd about decided you went under," Roberta said as Rachel burst out from the brush. She had backed the tow truck around with utter disregard for the dense brush, so that the big dual wheels rested on the edge of the firm ground. "Figured you got your mud-running days out of your system years ago."

"I wasn't expecting the hole," Rachel said meekly.

"Your mom, neither, I guess." Giving her a sharp look, Roberta hauled the big sling down from the tow arm. It wasn't all that warm, but she wore her summer uniform—khaki shirt with the sleeves rolled up. She had a tattoo on her right arm, just on her thick biceps—the initials SRF inside a wreath of dark roses.

Nobody in Blossom had a clue as to what those initials stood for.

Pulling a battered and mud-stained pair of hip waders from the bed of the truck, Roberta pulled them on, then slopped out into the mud, knelt down, and began to attach the sling. "We'll get you out, then I'll take a look at your mom's baby." She stood, wiping mud from her palms onto the waders. "Okay, hop in. This is a piece of cake."

It took her only a couple of minutes to haul the mired truck out onto solid ground. But it took Rachel considerably more time to maneuver carefully around the big tow truck. Finally she was clear. By the time she had parked out of the way, Roberta and her mother were conferring over the MG.

"Don't look like you did any damage." Roberta rose from where she had been peering under the car. "No oil leaking. No sign of any real damage. Hang on a minute." She went back to the truck, returning in a moment with a small chain saw. Yanking on the starter cord, she revved it to a shriek, then sliced neatly through the bent trunk of the hawthorn. It quivered with released strain and dropped flat beneath the car. "No sense in doin' more harm," Roberta said as she shut off the saw.

She hooked up the MG with a gentleness that was almost tenderness, Rachel noted with a smile. Roberta owned four or five Triumphs in various stages of reconstruction, and obviously had a soft spot in her heart for any species of sports car. She pulled the MG out of its nest of brush with deft care, and towed it past Rachel's truck and onto a fairly smooth stretch of the track. Then she crawled underneath once more, before she'd even let Rachel's mother get into it.

When she started it, the engine revved with a healthy roar. Roberta listened for a full minute, her head tilted critically. Then she gave Deborah a thumbs-up and a wave. "On the house," she yelled over the mutter of the MG's engine. "See you in town."

"Thanks," her mother said, then turned to Rachel. For a moment she seemed about to say something, then gave her head a small shake and merely waved. The MG crawled back down the track toward the main road—at a considerably slower pace than it had maintained on the way in. Roberta finished stripping off her muddy waders and turned to Rachel.

"That'll be fifty bucks." She held out a calloused and grease-stained palm.

"Fifty!"

"You're payin' for your mom," Roberta said laconically.

Rachel opened her mouth to protest, then closed it and fished her wallet out of her pocket. Pulling out two twenties and a ten, she laid them precisely in the center of Roberta's palm.

"Thankee," Roberta said, and her eyes twinkled. She lifted two fingers in a sort of salute, swung aboard her big truck, and trundled off down the track, the tow sling swinging at the end of its arm.

As Rachel followed her back to the main road, her cell phone rang. It was the mayor.

"Actually, I'm glad you couldn't make it," he said blithely. "I would have been late anyway. Can you come by now?"

"Sure," Rachel said, thinking she was about ready for *something* to go right today. "I'll be there in about twenty minutes, okay? I need to check in on Julio and Spider."

"See you there," he said and hung up.

CHAPTER

10

"You know, I've never owned a house before." Phil Ventura guided Rachel through the small house, toward the kitchen and dining area that took up most of the back. He eyed the yellow legal pad on the clipboard she carried warily. "I just sort of took landscape for granted—it was the landlord's problem. But then my sister brought my nephew out to visit. Aaron's four—and reading already." He gestured toward a picture on top of a plain Shaker-style chest, beaming with pride. Rachel admired the tousle-headed child with Ventura's grin and mischievous eyes.

"Looks like a handful to me," she said.

"My sis sure thinks so. Anyway, she really got on me about the backyard. Called it a wasteland." He made a face. "Well, the house was a rental for a lot of years, after all."

"You've done a nice job inside." Rachel looked around approvingly. The wood floors—freshly refinished—were enhanced by a couple of very nice oriental rugs. The furnishings—elegant and spare—reflected no particular style, but combined with the simple window shades, white walls, and a few lush plants to give the rooms an airy, spacious feel.

"I use the sunroom for my office." He gestured to the glassed-in porch with a tile floor that had been added on to the living room in recent years. Rachel spied a plain oak desk topped with a computer and an untidy pile of paperwork. "Here." He led her through a plastered archway and into the rear of the house. "Kitchen, dining room, and wasteland."

A set of wood-framed French doors opened from the large dining room onto a small, weathered deck with clumsy built-in benches. Beyond it, a square of weedy grass offered up yellow bouquets of dandelions to the sun, surrounded by a sagging wooden fence that looked as if it was being propped up by the riot of morning glory and tall weeds that grew along its rear section. A carpet of vinca edged into the struggling remnants of a lawn, and a lone birdbath offered scummy water to the disdainful sparrows scavenging beneath a plastic bird feeder hung in a dead pear tree. Three faded plastic tulips jutted crookedly up from the roots of the dead tree.

"I should have thrown the tulips away." Ventura cleared his throat apologetically. "But my sister was so horrified by them that I had to let them stay. I don't think she believes that they were here when I bought the house." He gave Rachel a weak grin. "Sally has much better taste than I. So?" He squared his shoulders like a patient bracing himself for bad news from his oncologist. "Can I do anything with this mess?"

"Oh, sure." Rachel spread her arms. "You can do anything you want. You don't have anything but space to work with."

"You make that sound like a blessing."

"It is." She smiled. "So what do you want the yard to be for you?"

"For me?" He frowned and wandered out onto the spongy deck, his eyes moving along the fence as he gingerly descended the sagging steps to the ground. "I don't know . . . I guess I want a place to relax. Where I can pretend I don't have neighbors, and I'm not mayor with a recall petition on my neck. And I'd like to be able to entertain out here. But it's probably too small for all that," he said ruefully. "I wish it was bigger. Maybe we could just plant a wall of bamboo along the old fence and hide everything."

"Then you still have a wall." Rachel climbed cautiously down the steps and went out into the middle of the yard, turning slowly so that she could take in the house, deck, and yard as a whole. "We can use a bit of fool-the-eye. An interesting array of plants will draw your eye away from what you don't want it to see. How about a bench beneath an espaliered camellia, a star magnolia or, better yet, vine maple. They're airy and graceful, and they have great color in the fall." She waved at the back fence, warming to her task, seeing the yard as a real garden.

"You can screen a lot with vine maple, without feeling crowded, and it's vertical. It'll give you the illusion of space."

"Cool." Ventura sounded more enthusiastic. "How about a bench? Or a fountain? Or something like that?"

"What if we extend the deck along the back of the house, and take out those benches?" Rachel paced off the rear of the house. "They block the view of the garden from inside. Wide shallow steps would transition from deck to garden more naturally. Maybe we could put a simple trellis and your bench at the midpoint of the back fence?" she mused, eyes half closed, summoning and rejecting images in her head. "It would be a place to go *to*. Put a flowering cherry at the corner of the deck here, for shade. Maybe two vine maples there, near the house, and in the corner. The arbor and bench between them tie it all together, and we can use some pavers to connect it to the deck. The trees will help do that, too." She nodded, taking notes furiously on the yellow legal pad on her clipboard. "In a yard this small, everything needs to tie together—right down to the pavers."

"What about flowers and stuff?" Ventura looked around. "I love color, but I have just about zero time for gardening."

"We can go with evergreen shrubs—nothing too thick or large. Maybe some salal. It does fine in partial shade. How about a compact rhodie and some deciduous azaleas for a little winter drama and spring color? Dogwood is another good choice for spring and fall color," she mused. "You're pretty protected from the wind here."

"Sounds great." Ventura was grinning from ear to ear. "Maybe Sally will give me a little respect for once. How soon can you start? And how do we do all this?" He frowned. "I don't have a lot of time . . ."

"You don't have to do it yourself." Rachel wandered along the weedy remains of a former tenant's old garden beds, clawing up the occasional handful of soil. Actually, it wasn't too bad. Someone, sometime, had put some serious work into it. The original mayor? she wondered. "There's a guy who lives just east of Blossom who does really nice decks. A couple of my clients have used him. We need to start with the deck and the paved paths. Then I can put in an irrigation system, work on the soil, dig the beds, and finally"—she grinned at his woeful expression—"I can put in the plants."

"This is not a weekend process." He sighed. "So much for impressing Sis with a Fourth of July barbecue."

"Oh, it should look pretty good by then." Rachel folded her pad closed. "We're not dealing with a five-acre estate here. If Beck isn't busy, he could get your deck done in a few days, and it won't take us long to get the rest of it finished." She winked. "Unless you have a lot more city work for me."

"No, no more city work after the park. Except maintenance. We need to talk about a contract for that." He looked away. "We better get that done while I'm still mayor. Hey, I promised you lunch." He forced a smile. "I never got time for it either—or have you already eaten?"

"Not at all." Rachel grinned, hoping the rumbling in her stomach wouldn't rattle the windows. "I'd love a sandwich, thank you very much."

"I'm glad somebody else besides me forgets to eat. Food's in the kitchen." He led her into the small, neat space beyond the dining room. Obviously newly remodeled, the white laminate counter gleamed beneath open shelves of cookware and colorful stoneware plates. An island with a wooden butcher-block top provided work space and obviously doubled as casual eating space. Two woven place mats with matching napkins were set out on the scrubbed surface, along with three white deli bags.

"I went to the Bread Box, just as you commanded." Still trying for a cheerful manner, he opened the bags. "I got the daily special—turkey, provolone, ham, and sliced tomatoes, with a pickled ginger mayo. They've got great stuff there." He unwrapped two sandwiches and set them on the plates, then took a white plastic container from the second sack. "Greek salad." He took the lid off and stuck a spoon into the container. "With a couple of brownies for dessert. And I can offer you a choice of juice, milk, beer, or even a passable pinot noir. I just opened it last night and I corked it well, so it should still be drinkable." He opened the refrigerator with a flourish.

"I'll take water, thanks." Rachel sat down on one of the wooden stools drawn up to the island and scooped salad onto her plate. Joylinn was generous with the feta and olives—the Greek salad was one of her lunchtime favorites. "Were you being serious about not being mayor much longer?" she asked as he set a tall glass of ice water in front of her.

"I don't know." Ventura pulled the other stool around to sit opposite her. "There's a recall petition circulating. That much is true." He regarded her levelly. "I don't know how many signatures are on it. Or how many will end up on it."

"I haven't seen it yet." Rachel ate a forkful of the salad, reveling in the salty tang of the feta set off by the thick, crisp spinach leaves. "I don't think you have to worry. Most people I've talked to think you're doing a good job." She grinned. "They just don't yell and scream about it, that's all."

"I hope you're right." The mayor took a distracted bite of his sandwich and put it down. "I feel like I'm public enemy number one at times." He lifted the top slice of bread and stared pensively at the layered meat and cheese beneath. "I think I'm in a prime position to become a scapegoat for everything that scares people out here—the declining produce prices, the influx of tourists, development—everything." He dropped the bread into place, glowering at his plate. "Sometimes I wonder how I ever made myself believe I could do this job."

"You're doing a great job." Jolted by his tone, Rachel pushed her plate aside. "Sure, a lot of people grumble—and they're the ones you hear. Things are changing, and a lot of folks are still doing things pretty much the same way Grandpa did them." She was thinking of her uncle, and shook her head to chase the thoughts away. "You need to give us more credit than that. Even the grumblers know that tomorrow is going to arrive, and it's scary, but we have to face it. You're getting us there a lot better than Andy Ferrel would have done.''

"Now, there's a man who really does think I'm public enemy number one. I'm a little surprised he hasn't taken a swing at me at one of those town meetings.''

"To be honest, so am I,'' Rachel said dryly.

Ventura gave her a lopsided smile and poured himself a glass of cranberry juice. "To change the subject before I start thinking about hiring a bodyguard—you never found my jacket, I take it?''

"Sorry.'' Rachel shook her head. "But I'm convinced Spider didn't take it. By the way, Julio, my assistant, wants a picture of it. He thinks it might turn up at a flea market or secondhand store if it was stolen.''

"I believe you about your Spider.'' Ventura gave her a sheepish look. "I felt bad after I asked you—yeah, I was sort of accusing your kid just because he's from the farm. Guess I'm not so politically correct as I'd like to think.'' He glanced at his watch and finished his juice.

"Tell Julio that if he can find my jacket, I'll give him a reward. My sis took a bunch of pictures last time she was here. Considering the weather this past month, I was probably wearing the jacket in a lot of them. I'll find you something.'' He finished one half of his sandwich in a few hasty bites and began to wrap up the other half. "I'm going to have to run. We've got a Council meeting scheduled for this afternoon— to discuss one more time the appointment of an interim council member to replace Bob. We didn't get very far last time. People mostly wanted to talk about who might have killed him.'' His brows drew together. "I'm losing faith in our chief of police. He doesn't seem to be making a lot of progress on this case.''

"He's working hard at it,'' Rachel said carefully.

"I'm sure.'' But Ventura's frown didn't soften. "You have to wonder . . . I mean, I don't think we're dealing with a stranger crime here. It wasn't any wandering transient who killed Bob. Maybe . . . Price is a little too close to people in this town.''

"That wouldn't stop Jeff,'' Rachel said sharply. "He'd arrest his mother if she committed a crime.''

"I'm sorry." The mayor blinked at her. "He is an honest man, I didn't mean that. It's just . . . sometimes you wear blinders, even when you think your vision is crystal clear. But that's neither here nor there." He got to his feet. "Don't hurry your lunch." He lifted a hand as Rachel began to wrap up her sandwich. "Just lock the front door on your way out."

"I need to get back to work, thanks." Rachel finished her water and put her glass on the counter with her plate. "I ate a lot of that salad. I think I'll save the sandwich for later."

"Take the brownies with you, too." Ventura rinsed his own plate and put the juice back in the refrigerator. "I'm looking forward to seeing your final plan for the yard. Can you contact that deck builder—what's his name?"

"Beck. He doesn't have a last name."

"Really?" Ventura looked dubious.

"He's kind of strange," Rachel said with a smile, "but he's an artist with wood."

"If you say so." The mayor shrugged. "Why don't you call me when you've got the plans, and we'll get together. The park is looking great by the way," he said as he picked up his car keys from the counter.

They left together, and Rachel found she had to stretch her legs to keep up with the mayor's long stride as they walked the four blocks down to Main Street. There Ventura turned right, toward City Hall, and Rachel headed left toward the Memorial Park, a block away.

Before she had gone ten steps, a gray Jeep Eagle sporting the words *Blossom Taxi, Independently Owned and Operated Since 1977, CASH ONLY* pulled over to the curb next to her with a screech of brakes. "Get in." Earlene Guarnieri leaned her head out the window.

"I'm just going—"

"Fine. I'll take you. Get in." An unlit cigar jutting from her mouth, Earlene glared at Rachel from beneath her rumpled gray hair.

"Is this about the tow this morning?"

"Nope."

For a moment Rachel eyed the older woman, poised between curiosity and annoyance. Then she shrugged, went around to the passenger side, and slid onto the front seat. The vinyl seat covers had been patched with duct tape, and a rosary of coral beads swung from the rearview mirror. "I didn't know you were Catholic," Rachel said absently, wondering what was going on. "I paid Roberta for the tow."

"I'm not. And I know you did." Earlene put the Eagle into gear and roared off down the street, laying down a thin veil of blue smoke. "Rings are going," she growled. "This isn't about the tow. This is about you and Jeff."

"Huh?" Rachel sat bolt upright on the seat. "What do you mean?"

"Don't play games." Her chin jutting out like her cigar, the older woman swung the car around the corner and up the next street with a race driver's precision. "Boy's clear as water. He starts walking around all closed up like a shuttered house, cold as a Gorge cliff, and I don't have to wonder too hard what's goin' on. You two had a fight, huh? Over that loudmouth fool uncle of yours?"

Rachel closed her mouth with an effort. "Is this the current gossip?" she asked bitterly.

"Dunno."

The purr of the engine filled the car. "All right," Rachel said after a moment. "Look, we didn't have a fight. Even if we did, it's our business, I think." Rachel crossed her arms and glared out the window as they roared up the county road that she and her mother had taken earlier. For a moment she thought Earlene was going to pull onto the same gravel road that had led her into the mud hole, but she roared on past, swinging the car onto an even narrower track between unkempt rows of apple trees a few moments later. "For your information, whatever is eating Jeff, he's not telling me about it," Rachel said at last. "He's not talking to me at all."

Earlene swung the car suddenly off the track, into a seemingly impassable wall of weeds. Rachel gasped in spite of herself. They bucked over rough ground for a few moments, crowded by young alder and hawthorn thickets. Then, without warning, they emerged onto a broad ledge of rocky ground studded with pink and yellow blossoms. It ended abruptly, a scant few feet in front of the bumper. A little breathless, Rachel stared down at the blue-gray sweep of the Columbia, seemingly beneath the front wheels.

"What is this?" Rachel muttered. "The official day for intense conversations at the lip of the Gorge?"

Earlene turned off the engine.

"I want to tell you a story." Earlene crossed her arms on the steering wheel, her rough voice loud against distant birdsong and the whisper of the wind. "About this skinny kid I caught swiping candy from the station one day. He'd been doin' it for a while, so we had this little talk. And he worked for us for a bit. Enough to pay for his candy and then some. He was good with a wrench—wanted to learn, that kid did. Wanted to be good at something. Wanted it real bad."

"Jeff?" Rachel asked softly.

"He was ten. Kept on workin' for us, on and off. Until his mama blew town and took him with her. Bad thing to do to the boy, I thought, but, hey, he wasn't my kid." She spat out the window, then returned her gaze to the river far below. "You know what that kid cared about more than anything in the world?"

"No," Rachel whispered.

"Family. He didn't have much of one. He'd look at his friends with parents, brothers and sisters, aunts, family picnics. Thought it was heaven. I told him better, but, hey, who was I? I didn't have any family to speak of neither." Earlene laughed a cracked laugh and spat again. "He believed what he wanted to. You get it yet?" She turned suddenly and stabbed a grease-stained finger at Rachel.

"I'm not sure."

"He's not gonna get between you and your family, girl. He figures your uncle maybe offed Dougan. *I* don't think Jack did it, but, hey, Jeff doesn't have anyone better in line yet. So he figures he should stay clear of you. 'Cause he's the enemy now."

This seemed to be a universally held opinion, Rachel thought bitterly. By everyone except her.

Earlene nodded and turned on the engine.

"So what do I do, Earlene?" Rachel swallowed, her throat tight. "He won't talk to me. And I can't stay out of this."

Earlene shrugged as she wrestled the car around in the narrow space. ''You'll figure something. If it matters.'' They crashed through the weeds again, then turned back toward town. Earlene didn't speak until she was pulling over in front of the Memorial Park. ''I got faith in you, girl,'' she said as Rachel climbed out of the car. ''You got your dad's brains and your mom's guts.''

''Thanks,'' Rachel said with as much irony as she could muster.

''You're welcome.'' Earlene nodded, her cigar bobbing, then pulled away from the curb in a fresh cloud of oil smoke.

Rachel coughed, laughed, and told herself her throat was only tight from the fumes.

CHAPTER

11

Rachel actually managed to get the drippers replaced, while Spider and Julio finished cleaning up from their day of work on the Memorial Park. They were almost finished, and she let herself enjoy a few moments of satisfaction as Spider swept up the last of the bark dust from the sidewalk. Imagining the new plantings leafed out, green, and irrigated-lush in the full of summer, she was pleased. The park would be a focal point for Main Street, instead of looking like an abandoned lot.

She noticed that every name in the memorial stone shone crisp and free of mud, moss, or insect leavings. Spider had spent several breaks with a toothbrush and a knife, scouring out every last letter.

She wondered briefly what those clean, furbished letters meant to him. Her cell phone rang then, and she reached through the truck window for it, eyeing the wall of gray clouds massing on the western horizon. More weather coming from the west. Rain. "Rachel here," she said.

"Rachel. Hi." Her mother's voice buzzed with static. "I . . . I just wanted to call. I didn't mean to rush off like that after Roberta hauled us out . . . but I . . . I just did."

"Mom, it's okay." Rachel felt a brief surprise at the strength of her relief. "I'm just glad you're not mad at me."

"I was afraid you'd be mad at *me*."

They both laughed then, in perfect unison. Rachel realized suddenly just how often that happened—that she and her mother found the same thing funny at exactly the same instant. "I think Roberta guessed we had a fight," Rachel said, smiling. "I don't think she approved, either."

"Probably not," her mother said gaily. "And I think both sisters are telepathic. Never underestimate how much they know about what's going on under the surface around here."

Rachel made a face. "I believe that," she said. "Earlene demonstrated it today. How's Uncle Jack doing?" she asked carefully.

"Not good." Her mother's tone sobered. "You know, sometimes I really want to grab that man by the hair and bang his head against the wall. Honestly." She let her breath out in a gusty rush. "Talk about obsessive. Maybe we need a tornado, or an earthquake, or a sudden freeze—something to take his mind off the murder and . . . off the murder," she ended awkwardly.

Rachel guessed Jeff's name had just been hastily deleted from her final sentence. She smothered a sigh. "Well, I think I'll kind of avoid the orchard for a few days," she said lightly. "Unless the tornado shows up."

"Actually . . . I was about to ask you for a tremendous favor."

Uh-oh.

"I think Jack's in a bad mood for visiting town, but he was all set to go into the Feed and Seed for some irrigation valves that just came in." Her mother was speaking rapidly, as if she was afraid Rachel would hang up. "I told him that Joshua was going to drop by and he'd bring them out . . . but I forgot that this is the day that Joshua went into Portland for the monthly get-together he does with those retired surgeon friends of his. He'll be staying over at the Heathman Hotel. Is there any chance you could bring the valves out, sweetheart? If Jack goes into town and gets into a fight with someone, it'll be just about the last straw for Catherine." Her mother sounded suddenly weary. "I don't think she's ever been as close to walking out on him as she is right now."

The idea of Aunt Catherine packing her bags and leaving startled Rachel. Aunt Catherine had been such a fixture during her childhood. She rarely argued with anyone and never raised her voice. When her husband was on one of his rampages, she simply retreated to the kitchen and made cookies, or baked a complicated casserole for dinner. She smiled and rarely laughed, but never got angry either.

"You're kidding," Rachel said.

"I think so." Her mother sighed. "But I don't want to push it. Jack's worse than he's ever been."

"I'll bring them," Rachel said. "And I've got a good excuse to hand them to you and take off—I've got a seven o'clock dinner date, and I don't think I should show up in my grubby jeans."

"A date with Jeff?" her mother asked a little too casually.

"Actually, no. It's with Ransom Loper, the man who wants to buy the old cherry orchard."

For a few moments, only static buzzed on the line. "Are you doing this because of what I said this morning?" her mother asked carefully.

"It's not that kind of a date." Rachel smiled. "And when have I ever done anything *just* because you asked me? Not that you asked me to go out on a date with someone besides Jeff, anyway."

"Well, I believe you have actually done one or two things just because I asked." Her mother's smile came over the phone. "But I'm relieved. I felt like such a . . . a *meddler*. You have to make your own decisions, and you need to listen to your heart, not your worried parent. You'll do what's right for you. I believe in you."

"Don't worry, I'll be fine, Mom." Even if she didn't have a clue as to how she really felt about all this. "And I'll be out with the valves as soon as I drop off Julio. They're loading the tools now. Love you."

"Love you, dear. I'll watch for you." Her mother hung up.

Her mother's light tone couldn't hide the strain in her voice. Rachel frowned as she replaced the phone in its holder, thinking once more about Earlene's words this afternoon. Family. She sighed. Time to talk this out with Jeff. Tonight.

Only the dinner date with Loper was going to make it too late to catch him before he went to bed. "I just need to be in three places at once tonight." She let out a gusty breath of exasperation, wishing she'd had the brains to ask Loper for a phone number so that she could call and cancel.

But maybe she'd find something out. "I hope so," she muttered. "Or it'll be a total waste of time."

Turning around, she discovered that both Spider and Julio were staring at her with fascinated curiosity. "Relax," she said. "Talking to yourself is only a symptom of insanity in one out of three cases." That earned her two identically knowing grins. "Just get the wheelbarrow loaded." She rolled her eyes. "And let's shut up shop. I see the farm van waiting for you, Spider." She nodded to where it was pulling into the City Hall lot. "Oh, yes, Julio, I nearly forgot. The mayor is going to give me a picture of him wearing his jacket. He said he'll give you a reward if you find it."

"Super!"

That seemed to be his favorite word this week. She shook her head as he drank the last of his water from his jug and stowed it in the bed of her truck. "And you will go see your *friend* tonight? Then he will not be sad and you will not talk to yourself." He grinned wickedly.

"Huh? What's this? Are you talking about Jeff?" Rachel narrowed her eyes at his mischievous grin. "How did he get into this conversation?"

"He came here. To see the job." Julio winked. "But you were not here. He was sad. I do not think our work made him sad."

Rachel glared at his smug adolescent grin. "Why didn't you tell me sooner?"

Julio's shrug was eloquent. "He left. In a car. And I *did* tell you. Now."

"Oh." Rachel sighed and closed her eyes against the first faint tickle of a headache. "You're right. You did tell me."

Sarcasm went right over Julio's head, most of the time. "*De nada*," he said cheerfully, then strutted off, calling to Spider to do a better job of tying down that wheelbarrow, *muchacho*. Rachel glared after him, wondering what had ever possessed her to hire an adolescent male. Shaking her head, she tossed her gloves into the toolbox. All they had left to do was set out the annuals, and finish spreading the last of the dust in the beds, and do the final cleanup. Then she could start working on the mayor's job.

She would have to talk to Beck first, make sure he would do the job. You never knew with Beck.

Mostly she wanted to talk with Jeff.

"Rachel?" Spider stood hesitantly at the rear of her truck. "You got a minute?"

"Sure." Rachel closed the toolbox and snapped the lock. "What's up?"

"I gotta go." He jerked his head at idling van. "But I . . . I called my mom yesterday. I told her I saw the jerk who stole her money. When she came out to visit last night—it was her day off—she brought this." He shoved a folded sheet of paper at her. "I asked her to. I told her you might be able to help us get that money back." His muddy eyes fixed on her face, and the fragile shadow of belief there silenced Rachel's denial.

"Let me see." She took the grimy square of folded paper and opened it up. The embossed letterhead—*West Coast Tomorrows—Your Tomorrow in Your Hands Today*—and creamy, expensive paper breathed success. *Dear Ms. Muir*, the letter began. So she hadn't kept her husband's name, Rachel thought, and read on: *I, too, have been impressed with the quick success of your investment with us. Don't be impatient with the current downturn. Everyone is suffering from the instability in the Asian markets. We're diversifying the portfolio in which you share an interest. You should be seeing more return on your investment shortly.*

The letter was signed by a Robert Desmond, President.

"May I keep this for a while?" Rachel refolded the paper and, as Spider nodded, slipped it into her wallet. "I don't know if there's anything I can do . . ." She watched the shadow of hope in his eyes begin to fade. "But I'll sure try."

"Thanks." He nodded once.

The parking lot of the Blossom Feed and Seed out at the edge of town was nearly empty, this close to closing. Rachel parked next to a woman who was loading sacks of rabbit feed into the back of a Subaru. She had moved to Blossom several years before to raise rabbits on a small acreage west of town. Rachel had heard that she sold them to a Portland organic meat market. She pushed a thick ginger braid back over her shoulder and gave Rachel a bright smile as she closed the lid of the trunk.

"Hi, Rachel." Brian Ferrel appeared on the loading dock above her. "Your mom called to say you were picking up those valves. Thanks for saving me the drive." He offered her a hand, pulling her up to stand beside him. "Marcy and I planned to have a picnic down on the river. She'd be ticked if I was late getting home."

"It should be lovely, if that rain holds off." Rachel followed him along the dock to the door, dodging the stacks of dog food, fertilizer, and mineral salt blocks that crowded the wooden dock. "Harvey parks his equipment here, doesn't he?" She nodded at the black dump truck whose gleaming nose was just visible beyond the end of the building. "I never really thought of it before, but I see his truck or his hoe here a lot."

"He sort of rents space here." Looking harried, Brian led her into the dim interior of the feed store. "He drives home in that old Chevy of his. He lives way out, so I guess it saves him gas. Once in a while Dad borrows the back hoe or the truck, or something. They've been doing it for years now."

"Nice system." Rachel stooped to pick up a tawny ball of baling twine that someone had knocked to the floor. The feed store had its own smell—a mix of chemicals and leather and dust, she decided. Pungent and soothing. She edged past a display of neon-bright halters that leaned against a precarious stack of tubes of cattle wormer. "You're gonna have an avalanche here in a minute, Brian."

"It's Dad." Brian reappeared from the stockroom with a hefty box in his arms. "I don't know what's gotten into him." His face darkened. "We had a fight about my stocking a new line of garden and pet supplies yesterday. Yuppie junk, he called it, and he threw a case of crockery pet bowls right off the damn dock. Broke more than half of them. I mean—hey—that's what people want to buy. Is it my fault?" He spread his hands. "I said that, and he called me a snot-nosed punk and stomped out. So now I'm shorthanded, because he won't hear of my hiring another clerk, even part-time—and I'm way behind. We got a new shipment of rat bait in, and I can't find it anywhere. Will Ferris came in asking for some, and there's none on the shelf, of course. So Will got ticked and told me he'd go over to Hood River for it."

Face tight, he carried the box up the narrow aisle. "I can't run this place by myself, and if Dad won't let me hire help, he'd damn well better stick around here, then. Hell, maybe I *will* quit and get a job in Portland."

"What's his problem?" Rachel asked as she followed him out into the bright light again. "More sales are good, right? Does it matter what you sell?"

"I didn't think so, but I guess I'm wrong. I guess it does." Brian heaved the box into the back of her truck. "This guy has a little store for sale outside of Portland. Calls it a farm and garden, but it's mostly dog food, garden supplies, and a little feed and horse tack. It'd be a stretch, but we could just about swing the payment."

"So you really want to leave?" Rachel asked quietly.

"I . . . I don't know." Brian looked away. "The store's losing money. If Dad won't let me change anything, it'll go down. And what else can I do around here, Rachel? Pick apples? Ah . . . maybe Dad'll cool off." Brian tried for a light tone. "Dougan's death really hit him hard, I guess. It wasn't so bad before—but then, they were old-time fishing buddies. From when they were kids, I guess."

"I hope you don't have to leave. Your dad sounds a lot like Uncle Jack, you know."

"That why you're in the landscaping business?" Brian asked grimly.

"Well, actually, yeah. Sort of." Rachel glanced at her watch and winced. "I got to run, Brian." She lifted her hand. "Hang on. Maybe they'll both mellow out."

"We can always hope, huh?" Brian shook his head and laughed. "Well, let me know when you go into the orchard business, okay?" He waved and vanished back into the cluttered depths of the warehouse.

Rachel drove out to the orchard through the thickening dusk, hoping that she could drop off the valves and escape without a confrontation with her uncle. The porch light was on, but the front room was dark as she pulled into the parking circle in front of the house. Dim light shone from the den windows—Uncle Jack must be in there watching the TV news. She got out and lifted the heavy carton of valves from the truck bed. The old farmhouse looked unaccountably strange tonight—as if it was a neighbor's house and not the place where she'd grown up.

Her mother came around from the back, hair loose over her denim shirt, slim and wiry in well-washed jeans. "Thanks, sweetheart." She took the box from Rachel, kissed her lightly, then carried it around to the back porch steps. "I hope you're not going to be late for your dinner date."

"I don't think so." She put her arm around her mother, frowning a little as the yellow wash of light from the back windows highlighted the shadows beneath her eyes, and the jut of her cheekbones beneath her skin. "You look really tired, Mom. Why don't you go back home?"

"I'm going to." Her mother smiled, her dark eyes sparkling with decision. "I decided to, right after I talked with you this afternoon. Poor Joshua. He's been so supportive, and so patient, but he's my husband. Jack's not sick. He's not dying. He's just having a major temper tantrum. It's Catherine I mostly worry about." Her mother sighed. "I'm going to see if I can coax her into coming into town with me, and at least spending a night with Joshua and me. I think it would help. I think she could talk about this a little more if she wasn't under the same roof with Jack." She kissed her daughter again. "In any case, it's not your worry right now. Go have your dinner. I'll call you. And thanks." She hugged Rachel briefly. "We *were* fey today, weren't we?"

"Crazy as bedbugs," Rachel said soberly, then they did one of their simultaneous laughs. She hugged her mother back, waved, and hurried quickly back to her truck, feeling better than she had in days.

All she had to do now was talk to Jeff. He'd listen. She'd make him listen. It might not be too late after her dinner with

Loper. Rachel bolted up the stairs to be greated by an impatient Peter at the door. He stalked past her as she opened the door, marched into the kitchen, and demanded his dinner now, and not a moment later, thank you.

Having learned from experience that ignoring him would cost her a pair of hose, she quickly opened a can of food and set it out on a plate next to his full bowl of dry food. "One of these days, I'll just stop feeding you canned food, period," she warned. "You'll have to eat dry food or starve."

It was an empty threat. She doubted very much whether he would do either. Smiling at her stubborn companion, she hurried into the bedroom, tossing jeans and work shirt into a pile, stripping off her socks with a grimace. She ran the shower hot enough to sting and to leave her glowing and breathless. She dressed quickly in a long-waisted print dress that made her look a little less stocky and low heels to add a little height. Loper was tall, she remembered. She did a fast job with her makeup and did what she could with her unruly hair. Grabbing a matching linen jacket from her closet—it was chilly and windy tonight—she hurried through the apartment and down the stairs. Not bad, she decided as she glanced at her gold "dress-up" watch. She wasn't going to be more than five or ten minutes late.

Loper was in the lounge at Fong's. He emerged as she stood in the red carpeted entry, searching for him among the diners. "You look stunning," he said, smiling. "That dress suits you."

"Thank you," Rachel said, feeling a twinge of guilt about her proposed fishing trip.

Once seated, Loper ordered champagne for both of them from one of Fong's smiling nieces. He was the take-charge type, Rachel decided. At least, he didn't bother to ask if she liked champagne. Which she did, so it was a small matter. He also ordered the dinner. This was probably considered to be a masterful manner, Rachel decided with an internal sigh. She kind of wished he had consulted her, though. He seemed to have a thing for sweet-and-sour preparations. The champagne came, along with a plate of sweet-and-sour shrimp and stuffed wonton as appetizers. She had never much cared for sweet-

and-sour food. The pot stickers and light-as-air spring rolls were Fong's standouts.

"To real estate." Loper lifted his glass to chime against hers.

"You must buy and sell a lot." Rachel smiled innocently as she sipped at her champagne. "My father always felt you should hang on to land. Pass it on to the next generation."

"Which is why your average farmer is so poor." Loper waved an admonishing finger at her. "How you make money on land is to buy and sell—keep your finger on the pulse of the market, unload when the prices hit the top, buy before a local gets discovered. Which is why I'm so interested in Blossom." He topped off his glass, set the bottle back in its ice bucket when she declined a refill. "You wait. Hood River's just hitting its popularity stride. And here we have small, cozy little Blossom—close enough to Hood River for the nightlife, but elite. Special. Actually, your mayor's annexation plan won't do me much harm in the long run. I may have to give up on some condos at the edge of town, but I bet you the property values will be fifty percent higher if you all can preserve your nice small-town ambience."

"Don't you need a lot of capital?" Rachel nibbled on a crispy fried wonton.

"You do it all on paper. Cash?" He laughed. "What's that? Money is power—but it doesn't have to exist as bills and coins. You can acquire a hell of a lot of power and money both in real estate—if you play your cards right."

"As you have?"

"Damn right. I do it from both ends—buying and selling, and also developing." His eyes gleamed with fervor. "By the time I'm done, I'll have a lot of clout in this town. You wait and see. Everything I need is here to turn little Blossom into an upscale vacation community for the Portland executive set. We'll offer exclusivity—small and private. Good security and private patrols. River frontage. Classy retail outlets. None of those factory-outlet monsters—we're talking Saks and Nordstrom's, and out-of-the-way restaurants that get reviewed in the top magazines. I've already got enough options to get the ball rolling."

"I thought Mayor Ventura was against that kind of growth." Rachel dipped a crisp wonton into a vinegary plum sauce and took a bite. Not too much hot pepper this time. Fong Senior must be in a benign mood tonight. On his bad days, you didn't dare order the Szechuan dishes. "Isn't he planning to keep condos and retail development under control with his new annexation?"

"He's not going to get his annexation," Loper said. He lifted his glass to watch the tiny streams of bubbles rise. "People around here know there's money in their land. They're not going to let him tell them what they can and can't do with it." He drained his glass. "The Council was all set to veto that annexation. If he appoints some yes-man in Dougan's place, I'm filing suit." He winked. "Maybe he killed Dougan, just so he could get his agenda passed."

"Dougan was going to vote for it." Rachel dipped another knot of crispy dough into the sauce. "Mayor Ventura says he came to his office to tell him. I guess it surprised him a lot."

"He's lying." Loper deftly snagged a shrimp with his chopsticks. "Dougan was against it." A phone beeped shrilly. Loper frowned and groped in the leather briefcase he'd set down on the floor beside his chair. "Loper here," he said into his cell phone. He frowned as the caller spoke, then glanced sideways at Rachel and away. "Can't I call you later?" He frowned again and rolled his eyes. "All right—just a minute, and I'll call you back." He hung up the phone and gave Rachel an apologetic smile. "Business never waits. Will you excuse me for a moment? I'll only be a minute or two."

"Take your time." Rachel poured hot tea from the white porcelain pot that the waitress had left on the table. "I'm in no rush." As he hurried off in the direction of the public phone on the wall near the rest rooms, she wondered what he had to say that he didn't want to say in front of her.

The waitress appeared, smiling and nodding, and set an oval plate decorated with a pink, green, and gold dragon and pagoda pattern at each place. Rachel's stomach rumbled as she whisked the covers from platters of lemon chicken and sweet-and-sour pork, and set them on the table. As she placed a bowl mounded with white steamed rice between the platters, she caught her toe on the briefcase parked against Loper's vacated chair. It tipped over, spilling a couple of maps and a handful of papers from its open top.

With an exclamation of horror, the waitress squatted to pick up the items.

"It's all right." Rachel quickly bent to reclaim the scattered papers. "I'll take care of it." She smiled to reassure the agitated girl, who retreated quickly with her now-empty tray.

Carefully Rachel gathered the papers—letters and photocopies of title deeds and tax statements, she noted—and slid them back into the briefcase. He carried a lot of stuff with him, she thought. His traveling office? A surreptitious glance toward the rest rooms gave her a glimpse of Loper's back at the wall phone booth. He seemed to be deep in an agitated conversation. Quickly she peered into the side pockets of the leather case. Nice leather, too. Expensive. She rifled through more papers, feeling intensely guilty, not really sure what she was looking for, or if she'd recognize anything if she did find it.

As she was about to close the briefcase and lean it back against Loper's chair, folded papers caught her eye. Nothing else in the briefcase was folded. She opened them quickly and glanced at them.

The top page turned out to be a letter written three weeks earlier to a woman named Diane DeLeon, promising her that a check was currently in the mail to her, that her investment was doing poorly at the moment because of the disruption in the Asian markets, but that it should improve shortly. The letterhead proclaimed *West Coast Tomorrows—Your Tomorrow in Your Hands Today*.

The name scrawled at the bottom was that of Bob Desmond. The other two letters in the bundle were similar to the top one—communication with apparent clients about their stock purchases.

"What are you doing?"

Rachel jumped at the sound of Loper's voice. "The waitress knocked your briefcase over." Forcing herself to move casually, she slid the folded letters back into place, patted the rest of the papers into a neat square, then stood the briefcase against the chair again. "I think I got everything. Poor girl, she was so upset." Rachel straightened, smiling up at the developer. "You sure carry a lot of stuff. But I guess you have to in this business."

"Yes, you do." He seemed satisfied by her explanation as he took his seat again, although he rifled through the contents as if to verify that they were all there. "Real estate requires a lot of paperwork. I don't want to run back to an office four times a day." Apparently reassured that nothing was missing, he set the case on the floor again and faced her with a smile that had cooled a bit. "Looks like the food arrived. I'm starved."

"Me, too," Rachel agreed, although her stomach fluttered with leftover adrenaline.

Loper scooped sticky lemon chicken and pork onto their plates. As they ate, he was more than willing to tell her about his exploits in the past—how he had evaded city planners bent on restricting his projects, or pulled off monetary coups. Her amazement wasn't an act. If he had accomplished half as much as he boasted, he had been a busy man indeed. She scooped up rice with her chopsticks, sticky with lemon sauce, wishing that Loper wasn't so fond of the sweet dishes. She'd take Kung Pao chicken over lemon any day.

She eyed Loper's expensive clothes and shoes and the gold Rolex watch on his lean, tanned wrist as he went on and on. He might very well be telling the truth about his successes. "Those two projects you've got planned near Blossom—the one on our old cherry orchard, and that one along Saddler Creek—they're both on land that the mayor wants to annex, right? My uncle is so *furious* about that." She picked up a piece of pork and did her best to leave as much of the gelatinous sauce behind as she could. "What are you going to do if he won't let you build?"

"I told you, they're not going to pass that annexation." Seemingly unconcerned, Loper sipped tea. "I know what your mayor is up to—he's playing politics. He's building a liberal track record so he can jump into state politics with a record to impress the liberal Portland vote. You wait. He'll finish his term, move to the Portland suburbs, and run for a House seat."

Loper laughed sourly. "He's just using this town."

"Really?" Rachel poured herself more tea as he refilled her champagne glass. "He seems so earnest."

"He's not a bad actor." Loper topped off his own glass and dropped the bottle back into the metal ice bucket again. "He'd be good in real estate." His lips tightened. "I'm not worried," he said shortly. "Let's talk about something else." His eyes strayed to his watch.

Whatever had gone on over the phone, it seemed to have made him anxious to end the evening, which was fine with Rachel.

He tried to kiss her in the parking lot, but he didn't try very hard and didn't seem very brokenhearted when she evaded him. His mind was clearly elsewhere, and when he pulled out of the parking lot in his gray Mercedes, he spun the wheels, scattering gravel across the driveway. She should probably be insulted, Rachel thought as she started the engine. Oh, well.

Peter wanted to go out when she got home and darted past her with barely a glance. Every so often, he went off for a couple of days, reverting to the stray-cat life he'd led before Rachel had started feeding him. When he finally returned— usually with a new scar or two—he would rub against her ankles, purr, and generally act the prodigal son for a day or two. Then he'd settle happily into tame-cat mode, until the next fit of wanderlust struck him. Rachel shook her head as she hung up her linen jacket. Without Peter, the apartment felt unbearably empty tonight. She checked her machine. No messages. It was late. But . . .

Too bad.

She picked up the phone and dialed Jeff's number.

It was busy.

Well, he wasn't asleep yet, anyway. He couldn't use that excuse. She put the receiver down with sudden decision and grabbed her jacket again. Her heart lifted as she locked her door and trotted down the outside steps. Stars blazed in the sky, barely dimmed by the sliver of waxing moon, and a chilly wind fluttered the hem of her dress as she opened her truck door. For all its temperature, it had a hint of soft spring to it instead of winter's bite.

The moon hung like a silver crescent in the sky, and Orion swung overhead. It was a beautiful night, but in spite of her determination, Rachel couldn't still a flutter of apprehension in her belly as she drove up from the river, along the twisting gravel road that led to Jeff's house, perched high on the rim of the Gorge.

CHAPTER

12

The drive to Jeff's house was a dark one. The splash of her headlights illuminated the straight trunks and dark green canopies of young cherry trees, which eventually gave way to a weedy stand of second-growth fir and scrubby alder. The trees seemed to close in on the road, and Rachel glanced uneasily in the rearview mirror as the asphalt turned into gravel, resisting the urge to step harder on the accelerator. There were some nasty potholes up ahead, where a natural spring turned the road to mud in the winter rains.

A gray shape floated soundlessly across the road in front of her, and Rachel gasped, ducking instinctively as it seemed to brush the windshield with silent wing tips. The truck jolted into one of the potholes at that moment, and Rachel nearly hit her chin on the steering wheel. An owl, she told herself shakily as her headlights splashed across a stretch of dusty brush. It was a great horned owl, out hunting for mice and rabbits. Nothing more.

With enormous relief, she reached the overgrown gate that marked Jeff's driveway, and turned onto the narrow lane. He had cut back the chest-high weeds that had nearly blocked the road when he moved in here, but the lane was still only wide enough for a single car. A row of poplars—planted as a windbreak by the original builder—fenced the lane on either side. They towered over her, turning the night utterly black beneath their upraised branches. More poplars provided a windbreak for the small house with its sagging barn. Rachel exited the lane and pulled up beside Jeff's new Jeep in the freshly graveled turnaround.

He was building a deck on the rear of the house, where you had a breathtaking view of the Columbia far below. A neat stack of lumber glowed pale and new in the faint moonlight. The porch light was off, and no lights showed inside the house. Rachel frowned and checked her watch. It wasn't quite ten o'clock. Jeff never went to bed before eleven, and he always left the porch light on. His Jeep was here. But he might be driving one of the official cars. Turning off the engine, she drew a deep breath and got out.

The unease that had nipped at her heels all the way up to the house breathed on her neck as she hurried up the newly paved walk that led to the front porch. It was too quiet. Even the nighttime insects seemed to be holding their breath. In the distance an owl called and was answered by another. Rachel shivered in her light dress as she reached the porch steps. Clutching her jacket around her, she fought the unease that tried to turn into out-and-out fright.

The front door stood open.

The fright won out, and she almost turned and ran. Then from inside came a whisper of sound. It might have been a moan. Might have been the house settling, or her imagination. Heart pounding, Rachel tiptoed across the porch and reached through the open door, holding her breath as she groped for the switch just inside. The porch lamp came on, blinding her briefly, driving back the scary dark with welcome yellow light. Now she could see the red splashes on the door. Her heart contracted to a hurting knot in her chest. Then she smelled the pungent turpentine odor—paint. Rachel stared down at her fingers, at the crimson smear on her palm where she had brushed the paint as she had groped for the light switch. Someone had used a brush to paint the word COP on the panels of the new front door Jeff had just installed. Thick crimson drops spattered the wide planks of the newly sanded wood floor inside.

"Jeff!" She dashed into the house, knocking the lamp from its perch on the low wooden table beside the sofa in her hurry to turn on the lights. She grabbed for the lamp as it toppled, and snapped it on. Harsh light dazzled her, and Rachel looked around with horror at the words PIG and STINKING COP slopped onto the white walls. She had helped paint those walls when Jeff had first moved in.

"Jeff, are you all right? Are you here?" Her voice came out thin and shrill with fear, and for a moment all she could hear was the rush of her own breathing. She turned slowly, dazed, searching the space. There was only this main room and the small bedroom. He had to be here. . . .

He lay curled on his side on the tiles he had laid just a month ago, behind the breakfast bar that separated the living room from the small kitchen area. His back was to her, and another crimson pool gleamed beneath his cropped black hair. It wasn't paint. She knew it wasn't paint even before she dropped to her knees beside him. The blood matted his hair and streaked his pale face. For an instant her heart seemed to stop. She touched his throat with trembling fingers, and he moaned softly. Rachel choked back a sob as she felt the reassuring pulse of a heartbeat beneath her fingertips.

Stumbling to her feet, she dashed for the wall phone at the end of the kitchen counter. Dimly she was aware of broken glass gleaming on the wooden floor at the rear of the house. Someone had smashed the glass in the door that led to the backyard. The door stood ajar, and beyond she could see the pale planks of the half-finished deck, and more splashes of paint. A wad of dark fabric lay on the freshly laid planks.

"Hello?" Rachel gasped into the phone. "Lyle? Is that you? Someone attacked Jeff. Here, at his house. He's unconscious. Yes, he's alive!" She struggled for breath, feeling as if all the oxygen had suddenly fled from the house. "Someone hit him on the head. I'm afraid to move him."

"I'll get an ambulance up there." Lyle's voice came over the phone, sharp with authority. "Cover him up and keep him quiet." The line went dead, and Rachel replaced the receiver, noting absently that her hand was shaking. No, she was shaking all over. The ambulance would have to come out from Hood River. How long?

She went back to check on Jeff, counting the rise and fall of his chest for a reassuring few seconds before she went over to the sofa.

Numbly she picked up the patchwork quilt folded across the back. He had found it at a rummage sale, had wondered about its history—who had sewn the tiny stitches, where the quilter bloohad lived. *How could someone sell this?* he had asked after he had paid for the quilt and was carrying it to the car. *It's part of someone's family—part of someone's past.*

Family. Rachel swallowed, her throat aching, as she knelt to lay the quilt over him, careful to keep the faded squares out of the blood. His eyelids fluttered, and he opened his eyes, wincing and raising a hand weakly toward his head.

"Lie still!" She took his hand, laced her fingers in his, and held it tightly. "There's an ambulance on the way."

"I guess they were still there." The words slurred a bit, and he winced as he tried a weak laugh. "You'd think I'd know better—so what do I do?" His eyes closed briefly, and he gave her hand a faint squeeze. "I go running in here like any pissed-off homeowner. Damn him. Damn him to hell." His voice faded to a mumbled whisper. "What a mess . . ."

Rachel clutched his hand, her throat tightening as fresh blood trickled down his forehead. How could there be so much *blood*? "The house will be fine," she whispered. "I'll help you clean it up."

"How come you're up here?" Jeff opened his eyes again, frowned, and made a move to sit up.

"Lie still!" Rachel pushed him gently down. "Just wait for the paramedics, huh?"

"How come?" His eyes never left her face.

Her throat felt thick again, and this time it wasn't fear that closed it. "Because I had to come tell you . . . that it's not between us. Uncle Jack. Your job—it's tough. It's hard on you. And on me right now. But it's not *between* us. Damn it." Finally, uncontrollably, she began to cry.

He held her hand tightly and reached up to touch her face

without speaking. Outside, tires crunched on gravel, and an engine throbbed and fell silent. A moment later, boots pounded the porch steps.

"Jeff? Rachel?" Lyle appeared in the doorway, his square face anxious. "What the hell went on here?" Staring at the dripping crimson words and the splashed paint, Lyle walked stiff-legged across the room. "What a mess." His expression disgusted, he squatted beside Jeff. "You see 'em?"

Jeff started to shake his head, winced, and lay still. "No. The guy was out on the deck. I opened the door, I remember. Started to go charging out there like an idiot, too mad to think." He gave a lopsided grin and narrowed his eyes with pain. "He got a good swing at me, I guess."

"Looks like you staggered in here before you went down. More than one of 'em." Lyle's eyes traveled the violated walls. "Different printing."

"Just one."

"How do you know?"

Jeff frowned. "I . . . I'm not sure. I keep thinking that maybe . . . I saw the guy. But I don't remember anything after I started out the back door." His face contorted in frustration. "I'm pretty sure . . . it was just one man."

"Looks more like kids." Lyle shook his head. "Teenage vandalism." His eyes slid briefly toward Rachel and away. "Couple of those Youth Farm kids. Betcha."

"I don't think they let 'em run around loose at night." Rachel bristled. "And that includes Spider."

"A jail's only as good as its guards." Lyle got to his feet and edged a crumpled pack of Camels out of his pocket. "Guess I'll go take a look around." He went out onto the deck in back, scrutinizing the broken-out glass without touching anything. "This your jacket?" he called back from the half-finished deck. "Denim? Looks kind of small."

"Not mine," Jeff mumbled. He looked even paler than he had, and beads of sweat glistened on his forehead. But when Rachel touched him, his skin felt cool. Clammy. She said a small prayer that the ambulance would get here soon.

Dimly she remembered a family story—a cousin of her father and uncle, a nice, hardworking family man who fell off a house he was framing out in Idaho and fractured his skull. He had become "strange," the story went. The word "strange" was never adequately explained, as she recalled, but since he had ultimately abandoned his family and vanished down the highway, carrying only his toothbrush and a potato masher—so the story went—"strange" had been kind of scary.

It scared her a lot, right now.

With enormous relief, she heard the grind of tires on the gravel drive and heard doors slam. A moment later, a pair of uniformed paramedics burst into the room. Gratefully she stood back and let them take over, holding her breath as they asked Jeff his name and what day it was, who was the President, shone a light into his eyes and took his blood pressure. They refused to let him sit up in spite of his protests. As they began to move him, he threw up. After that, he stopped protesting and lay on the stretcher, bone-white and clammy with sweat, saying nothing as they secured the straps across his body and carried him to the ambulance.

They wouldn't let her ride with them, so Rachel went back to tell Lyle she was leaving, and ran back to her truck. Nausea was a symptom of head injury—concussion. She remembered that much from the time she fell out of the apple tree and her mother had to take her into Hood River to the emergency room.

Fighting fear, she followed the ambulance. It passed through Blossom's late-night empty streets with its lights and siren mercifully off, took the ramp onto the interstate, and headed for Hood River and the hospital at the legal speed limit. Rachel told herself that was a good sign.

She wasn't sure she believed it.

The small emergency room at the hospital was nearly empty. An elderly man held a magazine rigidly in front of his face in one of the chrome-and-vinyl chairs. Rachel hurried past his unmoving form, frightened all over again by the hospital smell, the bright lights, and the pale green gowns and dangling masks on the hurrying staff who gave her only a passing glance. She was healthy. They were busy with the others, their posture told her.

She asked a kind-eyed receptionist about Jeff, and the woman made her wait for a few minutes, then brought her back to a curtained cubicle where a green-clad young woman with a French braid of silvery blond hair was asking Jeff all the questions that the paramedics had asked, while she shone another light in his eyes. He lay on a sheet-covered gurney, his face nearly as pale as the fabric.

"Well, we'll have to put a few stitches in your head," the woman said cheerfully as she unwrapped the black flap of the pressure cuff. "You're going to have quite a trendy haircut when we get through with you."

Jeff growled something, then smiled weakly as he caught sight of Rachel. The woman turned as he reached for Rachel's hand, an appraising look in her clear gray eyes. The small name tag on her scrubs identified her as Dr. Potter. *Doctor,* Rachel thought with a mild sense of shock. She seemed so *young.*

"We'll get Jeff here stitched up." Dr. Potter smiled. "He doesn't seem to be concussed, but I think we're going to send him into Portland for a scan. Dr. Goshwami, at Emanuel Hospital, is a top neurologist."

"To Portland!" Rachel looked startled.

"This is crazy." Jeff started to sit up, winced, and eased himself back down onto the gurney.

"You don't want to find out the hard way that we missed something," Dr. Potter said firmly. "Neither do we." Obviously the discussion was closed.

Jeff scowled, obviously ready to dispute this, or refuse outright. "Get it done." Rachel squeezed his hand tightly. "It's important. Please."

He gave her a surprised look, then nodded, his expression dubious. "I guess. God, it's going to take all night."

"Possibly." Dr. Potter gave him a sweet smile. "You might luck out. You never know."

"Doctor, I saw the man who hit me." Jeff fixed his eyes on her. "I know it. It's there, but I can't *reach* it." Frustration edged his voice. "Is that going to come back? That memory?"

"Someone attacked you?" The doctor frowned, absently tugging at a loose wisp of pale hair as she glanced at his chart.

"Oh. You're with the police." She sounded surprised, as if she hadn't realized that before. "Will you remember? I don't know." She tugged at her hair again. "You might. You might not. You don't seem to have any other memory lapses."

"Just that moment—I guess it was after he hit me, as I was on my way to the floor," Jeff said slowly. "I have this vague memory of looking up as I fell, twisting around . . . it's as if I can look at the scene but can't really *see* it."

"Don't try so hard." The doctor patted his shoulder as she tucked the chart under her arm. "It'll probably come back more easily that way."

"I sure hope so." Jeff stared morosely after her as she vanished through the pale green curtains. "I want to get that bastard—whoever it is. Whoever he was, he was smart to try to blame it on the Youth Farm kids." Jeff lay back, looking drained. "We've had two reports of petty theft that looked like maybe farm kids. Andy Ferrel swears he saw 'em in his barn. And the Whites—with the apple orchard the other side of the farm—said kids were sneaking into one of their outbuildings to smoke dope. Could have been a Blossom teenager," he mumbled. "But that's not what folks think." He pulled her hand to his chest, closed both of his hands over it. "Thank you." His eyes were fixed on hers. "For coming out. You got blood on your dress."

"It'll come out. I meant what I said." She leaned forward and kissed him, figuring that surely couldn't hurt his head.

The rustle of the curtains parting and a gently cleared throat made her straighten, cheeks heating. Jeff chuckled and held on to her hand as she turned to find Dr. Potter and a dark-haired nurse smiling at them. The nurse carried a steel tray with dressing materials, a syringe, a jar of suture, and a blue paper package on it. She set it on the metal stand beside the gurney and began to unwrap an array of steel instruments.

Deftly the nurse used a pair of electric clippers to shave the area around the gash in Jeff's scalp. As she cleaned the cut, evoking a trickle of bright fresh blood, Jeff clenched his teeth. He didn't make a sound, but his fingers dug into Rachel's flesh. The doctor closed the curved gash with deft, rapid stitches. "Men are so easy to work on when their girlfriends are watching,'' the doctor said with a wink at Rachel.

Jeff growled something unintelligible, which the doctor must have understood, because she laughed and shook a finger at him. The finished dressing—gauze and tape—gave Jeff a slightly disreputable, piratical air when they had finished.

''We've got an ambulance here for you.'' The doctor scribbled something on the chart, then turned to hand it to a blue-uniformed paramedic who had appeared behind her. ''I'm sure you're fine—but this way we can all relax.'' She smiled at Jeff, then at Rachel. ''Good luck,'' she said.

The ambulance team shifted Jeff once more to a stretcher and wheeled him back through the ambulance entrance to their waiting vehicle. Rachel went back through the waiting room to get her truck, feeling a brittle sort of energy that made her wonder just how safe it was for her to drive to Portland and back tonight. But Jeff would need a ride home. Because they'd find that nothing was wrong and . . . She halted in the middle of the waiting room. The old man was gone, his magazine discarded on the seat where he had been sitting. Next to it, her mother and Earlene Guarnieri were getting to their feet.

''They said you'd be right out—that they're sending Jeff to Portland for a CAT scan.'' Deborah O'Connor opened her arms to her daughter. ''Sweetheart, how is he? And how are you?''

''He'll be fine. They're just making sure,'' Rachel said. As her mother's arms went around her, she buried her face against her shoulder, feeling about six years old again.

Her mother held her tightly, murmuring soothingly. Earlene scowled at the door, affecting not to notice the receptionist's pointed glare directed at the unlit cigar in her mouth.

''I talked to Lyle.'' Earlene shoved her fists deeply into the pockets of her grease-stained coveralls. ''He told me the bastards trashed the house. Jeff worked damn hard on the old place. I kind o' hope I find out who did it before Lyle gets to 'em.'' Her shoulders hunched, thick with muscle and threat.

That would be a fitting punishment, Rachel thought fiercely. Her arm around her mother's waist, she nodded. ''He threw paint all over and scrawled . . . words . . . on the walls. Trying to make it look like kids did it.''

"Lyle said it was maybe punks from the farm."

"No." Rachel shook her head. "Jeff says it was a man. One man."

"He saw him?"

"No . . ." Rachel hesitated. If the person was the killer . . . If he thought that Jeff had recognized him . . . "Jeff didn't get a look at his face, but he's sure it was a man—by himself."

Earlene grunted. "You go on to Portland with your mom." She nodded brusquely. "Gimme your keys, and I'll take your truck home. I can walk down to the station, after."

"You're in no condition to drive," her mother said sternly, running her fingers through Rachel's tangled hair. "And no way you go to Portland by yourself."

"I'm not arguing." Rachel handed over her truck keys to Earlene, her knees suddenly shaky with relief. "Thank you so much for coming." She hugged her mother tightly.

"You should have called me," her mother said.

"I should have." Rachel swallowed, sudden truth squeezing her. "I guess I can't help it—thinking that you're against Jeff, too," she said in a small voice.

"I guess I was." Her mother sighed, sounding suddenly weary. "Well, I still am, a little bit, but not in the same way. But after our little mud bath, I did realize that you're a grown-up, and you get to make your own decisions. It's just . . . hard to let your child be a grown-up. Remember that when you're a mother," she said sternly.

"Yes, ma'am." Rachel hugged her.

"So, let's go, girl."

"Personally, I think you ladies need a qualified chauffeur," a familiar voice spoke up.

They turned, startled. Joshua stood in the doorway, his hands on his hips, smiling.

"Joshua!" Rachel's mother opened her arms to her stocky husband. "I thought you were in Portland."

"I was . . ." He glanced at his watch. "A little more than an hour ago."

"Oh, Lordy." His wife rolled her eyes as he kissed her. "Did you ever slow down to the speed limit?"

"Don't think so." He kissed her again, then held out a hand

to Rachel. "Poor girl. What a horrible scene to walk in on. Jeff'll be fine." He squeezed her hand, his gray eyes alive with sympathy. "I talked to Dr. Potter just now. She doesn't think there's any brain injury. She's just playing it safe. She's the daughter of an old friend of mine, by the way. He's one of the best cardio docs in the business, and his daughter's just as sharp."

As he talked he ushered Rachel and her mother through the glass doors and out to the curb where he had left the Jeep Cherokee he drove when he had too many passengers for his beloved sports car. "You just relax." He opened the front door for her. "See if you can sleep a bit. You look pretty shocky yourself."

"As if anyone could sleep while you drive...." Her mother muttered as she climbed into the backseat. "Remember, love, this is a Jeep, not an MG."

"Oh, all right, all right." He rolled his eyes in mock resignation. "And here I was all set to beat the ambulance, head start or no."

"Behave yourself," his wife ordered, then leaned forward to tickle the tanned back of his neck. "Put the seat back and sleep, sweetheart," she said to Rachel. "You may not get much more tonight."

Rachel did as she was told, knowing that there was no way she could sleep. Not yet. They drove down through the sleeping town, past puddles of neon light from the new shopping center, and took the ramp to the interstate highway. Joshua was recounting a long, convoluted tale of how he and Dr. Potter's father were interns together, and how they had once smuggled a cadaver into the staff lounge at the hospital where they worked. Halfway through the story, Joshua's reassuring words echoing in her head, Rachel actually fell asleep.

CHAPTER

13

Rachel's catnap in the car left her feeling as if she had been wrapped in a thick layer of plastic as she moved through the quiet hospital corridors in Portland. It had begun to rain as they drove westward down the Gorge. The water fell in twisting sheets, driven by a gusty west wind that forced Joshua to turn the wipers up to "high" and actually drive at less than the legal speed limit. Huge semi rigs threw up clouds of dense spray from their multiple wheels, turning the world briefly into a dangerous opalescent limbo.

Chilled and damp, Rachel huddled in a waiting-room chair, staring at the neatly stacked magazines on the plastic wood-grained table in the middle of the small alcove. A vending machine in the hall hummed softly, and she sipped absently at the frothy cup of overly sweet hot chocolate that Joshua had purchased from it. The magazines included tattered and thumbed issues of *Sunset Magazine, Good Housekeeping, Cooking Light,* and one aged copy of *Fishing and Hunting News.* It seemed out of place here.

Her mother sat beside her, not saying much, merely holding Rachel's hand. Every so often she squeezed it, with a warmth and sympathy that needed no words. Joshua sat on the other side of her, saying nothing, his own sympathy like a gentle

radiating heat. They had tried conversation and had mutually
desisted from the empty effort. Eventually a round-faced
cheerful nurse wheeled Jeff into the room.

She seemed very fresh and wide-awake for this hour of the
day, Rachel thought with a distinct lack of charity.

"We're all done with him," the nurse announced with a
dimpled smile. "You can have him back. Doctor can't find
any reason to hang on to him anymore."

"They decided there wasn't anything there, so nothing
could get hurt," Jeff said with a weak grin. In spite of his
attempt at humor, his face looked gaunt and sallow beneath
the bandages that crowned his head. Shadows darkened the
skin under his eyes.

"I'm so glad." Rachel took his hand, squeezing hard, her
heart full of feelings that she couldn't begin to sort out. "Let's
go home," she said, her voice choked.

"I got us some rooms at a hotel." Joshua put a hand on
her shoulder. "The two of you look as if you're going to fall
on your faces at any moment. Might as well fall into a bed.
We'll go back after you've had a chance to get some rest."
He gave Jeff a mock glare. "As a doctor—well, a retired
doctor—I prescribe at least twenty-four hours of rest and re-
laxation in town here. That's an order."

"Yes, sir," Jeff said, so meekly that Rachel stifled a giggle
with alarm.

A giggle would do her in, she thought. Utterly. So she didn't
say anything and kept her grip on Jeff's hand as the nurse
wheeled him through the maze of corridors. They passed
through the automatic doors of the small tiled reception area
where the ambulance had brought Jeff. He made no effort to
remove his hand from hers. Rachel felt a small sense of shock
at the orange rim of the sun just visible beyond the roofs and
treetops to the east. Morning. Exhaustion seemed to fill her
like water running into a bathtub, and her legs began to trem-
ble. Joshua had the Jeep waiting at the curb, and she climbed
in after Jeff, collapsing gratefully onto the backseat.

The brief drive to the hotel was a blur. Joshua parked in
front of a long wing of windows fronted with small railed
balconies, and helped her out of the car. "I got three rooms.

They're connected by doors." He kissed her on the cheek. "So you can keep an eye on Jeff."

"Thank you so much," she said, and meant it from the bottom of her heart.

"I need to call Lyle." Jeff looked around restlessly at the double bed, chair, and tables that filled the carpeted room. "See if he got anywhere."

"I bet Lyle is asleep and wouldn't be very happy to hear from you." Joshua put a hand firmly on his arm. "Let him do it, Jeff. Get some rest. That's another order."

"All right." Jeff looked away. "I guess I could let him do his job, huh?" He slumped onto the bed.

"You can have the next room." Joshua handed Rachel a key and laid a second one on the nightstand beside the big bed. "There's a nice coffee shop and a restaurant in the lobby. We're right next door, on the other side of Jeff."

"I'm so glad you're all right, Jeff." Rachel's mother leaned over and kissed him on the cheek. "I was frightened."

"Thank you," Jeff said. He took her hand. "For everything you've done. I . . . I'm sorry . . ."

"No." Deborah shook her head. "No need for that. Not tonight. Not ever." She smiled at him, a trace of tears making her eyes brilliant. "You do your job well, Jeff. You have to. Good night." She took Joshua's hand, smiled at both of them again, and exited with her husband into the adjoining room.

Rachel helped Jeff get into bed—which he allowed rather than really needed—then kissed him lightly.

"I'm sorry you had to be the one . . . to find me," he mumbled sleepily. "Pretty messy."

"It scared the daylights out of me." She smiled as his eyes closed, and laid his hand gently on the flowered spread that covered the bed.

In her own room, sun streamed through the windows, and her earlier sleepiness had vanished, leaving her filled with a brittle, restless energy. She closed the blinds, turned the flowered spread down, and plumped the pillows, but then went back into Jeff's room and sat down on the edge of the bed. His chest rose and fell with the reassuring rhythm of sleep. She watched him breathe for a long time, letting the jumble of feelings in her chest untangle themselves slowly.

"I'm afraid," she whispered after a while, touching his lean, long-fingered hand. A small white scar curved across the back, like a shallow, cursive *S*, just below his knuckles. He had cut that left hand one afternoon, when the two of them and their friends Sandy and Bill had been exploring the old abandoned Hansen place. He had bandaged it himself, afraid to tell his mother, because they weren't supposed to be in the Hansen place, with its glass-strewn floors and broken chairs and tables. Who could have foretold that years later he'd live there? The scar looked bright against his tawny skin.

His hint of Paiute blood showed up in the summer when he got a little sun. Gently she ran her finger along the white line of scar tissue. Once she had asked him about his Indian blood. He had joked that he was as Indian as the Lone Ranger, but he would never talk about it after that. Like Spider, Rachel thought suddenly. A kid with a Vietnamese last name who is more white than Asian, his face a legacy from a crazy, vanished father. Family, she thought bleakly . . .

"Mom hurt so much when Dad died." She spoke to the sleeping man, her words a whisper that barely stirred the air. "It was as if someone had cut something out of her." Her mother had folded in on herself, closed up like a box. Although she had smiled and packed lunches, worked in the orchard, and asked about schoolwork, it was as if she had retreated inside a house and pulled down the blinds. "It was as if she was wounded," Rachel whispered. "She loved him so much." Her finger traced that line of white from one end to the other, back and forth, back and forth. "I guess it scares me." She swallowed. "That I could be that hurt. If I let myself admit that . . . I love you." Her voice faltered on those final words. Gently she laid his hand down on the comforter, and as she did she thought she might have felt the slightest pressure from his fingers. But when she looked at his face, his eyes were closed, and he breathed with the slow even rhythm of slumber. Tiptoeing out of the room, she left the door open, so that she could hear any sound he might make.

Still unable to sleep, she lay on the bed and listened to the sounds of travelers departing—car doors slamming, motors revving. The bright sun crept slowly across the floor—an edge of hard light beneath the hem of the drapes. She thought about going down to the coffee shop, but she wasn't really hungry and she didn't want to leave Jeff. But she finally must have drowsed, because when she opened her eyes, Jeff was sitting in one of the room's upholstered easy chairs, watching her with an enigmatic look on his face.

"Good morning." He smiled. "Or good afternoon, rather. It's past twelve."

"I fell asleep after all." Rachel sat up and yawned, stretching, feeling the effect of the last eighteen hours in her shoulders and back. "How are you feeling?"

"Fine." He grimaced and touched the bandage on his head. "Except that this itches. And I had to wear a shower cap to take a shower."

He sounded almost cheerful. Rachel got up and reached for his hands. "I am so glad you're all right." And with those words, the tears that she had been holding back all night burned her eyes once more. Jeff's arms went around her, and for a while she merely buried her face on his shoulder while he stroked her hair and back, willing herself not to dissolve into tears.

"Let's go get some coffee." She straightened, sniffling a little, a lump still painful in her throat. "I think I need some."

"Some breakfast, too." He twined his fingers in hers and squeezed. "I think lunch yesterday was the last time I ate."

She hadn't been hungry before, but now her stomach rumbled loudly, and they both smiled. Her mother and Joshua weren't in their room, so Rachel scribbled them a note on the hotel pad that had been left with a convenient pen on the oak-veneered dresser, and they walked down the long carpeted corridors to the central lobby of the hotel. A low wall with a built-in planter full of silk foliage divided the tables from the rest of the lobby. A buffet table in the center of the area offered a variety of salads, and the tables were moderately full. Joshua and her mother sat in a booth in the far corner, and her mother waved vigorously as she spotted them.

"You look pretty good." She eyed Jeff critically as they made their way past other diners. "That bandage suits you."

She twinkled up at Jeff. "Makes you look rather rakish."

"The newest thing in headgear," Jeff drawled as they sat down. "All the teenagers will be doing it." He eyed their plates, which were both loaded with a variety of salads. "Food. I'll take it, whatever it is."

"The salad bar." Joshua nodded. "Try the shrimp and noodle salad. It's got a nice spicy Thai sauce. The chef used fresh ginger."

The waitress appeared at the table to take their order, and instructed them to take a plate from the pile at the end of the salad bar and help themselves. Ravenously hungry, Rachel and Jeff immediately departed in search of food.

The salad bar was indeed a delight. Rachel loaded her plate with various green and pasta-based salads, and piled two fresh rolls on top of it all. Jeff's plate was even fuller than hers, if possible, and she laughed as they carried their food back to the table. "People will think we haven't eaten in a week." She set her plate down on the table and grinned at her mother. "I love salad bars. No guilt."

"Unless you load up on a gallon of dressing." Joshua eyed her plate and nodded. "I don't think you need to feel guilty at all, my dear. Have you talked to Lyle?" Josh turned his attention to Jeff. "I wonder if he found out who attacked you yet."

"I called him when I woke up." Jeff's lips thinned briefly. "He doesn't know anything more." He set his fork down. "I saw the guy. I know I did. But I just can't remember . . ."

"It'll come to you." Rachel reached over to touch his wrist. "Remember what the doctor said? Don't try, and it'll come back."

"She said *maybe*. Let's hope it does." Jeff forced a smile. "I owe somebody for that crack on the head yesterday." He began to eat, and for a few minutes conversation languished as everyone concentrated on their food.

"Are you going to want to go back to Hood River right away?" Joshua reached for his glass of iced tea. "As your non-doctor, I'd recommend taking the day off. Rest. Relax by the pool—they do have one here. We could have dinner tonight, maybe listen to some music, and go back in the morning."

"That sounds like fun." Jeff smiled. "I actually did plan to spend the day in Portland—but I need to get back tonight. I called Spider's mother." He turned to Rachel. "I thought I'd go talk to her about this investment scam Spider told you about."

"You never stop working, do you?" Rachel asked, her eyebrows rising. "So, how did you get her number?"

"I can't stop working until this case is closed." He regarded her soberly. "Actually, I talked to her right after you told me about the scam. Your friend Bard gave me the information—although a bit reluctantly, I have to say. I got her number from Lyle when I woke up. I was lucky to catch her at home. She works at a beauty parlor, but she's off this afternoon. I told her I'd come by around three."

"You did all this this morning?" Rachel sighed. "You're supposed to be resting and recovering, remember?"

"I am recovering." Jeff forked up a tiny pink shrimp. "This is the best way to do it."

"Do you want to take the Jeep?" Joshua leaned back to let the waitress remove his plate, his tone resigned. "I'll have an espresso please," he told her, and turned his attention back to Jeff. "Since I realize that there's no point in arguing with you, Deborah and I might take the hotel shuttle into town. I'm sure we can find plenty to do while you're interviewing this woman."

"I thought you were on my side on this rest issue." Rachel glared at him.

"I think he's right about speeding his recovery." Joshua patted her hand. "And I learned long ago which battles to walk away from."

"Which is why I love you." Rachel's mother leaned over to give her husband a demure kiss on the cheek.

"You love me for my MG. Only now you have one of your own." He grinned back at her, then sobered. "I think we'll worry less about you and Jeff both, once this murder is solved."

Rachel shivered, because he was right. Whoever attacked

Jeff might have intended to kill him. And they might try again. "Okay, I'll be quiet," she said meekly, then gave Jeff a sideways glance. "But I get to come along, okay?"

He opened his mouth to refuse, then closed it and nodded unexpectedly. "It might be better if you do," he said. "Maybe she'll be more comfortable with you there. Her name is Amy Muir. She took her own name back after her divorce from Spider's father."

"We'll meet here later, then," Joshua said cheerfully. He glanced at his watch. "How about six o'clock? We can have a quick dinner and get back to Blossom at a reasonable hour."

"Sounds good." Jeff looked over to Rachel. "Are you ready to go visiting? It's close to three."

Rachel rolled her eyes and observed her mother's smile. Whatever anger she had felt toward Jeff for his suspicions about Uncle Jack, the past night seemed to have laid it to rest.

"Good luck with your interview." Deborah took Joshua's arm as they rose. "Me, I'm going to Powell's Books as long as we're in town."

Josh rolled his eyes. "I knew it. We already need another bookcase." He handed Jeff the Jeep's key. "It's parked right outside our rooms. See you at six." He lifted a cautioning finger. "But if you start getting headaches, or get tired, quit and go lie down. Even if the scan was negative, you still got quite a bump on the head. You nag him," he said to Rachel with a wink. "Since I won't be there."

"I will." Rachel crossed her arms. "I certainly will."

14

Amy Muir lived in a rather run-down neighborhood east of Portland. The ramp from the freeway led them into a maze of narrow streets, many of them unpaved and full of puddles from last night's rain. Some of those puddles were deep, Rachel discovered. The houses that fronted these streets offered small muddy yards crowded with rusting cars on blocks, motorcycles in various stages of disassembly, and a few elderly speedboats on trailers, sadly in need of paint and repair.

Rachel eyed the picture windows that most of the houses seemed to possess as she drove slowly down the decaying street. Grimy drapes and even bedsheets protected the interiors from the gray spring light. No young children played in the wet streets, but a foursome of teenagers in colorful T-shirts and baggy pants tossed a muddy basketball at a battered hoop nailed to a light pole. Two were Asian—perhaps Vietnamese or Cambodian, Rachel guessed. The other two were white. All displayed skateboarding logos on their shirts, and their jeans sagged to show their underwear.

One of the kids reminded Rachel sharply of Spider, with the same mixed-race golden skin and almond eyes. His hair was buzzed close on the sides and bristled in a stiff bleached-

mahogany brush on top. He stared back at her, his face closed
and expressionless.

"Glad it hasn't rained much," Jeff muttered as she maneu-
vered between two derelict cars that nearly blocked the street.
"We'd need to use four-wheel drive for sure."

"Or waders. There. That's the house." The street had no
sidewalks, so she pulled as far off the street as she could. A
weedy yard surrounded a tiny cottage, fenced by battered
chain link. Although the house was badly in need of paint,
someone had tried to do a little gardening in the front yard.
Cold, unhappy pansies stubbornly lifted bedraggled purple
blossoms along the fence, and a scummy birdbath stood in the
middle of the yard. Three small boulders at the corner of the
street and driveway had been painted blue to match the trim
on the house. Rachel made a face.

"Not the best landscaping job, eh?" Jeff got out, locking
his door.

"Hey, it's better than most of the places on this street."
Rachel waited for him, oppressed by the muddy poverty of
this neighborhood that once must have been a nice place to
live. You could see the traces of gardens and landscaping in
the struggling shrubs and broken paving stones. Pale, sun-
faded drapes in the front window of the house twitched, and
the door opened as they reached the concrete step. More pansies sulked beside the door, waiting for sun and warmth.

"You must be the man who called." The petite woman who
stood behind the warped screen door peered warily at them
from beneath a spectacular mound of brightly auburn, country-
western curls.

"I'm Jeff Price, with the Blossom police." Jeff nodded.
"This is Rachel."

"Hi," Rachel said. The woman's hair was impressive both
in color and height. The mass dwarfed her small, fine-boned
features, and not a wisp moved as she nodded. She was
dressed in a sequined fuchsia sweat suit and wore matching
velour bedroom slippers. Her face was heavily made up. Blue
shadow on her eyelids clashed with the sweat suit fabric, giving her eyes a neon-lit glow.

"Police." She sighed. "It's always the police. Come in."

She unlatched the screen door and pushed at it tentatively, as if she wasn't quite strong enough to open it. "I guess you have to come in."

"As I told you, we're not here about Spider," Jeff said as they entered the main room of the house.

Spider's mother nodded, but her eyes doubted as she stared at Jeff's bandaged head. "He didn't do that, did he? That boy! Have a seat." She touched her towering hair as if to make sure it was still in place, then waved at a sofa and matching chair, worn on the back and arms, slightly dusty. The house smelled of musty fabric, bacon, and cigarette smoke.

A breakfast bar separated the narrow kitchen from the long front room. Dishes filled the sink, and a frying pan and teakettle occupied the cold burners. A laundry basket full of tangled clothes partially blocked the hallway that opened into the living room. Dusty, framed photographs cluttered the end tables on either side of the sofa—pictures of Princess Diana, Rachel noticed. And one picture of Spider looking very young and serious, posed stiffly against a marbled blue background. School picture? A velvet painting of Jesus hung on one wall, but other than that, the walls were bare.

"What did he do now?" She seated herself gingerly on the edge of a cheap bentwood rocker, reaching for the package of Virginia Slims beside an overflowing ashtray. Her long copper-colored nails matched the color of her hair perfectly. She snapped a cheap disposable lighter and inhaled deeply. "I thought he was making out okay at that fancy farm thing. He even wrote me a letter." Her words emerged on puffs of smoke. "It's a nice letter. Do you want to see it?"

"Spider's doing very well." Rachel glanced at Jeff and received a brief nod. "He works for me. Doing landscaping. He works very hard, and he's a nice kid."

"Landscaping?" Amy Muir swept her up and down with a sharp appraisal. "That's like yard work, isn't it? I never could get him to do the yard work around here." She made a face. "Not that I get much of it done either. I try, but I work six days a week—they only hire part-time at these walk-in places, you know. They don't want you to get too many regular clients, or you might up and leave with 'em. So you got to work two places, if you want to make any money, and it seems like there's never enough time. As you can see.'' She touched her hair again with one hand and waved at the kitchen with the other. ''It's not like this usually, you know. I keep this place really clean, but I had this cold, and I just sort of got behind. You look like you had a hard day, too, honey,'' she said with a touch of venom.

Rachel glanced down at her dress. She had slept in it, and it looked like it. Once again she noticed the rusty stains on the hem, mercifully concealed by the print. Jeff's blood. She swallowed.

''We're interested in your investment.'' Jeff leaned forward. ''The one that didn't work out. Spider told Rachel about it.''

''You mean John. His name is John, with an H. Yeah, he asked me to bring him that letter I got.'' Amy's fingers crept back to her hair. ''Carrie—we play bingo every Thursday together—she made a ton of money out of that club.'' She sighed. ''I guess you got to take your chances. That's what she said. That it's a high-risk thing. But you get a lot back if it works out. I should've stuck with the lottery.'' She laughed and patted the frozen curls at the base of her neck. ''I won a hundred bucks last month.''

''We think your investment club might have been something called a Ponzi scheme. That's an illegal scam,'' Jeff told her. ''That's what we're trying to find out.''

''Ponzi, huh? Never heard of it.'' Amy sighed, her hands fluttering to her knees like weary birds. ''I thought it sounded too good to be true.'' She added more smoky words to the thickening atmosphere. ''But Carrie made a ton of money.'' This was her rosary: Carrie made a ton of money. She leaned over to stub out the long butt of her cigarette. ''How could she make money if it was a scam?'' she asked wistfully.

''The first people in get paid by the money that the newest victims put in,'' Jeff told her patiently. ''But there's no real investment. The person who starts it gets most of the money. Do you have any more letters or receipts from this investment club?''

''Oh, yes.'' Amy got slowly to her feet. ''I keep real good records. Last year my bank shorted me fifteen dollars, and I caught it right away." She disappeared down the dark hallway, only to reappear a few minutes later with several sheets of paper clutched in her hand.

"I met Mr. Desmond." She handed them each a sheet of paper. "He was sweet, you know? But married. All the good ones are." She lit another cigarette. "I didn't keep the flyer Carrie gave me. But it told how investing isn't just for the rich, and how the club would put your money together with other people, so that you could really buy really good stocks. It told how all these people like doubled their money in just a couple of years. It invests in real estate mostly, you see. Risky, but you can really clean up," she said proudly.

Rachel swallowed a sigh as she scanned the document in her hand. Formatted to look like a statement from an investment firm, it listed shares held in a venture called West Coast Tomorrows and dividends returned. According to the statement she held—for October two years ago—Amy had made one hundred dollars on her five-hundred-dollar investment in the space of thirty days.

"That was before it started losing. I guess the housing market went bad. The club issues this newsletter that tells you what's going on." She shrugged. "I guess it was just bad timing. I made a hundred dollars before it went bust," she said hopefully. "If I'd started sooner, I could have made more than Carrie." Her expression faltered. "But you say Mr. Desmond is a crook. He was so sweet . . ."

"I'd like you to take a look at this." Jeff pulled a folded sheet of fax paper from his pocket.

"You *were* busy this morning," Rachel murmured, which earned her an innocent look as he handed the faxed photo of Bob Dougan to the frowning woman. "Does he look familiar?"

"Oh, sure. That's Robert, all right. I'd know him anywhere. He took me out to dinner at the Copper Penny. We had such a good time together." Sadness gleamed like a slick of oil on Amy's vague gray eyes. "I could've used that money to lease a station in a really classy salon. But I didn't. It was for John so he could maybe go to Portland State, do something besides work a drill press like my dad did, and like Sam did. Sam was

John's dad. He was crazy, but he was sweet. He never raised a hand to me or John. And he'd bring me flowers. For no reason, you know?'' She sighed. ''You know, if he walked back through the door this minute, I think I'd take him back.'' She laughed a small, smoky laugh. ''I guess I'm just as crazy as he is, huh?'' She handed the flimsy sheet back. ''Is Robert going to jail?''

''He's dead actually.''

''Really.'' Amy glanced at the colorful picture of Jesus with an air of disappointment. ''Well—God giveth and God taketh away. That's what my pastor always says, you know. Robert liked my hair. He thought I was ten years younger than I am.'' Her drab eyes kindled briefly. ''I bet Carrie's gonna be surprised when her checks stop coming!''

Rachel wondered privately if Carrie had really made much money, or if she had simply boasted to earn the admiration and envy of her friends. ''How old was Spider . . . John . . . when his father left you?'' she asked.

Amy turned to face her, hands refolding themselves. ''Ten.'' She sighed. ''Sam had been getting crazier and crazier—he started missing days at work—taking John on these long trips without telling me—just driving off to visit some stupid little cemetery out in the middle of nowhere. I told him just to forget it, but, no, he had to find his dad's name on some piece of rock somewhere.'' She shook her head. ''I don't think the guy died. Not for a minute. He probably had a wife and kids at home. Like he was really gonna bring some Vietnamese hooker and her kid home after the war. Oh, sure. One time they went clear to San Diego—were gone a week without a word. That's when I filed for divorce.'' Brief anger flared and faded almost instantly. ''But, you know, he was a good dad to John. He really loved him. He was so gentle.'' She smiled, her expression sadly wistful. ''I think it was one of the things that really turned me on to him at first—he was so gentle. Sweet and kind of exotic, you know?'' Her smile grew rueful. ''Most men I knew weren't sweet, and they for sure weren't gentle. I guess I was giving my dad what for, too. Marrying a gook . . . That's what he called Sam.'' She giggled. ''He just about had a heart attack. But I was eighteen, and he couldn't just beat me up and lock me in my room anymore. And besides. It was too late. I was already pregnant.''

"With John?" Rachel tried to add the numbers up, because Amy looked as if she was older than the bright hair suggested.

"With his brother, Sam." The woman looked down at her hands with their gleaming, perfect nails. "He died," she said. "When John was a baby."

"I'm sorry."

"That's why I started saving that money. It wasn't easy after Sam left, either." She lifted her chin. "Some weeks, it just doesn't seem like there's enough, never mind extra. But I always put at least five dollars away. Every week." Her eyes flashed. "I was a good mother. If John hadn't hung out with the kids he did . . ." She looked away. "It wasn't my fault. When you work two, three jobs, how can you be home all day, too? Tell me how I could've stayed home to look after him, huh?"

"John's a good kid." Impulsively Rachel reached for the woman's hand. Her polished nails felt like plastic against her palm, the fingers stiff and cool as a doll's. "He'll do okay. I believe that."

"I gave him good values. It was his friends who got him into trouble. Smoking pot. Drinking. Stealing cars. That's why he's there, you know. He was riding in this stolen car. And he'd been arrested for shoplifting already. They were all drunk." Amy stood, fingers checking her hair automatically. "And now . . . I've got no money for school. Even the state schools—do you know what they cost? Or can I get my money back from this scumbag?" Her face brightened briefly, then fell. "Oh, yeah, he's dead, right? So I can't get anything, I bet."

"We'll look into it." Jeff put a hand on her shoulder, his eyes dark with compassion. "There might be some way you could collect. May I keep your statements from the club for a while?"

"You really think I could get the money back?" She blinked briefly and rapidly. "I've got more papers. I'll get 'em for you." She shuffled away to return a moment later with a handful of neatly paper-clipped pages. "This is all of 'em, I think. I didn't get one last month."

"Thanks." Jeff touched her arm again. "I'll be in touch with you."

"Sure." She shuffled to the door after them, leaning against the frame as they exited. "When you see John, tell him I had a nice visit and I really liked the letter. I've got to write back to him. I keep meaning to. . . ." She made a vague gesture. "I've never been good at writing letters."

"I'll tell him," Rachel said.

Side by side, she and Jeff followed the cracked concrete walk to the street. They drove in silence back through the decaying streets, out to the main street that led to the freeway. "Is there any way that she could get Spider's money back?" Rachel asked as she turned onto the freeway.

"I doubt it." Jeff stared out at the traffic. "Maybe if she sued his estate. But I think she'd need more than she's got to prove that Dougan was behind this. From what I've been able to find out, he covered his tracks pretty thoroughly."

"Ransom Loper has that evidence!" Rachel sucked in her breath. "I completely forgot. Last night—I saw some papers in his briefcase. Letterhead from this club of Dougan's. Loper got pretty pissed when he caught me looking. I think maybe he was in on this thing. I'm sorry." She eyed him anxiously. "I told you I couldn't really keep out of this."

Jeff frowned at a passing semi, his shoulders rising and falling with his slow exhale. "I could shake you, but then we'd both end up dead." He sighed, then gave her a crooked smile. "So how did you manage a look at Loper's briefcase? You weren't breaking and entering, were you? No, don't tell me, if you were."

"I wasn't. He invited me to dinner, and I went." Rachel gave Jeff a sideways glance. "I keep thinking that Dougan's vote change would have sure messed up Loper's plans. It would have probably hurt him more than it would've Uncle Jack."

"It probably would have, considering his track record." Jeff paused while Rachel negotiated the car through the freeway interchange that would take them back to their hotel. "He's lucky he still has his contractor's license, and he's under some major financial pressure, according to what I've been able to discover. Which could fit with his getting involved in a Ponzi scheme.'' He didn't look at her. ''Actually, Ransom Loper has been my number one suspect for some time now. His alibi for that evening is shaky at best. He says he was at his motel, but nobody can confirm it.''

''You know—he really seemed to be certain that Dougan wouldn't change his vote, not matter what anyone says. I don't think he was acting. He was *sure*.'' She hesitated. ''Why didn't you say something about Loper to Uncle Jack?''

''I don't think Loper has a clue that I'm seriously interested in him, and I want to keep it that way.'' Jeff's lips tightened. ''And would it have made any difference to your uncle if I'd told him he wasn't my only suspect?''

Maybe. It might have made life easier for Jeff, Rachel thought. But Jeff wasn't going to compromise his investigation for that kind of reason. ''Jack would still be storming. You're right.'' She reached over to touch his knee. ''You mad at me for having dinner with Loper?''

''If you mean am I jealous—a little.'' He took her hand and squeezed it. ''Mostly you scared me. This guy has some very shady history.'' He placed her hand back on the wheel, his fingers lingering on her knuckles for a moment. ''If I stop asking you to stay out of this, will you leave him strictly alone?''

''No problem. He's not my type.'' She smiled at Jeff. ''You've been getting such a shitty deal in town. I'm so sorry.''

''Mostly folks are blaming Ventura.'' Jeff shrugged. ''I just get the fallout. Have you found that truck key yet?''

''No.'' Rachel sighed. ''I must have dropped it right there by the truck. So anybody could have picked it up. Was Loper at City Hall that day?''

''Yes.'' Jeff nodded, his jaw tight. ''I have a lot of circumstantial evidence against him like that. Not enough for an arrest.'' He gave her a sour grin. ''I have almost as much evidence against your uncle. Nothing concrete on either of them. By the way, Dougan's bank account shows a cash withdrawal of ten thousand dollars the day of the murder. We couldn't find any trace of the money. It might have been a payout for his Ponzi scheme.'' Jeff's expression darkened. ''If I could only remember who hit me . . .''

''You will. Anytime now.'' She touched his leg again, feeling the tension in his muscles.

''I hope you and that doctor are right,'' Jeff muttered as Rachel turned onto the ramp that led to their hotel. ''I really hope so, because right now that's the only concrete break I can see.''

At the hotel, they found Joshua reading *The New York Times* in the room. A violin concerto murmured from the radio, but he turned it off as they entered. ''Well, we never got closer to town than the fancy mall across the street from here. They had bookstores. And an antique merry-go-round. Your mom looks great on a carved wooden horse.'' He grinned as he folded the newspaper. ''So are you chafing at the bit to get back to Blossom?'' he asked Jeff.

''Hey, I thought we were pressuring him to take another day off.'' Rachel shook her head. ''What kind of backup are you?''

''Well, I'm sure Jeff is anxious to get back.'' Joshua gave her a benign smile. ''And this way I'm saved from the bookstores. The Jeep only has so much cargo space. We might have to rent a trailer.''

Rachel laughed but gave him a sharp look, wondering what had really initiated this about-face.

''I saw you drive up.'' Deborah entered before Rachel could say anything, wearing a one-piece swimsuit, a hotel towel draped around her shoulders. ''They have a rather nice pool here.'' She smiled and kissed her daughter. ''So how did it go?'' she asked Jeff. ''Your interview?''

''Pretty well.'' He eyed Deborah's petite figure with admiration. ''Somebody thought to pack last night.''

''Oh, I bought this today.'' She stroked the satiny fabric appreciatively. ''Figured I might as well enjoy the pool, long as they had one.''

''We could put one in, dear.'' Joshua rose to kiss his wife on the nape of her neck. ''You get to keep it clean.''

"Exactly." She turned to grin at him. "Which is why I think I'll stick with the river for my swimming, thank you." She turned back to Jeff and Rachel. "How about if we have a quick dinner before we go? Rush hour is starting about now, anyway. This *is* the big city."

"I wouldn't mind heading back tonight," Jeff said slowly. "I've got a few things I want to check out first thing in the morning."

Like Ransom Loper before he decided to leave town, Rachel thought grimly. She watched Joshua and her mother exchange looks, then plaster identically innocent expressions on their faces. "We found this lovely Mongolian Grill," Deborah chirped. "It's in the mall. We can eat there and then head back."

They checked out and went across the road to the restaurant. The food—cooked to order on a massive grill—was delicious, and they lingered for a while, talking about Blossom politics and the influx of new residents to the Gorge. "It'll be dark by the time we get back." Jeff eyed the declining sun as they exited the restaurant.

"It won't be too late." Joshua unlocked the car. "Even if I obey the speed limit. All aboard."

Rachel had a feeling that he and her mother had orchestrated the dinner carefully—that they had a schedule. For the life of her she couldn't figure out what they were up to. They certainly weren't giving anything away. She took Jeff's hand as he settled on the seat beside her, momentarily overwhelmed by memories of last night. He squeezed her hand reassuringly and kept hold of it as Joshua threaded the maze of freeway ramps to head east.

The meal, and her lack of sleep, caught up with Rachel as they left Portland behind. "Put your head on my shoulder," Jeff murmured. "Catch a nap."

"I'd better watch it next time I drive this highway," Rachel said with a yawn. "This is becoming a habit." Jeff chuckled, and she fell instantly asleep.

CHAPTER

15

The early spring evening fell before they reached Blossom. In the full dark, beneath a scatter of stars and tattered clouds, they turned onto the road that led up to Jeff's cliff-edge house. The drive back had been good, Rachel thought. Jeff and her mother had chatted, and there had been no tension in Deborah, no reserve. For her, he was no longer the enemy.

Toward the end of the drive, Jeff grew quiet. His profile stark against the fading sunset light, he had watched the broad Columbia roll by, beyond the Interstate. Rachel reached over and took his hand. "Work party tomorrow," she said. "We'll get the house cleaned up in no time."

"Mind reader." He nodded and smiled, but the line of his shoulders didn't relax. Rachel sighed and sat back against the seat as they rounded the turn at the top of the slope and pulled into the small gravel lane that led back to the house. Joshua began to whistle softly as they crept along the narrow corridor between the rampant brush. When Rachel gave him a suspicious glance, he fell instantly silent, his round face blandly innocent as they pulled into the clearing.

Cars packed the grassy space in front of the house. Rachel sat forward, a slow smile starting from deep inside. In the front seat, Joshua and her mother wore a matching pair of grins.

Earlene stood on the porch, a beer in her hand, waving.

"Nice timing." She came over to lean against the Jeep's roof. "Get here after all the work's done, huh?" She winked at Jeff, who looked stunned. "Well, you're just in time to party, boy. Least you didn't miss that."

"What . . . ?" He fumbled with the door handle, pushed the door open, and stood, still clutching the handle. More people were spilling out of the house—Joylinn Markham from the Bread Box, Roth Glover, even Mayor Ventura was there, dumping a bucket full of soapy water into the weeds, then waving cheerfully. Julio was there, too, hanging back shyly at the edge of the throng that crowded the doorway. "What are you doing?" Jeff croaked.

"You never invited us over for a housewarming," Earlene drawled. "Damned unsocial of you. So we invited ourselves. Place was a mess. We sort of cleaned up a little while we was waiting for you to show." Her grin revealed uneven teeth as she shoved the freshly opened beer into his hand. "Come on in. It kind of smells a little, so we moved the food out to the deck. Nice job there, by the way. Didn't know you were as good with a hammer as you are with a wrench."

Holding the beer by the neck, moving like a sleepwalker, Jeff climbed the steps. The small crowd parted in front of him as he crossed the porch, touching him, congratulating him, welcoming him back.

"Lyle was out here for a while, too," Earlene went on, obviously enjoying the drama of the moment. "He figured he'd better get back to town before you caught him goofin' off."

Jeff stopped in the doorway, leaning one hand against the frame.

All signs of the vandalism had vanished. The walls gleamed, spotless, and the smell of fresh paint filled the room. Everything stood in its place. He cleared his throat and turned back to the residents of Blossom who crowded his porch. "I . . . I'm not very good at doing speeches." His eyes moved from face to expectant, grinning face. "I guess . . ." His voice caught, and he cleared his throat. "About all I can say is . . . thanks. I . . . I didn't expect anything like this." He lifted the

beer in salute. "Here's to all of you. Thank you, my friends."
He cleared his throat again, blinked, and took a long swallow.

Everyone applauded, and Earlene slapped him on the back—
moderating her usual bear-paw blow to a mere tap. "Come
on out to the deck. Joylinn brought quite a spread. Hell, everyone pitched in with somethin'. Me, I brought potato chips.
That's 'bout my level of cu-lin-ar-y skill." She winked at Rachel.

Everyone trooped out onto the deck, pressing close to ask
Jeff about his head, express their anger over the assault, and
clap him on his back or shoulders. Jeff answered questions
and laughed at the jokes, more relaxed than Rachel had seen
him in days. Outside, a sheet of plywood set on two sawhorses
and covered with a gingham tablecloth groaned beneath a
bountiful potluck. Piles of paper plates and plastic forks waited
at one end of the table, and a couple of ice chests held pop,
juice, and beer. Rachel went over to hug her mother and
Joshua as everyone crowded around the table.

"Did you set this up?" She tilted her head at the grinning
Joshua. "I wondered why you changed your tune about Jeff
staying overnight in Portland."

"Earlene got everybody organized, I think. She called us
while you two were out." He exchanged smiling glances with
his wife. "But she said that people just started showing up
this morning, once word got around. I told her we'd get the
guest of honor here for the after-work party." He sobered. "I
think maybe Jeff needed to be reminded that folks are his
friends—even when they're not happy with what he has to do
in his job."

Rachel nodded, her heart full. It was indeed a timely re-
minder, she thought as she looked around the picnic throng.
Her uncle Jack was not among them. She stifled a sigh. Neither
was the former mayor, although his son Brian was talking
animatedly to Jeff over a plate full of cold cuts and Joylinn's
dark rye bread.

"I'm sure glad Jeff is okay." Phil Ventura wandered up,
carrying a sandwich in one hand and a can of pop in the other.
"By the way . . . your deck guy showed up this morning."

"Beck? Already?" Rachel nodded as her mother and

Joshua headed for the table. "That's good. He didn't make me any promises when I talked to him." In fact, he had sounded quite oddly reluctant, and she had wondered if he was one of the mayor's detractors. She had never known Beck to take any interest in politics.

"I'm glad you told me he was a little . . . eccentric." Ventura went on with a doubtful smile. "I looked out the window this morning, and here's this half-naked wild man complete with gray braided hair and a string of beads sitting in the middle of my backyard in the lotus position. I was about ready to call Lyle."

"Beck wears a shirt when it's below freezing," Rachel said with a straight face. "I think. And you should definitely ask to see the beads next time you run into him. He carves one out of the wood he uses on every project. I guess it's kind of a record. Just don't ask unless you have time, because you'll hear about each one." She shook her head. "He always visits a site before he starts a project—whether it's furniture or a barn he's building. He told me once that he has to match the soul of the wood to the soul of the place where it will live, or the harmony will be destroyed and it will fail."

"He looks—and sounds—like a refugee from the sixties." Ventura grimaced.

"Actually, he's barely thirty—not much older than me." Rachel shrugged. "He joined the army right out of high school. I heard he got sent to Iraq during the Gulf War, but he won't talk about his military time at all. Relax." She smiled at the mayor's dubious expression. "Beck is about the sweetest person I've ever met. I've never heard him say a single negative thing about anybody. Ever. He won't even swat a mosquito. He says that evil only happens if we believe in it. Trust me—you'll be glad I got him when you see your deck. He's an artist."

"Okay, I'm convinced. I think." Ventura still looked wary. "So that means you'll be getting started soon? Hey—" He broke off suddenly. "That's the same vine that's growing on my back fence." He walked over to the edge of the deck, pointing out a twining vine that sprawled over a pile of neatly cut branches that had been stacked at the edge of the yard. "It had pretty little purple flowers last summer and red berries in the fall. I thought you could leave it to grow up a trellis, or one of the trees, or something.'' He turned to her. ''What do you think? And do you know what it is? Somebody's leftover garden plant?''

Rachel hopped down from the deck and walked over to lift a spray of dark green leaves. No buds yet, she noticed. They would come later, in the summer. ''They looked like purple tomato blossoms, right?''

''Yep.''

''It's a member of the nightshade family.'' She straightened. ''It's—a relative of the tomato and potato. Locally we call it Deadly Nightshade. It's also called Bittersweet Nightshade.'' She shook her head. ''Your nephew is going to be playing in your backyard, isn't he? The berries are kind of tempting. And it can live up to its name.''

''Oh, no.'' Ventura stepped back, as if the nightshade plant was a snake that might suddenly strike at him. ''No way I keep it if it could hurt Aaron.'' He glared at the plant. ''You know, that thing is a good metaphor for what's going on here.'' He glanced up at her, his expression thoughtful. ''Somebody in this town looks like a harmless, upstanding citizen. Only he or she is not.'' He looked back at the deck with its knots of chatting people. ''I wonder if the person who murdered Bob Dougan is up there,'' he said softly. ''Eating and smiling. Creepy. Kind of horrific actually.'' He gave her a crooked smile. ''Sorry. I've been feeling a bit guilty. I . . . might have saved Dougan, I guess.''

''How?'' Rachel pulled up the nightshade plant and dropped the tangle of bruised leaves and stems onto the pile of firewood. ''You weren't even there.''

''I was supposed to be.'' Ventura gazed moodily at the dying plant. ''Roth Glover wanted to talk about the annexation vote after he closed up the store. I guess I was tired of the whole damn wrangle and . . . I forgot.'' His lips tightened. ''If I'd been there . . . if we'd been in my office with the lights on . . . It overlooks that alley where Dougan died.''

''It probably wouldn't have made any difference.'' Rachel

shook her head. "You might not have heard anything. Or you could have already left by then."

"Yeah, I know." Ventura straightened his shoulders. "One of those 'what if' moments that haunt you at two in the morning. Come on." He smiled and gestured at the deck. "Let's go get some food before it's all gone."

The floodlights mounted on the house washed the deck with yellow light. The tall cedars to the west of the house rustled in a rising, chilly wind. Rachel was glad of her jacket. She ate a piece of smoked sturgeon that Ralph Glover, Roth's brother, had pulled from the Columbia and smoked in the smokehouse their father had built behind the house. He still lived in the house where he and Roth had been born. Rachel watched the residents of Blossom taking their leave, packing up their plastic containers, bowls, and casserole dishes, and wondered if the next generation would be able to do that. Or if they would want to. Her cousins had left Blossom as soon as they had graduated from high school. Her mother was right, she thought. They wouldn't be back. There wasn't much here for them.

The deck had nearly emptied. Over in the far corner, her mother stood with Jeff, petite next to his height, talking earnestly. The breeze gusted with the approaching evening, bringing Rachel scattered handfuls of her words.

"... doesn't hate you, Jeff. He was ashamed afterward. But he's so damn proud. Such a hard pride ... You'll have to say the first words ..."

Uncle Jack. His absence would not have gone unnoticed. For the first time in her life, Rachel was ashamed for her uncle. The wind carried Jeff's reply away, but he bent down to kiss her mother gently on the top of her head.

Joshua wandered by with a trash bag in one hand, picking up the odd abandoned plate or plastic cup. He paused, his eyes on his wife and Jeff. "Families," he said and shook his head. "We hurt the ones we love most." He let his breath out in a rush as he snagged a mustard-smeared plate balanced on the unfinished railing. "Maybe the hurt has to balance the love. Or something." He smiled ruefully. "Hell, I'm a retired surgeon, not a philosopher. Ready to go, love?" He turned to

Deborah, who was walking toward them with Jeff, his arm
around her shoulders. "I thought we might take an evening
spin up the river." He winked at them. "I need to unwind
after all that restrained driving."

"You're speaking in front of the chief of police," Deborah
said with mock severity. "Yes, I'm ready to go." She leaned
forward to kiss Rachel. "Long day, dear. I think you both
need some rest."

"Me, too, Mom." She smiled fondly after them as Joshua
hopped off the deck and reached up to boost Deborah down,
who giggled as he twirled her around in a ballet-style lift before setting her on her feet. "Honestly, I don't think those two
will ever grow up."

"Is that such a bad thing?" Jeff gave her a quizzical look.

"Not a bit." She tucked her arm into his. "I hope I do as
well when I'm her age."

"I have faith in you." He put his arm around her. "Leave
the rest of the cleanup. There's hardly anything left to do.
Let's go sit and watch the stars."

Someone had washed the few dishes of Jeff's that had been
used, and had stacked them neatly in the kitchen dish drainer.
Rachel glanced at the tiles where Jeff had lain, and suppressed
a shiver. He took her hand, squeezed it, and they walked hand
in hand through the house and across the mown yard that had
been a forest of weeds a year ago and would be a garden next
year, Jeff had told her. He had built two chairs from clear
cedar boards, sanded them until they had the feel of satin
against your palm, and had set them up on a needled shelf of
ground beneath the trio of huge old cedars that protected the
house from the afternoon sun. From this cliff-edge space, hidden from the house by a tangle of elderberry, you could see
up and down the gigantic gash in the earth that was the vast
Columbia Gorge.

This was where Jeff came to think. Rachel settled into one
of the chairs, still holding his hand. The wind had blown the
last rags of cloud from the sky, and the Milky Way sparkled
overhead, like a sequined scarf tossed carelessly across the
darkness. Orion was already disappearing below the horizon,
giving way to the summer constellations.

"What happened between you and Jack?" Rachel asked as she searched for the Pleiades.

"Look!" Jeff pointed. "A shooting star." The brilliant streak seemed to arrow down into the distant darkness of the river, far to the east. "Sometimes you give things weight when you talk about them." His words came to her gently on the chilly wind. He lifted her hand to his lips and kissed her palm gently. "Let's not give it any more weight than it already has."

"Okay." Rachel took his hand in both of hers and pressed it to her face. "I won't ask again."

After that they merely sat, watching the stars wheel slowly and inexorably above the river of darkness and wind that was the Columbia Gorge.

CHAPTER

16

Julio had Sundays off—which was a good thing, because Rachel didn't wake up until the morning sun was full on her face. Which made it nine o'clock, at least. She had gotten to bed very late—driving home in her truck which Earlene had apparently driven to the potluck and left for her.

Rachel sat up, yawning, pretending she didn't notice the glowering Peter perched outside on the sill of her window. How he got up there, two stories from the ground, she didn't have a clue. But he would be there anytime she slept in, sitting bolt upright on the narrow strip of painted wood, glaring at her through the glass, letting her know that he was risking life and limb to announce his imminent demise from starvation.

Carefully she raised the window, and he leaped to her bed, his tail stiff and vertical. "Come on. I get a morning off once in a while."

Peter's flattened ears told her he disagreed.

"All right. All right. I'll feed you." Yawning, feeling as if she still hadn't quite caught up with her sleep, she padded into the kitchen barefoot, measuring coffee and water into the pot before getting a can of cat food down from the cupboard. She and Jeff had agreed to meet for a late lunch at the Bread Box. The morning was her own.

"Here, cat." She set the plate of food on the floor and sipped her coffee. Peter stalked over, whiskers twitching suspiciously. He sniffed at the food, ears still back, then—finally—began to eat. Shaking her head, smiling to herself, Rachel took her coffee into the bedroom and got dressed.

She had decided to go see Beck this morning. Fixing herself a piece of toast spread with a very miserly film of peanut butter (to atone for Earlene's potato chips), she let Peter out and hurried down the stairs to her truck. Her landlady, Mrs. Frey, who lived downstairs, was already out in her rose garden, her pale withered face shaded from the sun by one of her huge straw hats—this one decorated with seashells and a faded ribbon bow.

"That cat is after my chickadees again." Mrs. Frey waved a trowel threateningly at Peter, who had taken up position on one of the beams that supported the stairs—where he had a clear view of the concrete birdbath in the center of the rose garden. "You get one of my chickadees, cat, and I'll take the rake to you!"

Peter yawned, and Rachel suppressed a smile. The war between her cat and her landlady was of long standing, and based more on affection than outrage, she guessed. The chickadees seemed to survive and prosper, in spite of all Peter's attention and Mrs. Frey's threats. "I really tried to put a bell on him," she told her landlady contritely. "But he takes off a collar in no time flat, and I'm afraid to put them on too tight."

"Of course not!" Mrs. Frey looked horrified. "He might hang himself. No, I've put my feeder way up high." She pointed with the trowel, scattering bits of dirt. "My nephew Crane fixed a nice tray underneath to keep the seeds from falling to the ground, last time he visited. That way the poor birdies won't fly down to get them where That Cat can . . ." She broke off and shuddered, absently polishing the rest of the dirt from the trowel with the oversized University of Oregon sweatshirt she wore. From the look of it, she used it for that purpose regularly. "I heard about somebody breaking into your poor young man's house." She shook her head, which made the seashells on her hat brim clack together. "I don't know what we're coming to, here. Crime in the streets—

that's it. My Lincoln rose is just coming into some perfectly
lovely buds.'' She pointed with the now-gleaming trowel, toward a tall stately bush covered in dark, bloodred buds. ''You
pick the best one for him. Nothing like roses to cheer a person
up, I say.'' She followed Rachel to the truck, shells clacking,
waving the trowel for emphasis. ''Mind you cut the stem long,
dear. That variety has such lovely long stems. And cut it on
an angle—it will last longer that way. Put it right into the
water. Don't let it dry out, even for a moment.''

''I will,'' Rachel promised. ''And I'll be careful.''

''I know you will.'' Mrs. Frey beamed at her. ''You value
roses. Like my nephew. Crane always helped me in the garden
when he was out here summers as a boy. He was wonderful
with roses. He has a lovely garden in Berkeley, you know.
Although they go in for the oddest plants down there. Exotics.''

She clearly didn't approve of exotics. ''San Francisco has
a very mild climate.'' Rachel opened the door to the truck and
got in. ''Thank you so much for offering me that Lincoln bud.
I'll definitely pick one for Jeff. He'll be very pleased.''

''You make sure you do, dear.'' Mrs. Frey waved her trowel
some more. ''And when that nice young man asks you to
marry him, mind you say yes. You don't want to pass up
something that good for some dream that might never show
up. Trust me.''

''I . . . I'll keep that in mind.'' Rachel managed to keep a
straight face, but just barely, and she could feel her cheeks
heating. Apparently Mrs. Frey noticed, too, because she cack-
led with laughter, then went back to her rose garden, shaking
the trowel at Peter and threatening mayhem should he touch
her chickadees.

Still smiling, Rachel drove through Blossom and turned
onto the winding county road that led up from the river and
onto the shoulders of Mount Hood. So Jeff had been given
official sanction by her landlady. Mrs. Frey might watch over
her a bit more than she would have wished, but she was a
good person, Rachel reflected. Nosy, but not too intrusive.
Ahead, bright spring sun glittered on the snow that still
cloaked the mountain's peak. Rachel slowed to enjoy the view.

Apple trees marched in neat rows on either side, their clustered buds showing the first faint traces of pink. Fuji? Fuji was
a popular apple these days, bringing a good price. A lot of
growers had young plantations of Fuji and Gala. The old
standbys—Red and Yellow Delicious—had been the work-
horse varieties for years. The Yellows, in particular, had found
a good market overseas. But in the face of the shaky Asian
economy, the growers who had had the foresight to diversify—
to court the upscale ''gourmet'' apple market—were the only
ones doing well. The loss of Asian sales had hurt the family
orchard.

They still grew the old standbys, plus Bing and Royal Anne
cherries. It was only her own experiment with espaliered cul-
tivars that offered the popular new varieties. Aunt Catherine
sold that crop at the Hood River farmer's market, which meant
that Uncle Jack discounted them utterly, although Rachel knew
that they fetched more per pound than the main-crop apples
did. If she ran the orchard, she'd put in several new varieties,
on trellis wires to make picking and spraying easier. . . .

Daydreaming, she nearly missed Beck's narrow driveway.
Braking hard, she scattered gravel as she made the tight turn
onto the unkempt dirt track.

Branches brushed the side of her pickup as she eased the
truck along the muddy ruts. In places you could still see the
original gravel, but mostly it had sunk into the mud. You
didn't drive down Beck's driveway when it was really wet.
You parked on the main road and walked in. Wearing boots.
That suited Beck just fine, Rachel thought with a smile, although she sometimes wondered how he got the wood in for
his projects. Maybe he stored it in his big metal-sided shop,
like a squirrel storing filberts for the winter. She negotiated a
tight turn that became a small lake when it rained, and
emerged into the small clearing that Beck called home.

She always had the feeling that the clearing was a transient
space—that one day she would arrive and it would simply
have vanished, taking all signs of Beck with it—like the lost
Scottish village of Brigadoon. He didn't quite belong to the
real world—seemed more like a refugee from some gentler
place. The tall pole-built shop covered with green-painted

metal siding dwarfed the tiny cedar-shake house—a cabin really—that leaned companionably against the bole of an enormous old willow. Rambler roses climbed across the cabin's
weathered face in the summer, curtaining the windows with
scarlet blooms and thick mats of leaves. Now young thistles
thrust upward in dense green clumps beside the front door. A
trickle of smoke rose from the fieldstone chimney. In good
weather, Beck cooked on a propane stove in the pole building.
In the winter, an ancient sheet-iron woodstove heated the
house, filling it with the scents of the stew and coffee that
always simmered on its rusty cooktop.

Rachel stopped the truck at the end of the driveway. Beck
stood in the middle of the yard, shirtless as always, dressed in
a pair of faded cutoff jeans and ragged running shoes. Strands
of polished wooden beads gleamed on his sun-bronzed chest,
and his lanky muscles looked like rope wrapped around his
bones. He had woven a red ribbon into his thick gray braid.
Around him in a loose semicircle, eight black cats crouched
on the grass like miniature black panthers in a circus act, their
tails lashing, staring up at him. For a few moments, the tableau
held. Then Rachel turned off the truck's engine, and the cats
immediately streaked for the brush, vanishing into the shadows
before she even had time to open the door.

"The cats told me you were coming." Beck wandered over,
his braid swinging between his shoulders. His pale blue eyes
seemed to glow with their own inner light, and Rachel sometimes wondered if he saw the same world as everyone around
him.

"Hi, Beck. I hear you went to look at Mayor Ventura's
yard yesterday."

"I went." Beck leaned his skinny butt against the fender
of her truck. "Thought I wouldn't. Finally did. Guess I'll start
pickin' out the wood tomorrow. Yard's closed today."

Rachel nodded, pleased because you never knew if Beck
would take a job or not. She had long ago given up trying to
figure out how he decided these things. "You going to use
cedar?" She crossed her fingers. Beck was willing to follow
her plans—garden and deck design held no interest for him—
but sometimes he didn't agree with her choice of wood. If he

didn't think cedar fit the soul of that yard, then he wouldn't use cedar, and all the coaxing and ranting in the world wouldn't change his mind.

"Cedar. Tight knot." He nodded. "Red, I think. Got some nice red down 't the yard. Young and feisty. Fits."

"Good!"

"Heard the Evil One did some bad stuff in town. Hurt folks." Beck turned his piercing eyes on her, clearly troubled. "He's hangin' around, that One. You watch out for Him." He turned and spat on the ground. "You be careful in that mayor-guy's yard, you hear? Evil One's been hangin' around there. I smelled Him—like the stink of somethin' dead."

Uh-oh.

"But you're going to do the job anyway, right?" Rachel forced a smile, stifling another pang of anxiety. "Why would the Evil One bother you?"

"Told you. I thought about it." He shrugged. "He ain't gonna bother me. He knows I know Him. He sneaks up on folks—that's His power. You can't see Him, so He can get you. He can't sneak up on me. I got the eye to see Him." A worried look crept into his eyes. "You watch for Him, you hear? Maybe I'll be there when you are. I can watch out for Him, for you. If I'm not there—you be careful." He frowned at her, arms folded tightly across his chest, the string of hand-carved beads gleaming like polished agates against his sun-bronzed skin. "You be real careful," he repeated.

"I'll be careful," Rachel reassured him, a little touched by his evident concern.

"What you do is you look folks in the eyes." He tugged at his braid, his eyes darkening like a cloudy sky. "That One can look like anyone. You. Me. You look that person in the eyes—then you can tell. See Him hiding there. Wearing that person's skin, just peering out at you and laughing."

"I'll do that." Rachel tilted her head, thinking that Beck could be very scary if you didn't know that he wouldn't even kill a slug on purpose. More than one client had refused to allow him on the property after meeting him. "How do you know he's looking out at you?" Rachel asked, fascinated in spite of her worries about the Ventura job. Beck had never been this explicit about his personal bogeyman before.

"He can wear a face, but He can't hide His nature, see." Beck peered into her face. "You look way deep, you can see the flames leapin'. The Evil One killed that guy in town, back a few days. Everyone's lookin' for a human killer, but they're wrong. You be careful." He touched her arm with a restrained urgency, then turned and strode rapidly off toward his shop, his long skinny legs moving in stiff strides, like a wading heron. A couple of the black cats emerged from the brush and scooted into the building on his heels.

Rachel went back to her truck, feeling chilled, in spite of the rapidly warming day. She shook her head, wondering once more what events in his past had made Beck become the man he was. Well, at least he was willing to build the mayor's deck, in spite of the stink of the Evil One.

As she reached her truck, Rachel noticed a narrow trail leading back into the tangle of second growth and underbrush along the drive. On impulse, she turned down it, treading the beaten earth softly as it wound between the low branches of young firs. It ended at the edge of a small grove of old cedars. Three of the trees stood upright, their lowest branches above head height, their trunks thicker around than she could reach, the needled ground bare beneath them. The fourth cedar had fallen in some windstorm years ago. It still lived, but the upper branches had swelled into young trunks along its length, thick as her thigh. Their green fronds formed a fence that closed the space between the trees into a kind of private cave, dense with shadow. The sun would never really shine here, Rachel thought. A scatter of brilliant yellow mushrooms sprouted at the base of the largest tree.

In the exact center of the space lay a small wooden platform. About the size of a tabletop, it had been made of strips of wood, their various shades and grains forming a rich tapestry of color, polished to a sheen. A small crude vase—the kind of thing a grade-school kid might pinch up out of clay for an art project—held a sprig of willow, its new green leaves just bursting from the scales on its golden stem. A cheap dime-store glass held a thick red candle, like people put out on their tables at Christmas time. About half of it had been burned, but the wick was short and neatly trimmed.

The skull of an animal lay next to the candle—yellowed canines curving from the polished ivory bone, suggesting fox perhaps, or a small coyote. Next to it stood another glass, identical to the one that held the candle, only this one was full of marbles—cracked cat's-eyes, swirled aggies, and spheres of clear blue and green that had been cracked and crazed clear through so that they glittered with crystalline fracture lines.

It wasn't the clutter of objects that held Rachel's eye. A carving stood in front of the wooden platform—the beginning of a carving, at least. A thick round of wood—a section of trunk, minus bark and cambium—sat on the ground. From it a face had begun to emerge, as if the wooden round was made of ice and was slowly melting to reveal a face that had been frozen deep within it. Rachel went over to it, walking almost on tiptoe, the hair prickling on the back of her neck. A thick silence filled the space beneath the cedar branches, so that the scuff of her shoe soles on the brown needles sounded loud. The carving was stunningly powerful. She touched the satiny wood, finding not the slightest nick or rough spot to suggest that a tool had etched this face from the piece of tree trunk.

"This is private."

Beck's low voice startled her so that she jumped and stifled a gasp. She turned and found him standing at the end of the path, framed by the sweeping green fronds of the cedar. The soft twilight highlighted the ropy bulge of his muscles, and his expression. He stood straight, his hands loosely at his sides, balanced lightly on his feet. Rachel swallowed, thinking for the first time that she could be afraid of this man. "I . . . I'm sorry," she faltered. "I didn't mean to pry. I just saw the path and went down it."

"It's private." He moved toward her, and she stilled an impulse to back away. "I don't mind you being here." A filtered bit of sunlight caught his face, replacing the shadowy and unreadable features with his familiar gentle expression. Suddenly he was just Beck again. No one to be frightened of. Rachel let her breath out in a rush, realizing that her knees felt shaky, wanting to giggle.

"I'll go. I didn't mean to pry."

"It's all right." He smiled at her shyly and touched the beads on his chest. "I don't mind. Don't tell anyone else."

"I won't." She looked down at the platform, realizing he had made it, seeing not the slightest sign of a metal nail or screw in the construction.

He followed her gaze. "That was my dog." He picked up the skull and polished a bit of dust from the curve of bone with the hem of his cutoffs. "I found it. He died a long time ago." He set the skull down carefully next to the clay vase and the candle. "Couldn't let it just lie there. He was lonely."

"You carved that face." She moved to look at the sculpture from a new angle and realized with a sudden jolt that it was Beck's own face emerging from the tree trunk. She recognized the cant of the one eye that had been carved, and the bit of cheekbone revealed beneath it. Beck nodded, as if she'd spoken out loud.

"I'm working on it," he said. Then he paused, his gaze on the cedar branches, a faraway look in his eyes. "Funny thing. I woke up one day and discovered I was lost. Not in the woods, like, but just *gone*. I was still alive, walking and talking and eating. But hollow." He tapped his chest lightly. "Like an old log. I don't remember what used to be in there. It was all just empty darkness. I think the Evil One took me away. For a long time, I was just lost." He studied the sculpture for a moment. "Then one day I felt me, and knew I was out there somewhere. Hiding. So I went looking." He nodded at the trunk. "I looked for that tree for a long time. The Evil One is looking, too. That's why I don't let anyone know it's here."

"I won't tell anyone." Rachel touched the sleek curve of the sculpture again. "It's beautiful. It's really powerful."

"It's just me." He looked at her and smiled. "I don't mind you coming to look. I don't think the Evil One could ever wear your shape. There's no place for His hellfire in your eyes."

"Thank you," Rachel said. She smiled at him. "And thank you for letting me look at this."

"You can come back." He bowed his head gravely, as if he had just offered her a gift.

"I will," she said. "I'd like to see this again."

He walked back to the truck with her, behind her on the narrow path. He didn't say anything else, just hummed a low, intricate tune that she didn't recognize. At the truck he nodded to her again, smiled, and wandered back across his yard, accompanied once more by his black cats.

Strange, gentle man, Rachel thought as she climbed into the truck. She wondered what his rambling tale of lost and finding had meant. She would probably never know. Maybe no one would. Glancing at her watch, she decided that she just had just enough time to drop by the Rhinehoffer's nursery before meeting Jeff.

CHAPTER

17

Daren Rhinehoffer greeted Rachel cheerfully in the small graveled lot beside the nursery office. His small son grinned and drooled in a frame backpack seat, both his chubby fists clenched in his father's rusty hair. "Iko is up in Seattle, at the big Northwest Garden Show," he told her when she asked about his wife. "I get to be a single dad for a few days." He grinned. "You know, we should team up and enter the show next year. We'd do a great display." He winked. "Bring us both some business—or at least some serious attention. With your design sense and a focus on native landscaping, we'd be a standout."

He was serious. "I . . . hadn't really thought about it." Rachel shook her head. "I mean . . . I'm a tiny business."

"So are we. Some of the smallest landscapers put on the best show." He grinned. "Think about it and let me know. Lots of Portland folks look to that show when they're thinking about spending money on landscaping. And lots of 'em are moving into the Gorge. But let me know soon, if you decide to do it." He nodded. "We'd need to start working on next year's show right now."

"I'll think about it," Rachel said slowly. It would cost money to pull that off, but it might indeed jump-start her business if they really did do a bang-up job. "Meanwhile . . . I'm here for some stuff for our mayor's backyard."

"You're really becoming the Blossom City Landscape Department, aren't you?" Daren chuckled, then winced as his son yanked at his hair. "Ouch, kid. I'll be bald soon enough." He reached up to gently pry his son's fingers loose. "I think I noticed the Memorial Park for the first time yesterday. Nice job."

"Thanks." She smiled, because praise from Daren meant something. "And the mayor's yard is a private contract. No city graft here." She tickled the chubby boy until he giggled and gave her a gaping and delighted grin. "I'm going to need five vine maples to start with. Nice-sized ones, if you have them."

"Ouch." Daren grimaced. "We can see what I've got left. Your uncle dropped by yesterday with a petition to recall the mayor." He gave her a brief sideways glance as he ushered her along a gravel path that led between long tunnels of greenhouse plastic supported by arches of heavy PVC pipe. "I didn't sign it—and he had a few words to say to me." He clucked his tongue. "He's getting a little bent out of shape over this, isn't he? I mean—I heard he was kind of a suspect, but nobody really thinks he killed Dougan, do they?"

"No." Rachel pressed her lips together. "And I'm sorry if he was rude. You're right about him getting too upset over this."

"It's nothing for you to apologize for." He shrugged, then patted her arm. "I don't figure you're responsible for him." He stopped at the edge of a long raised bed. Three spindly vine maple saplings leaned forlornly among the churned earth. "That's all I've got left," he said. "The Portland paper ran a big feature on natural landscaping in their garden supplement. They listed us as a supplier—although we don't do catalog sales at all." He sighed. "After all the calls we got, I'm almost tempted. But anyway, this landscaper from Portland came out and bought us out in a lot of species."

"Salal, too?" Rachel asked plaintively.

Daren nodded. "Sorry. Too bad you didn't start the job a week ago."

"Just my luck." She sighed, hating to disappoint a client. "I'll probably have to go halfway to Seattle for them now," she said glumly. That would sure eat into her profit on this job. "Or maybe he'll have to settle for a star magnolia."

"Well . . . maybe not." Daren reached up absently to hold his son's hands. "A friend of ours has a small nursery down near Canby. She's just starting out, concentrating on native species. She might have a few nice trees. She was just complaining to me that she didn't even get a nod in that feature. And I've got to take some azalea and rhododendron down to her for her retail shop. I'll be coming back with an empty trailer. Want me to call?"

"Please. Bless you, Daren," Rachel said as they headed back to the office. While he called, she picked up a handful of bright orange tags from the office and wandered through the rest of the nursery, flagging the azaleas and rhodies she wanted, along with a well-shaped flowering cherry cultivar. Daren and Iko specialized in azalea, so she had a nice selection of deciduous azalea to choose from. "Red osier dogwood," she told him as he reappeared. "That'll be everything—except the salal and vine maple."

"Cindy has both. And there are your dogwoods." He pointed. "I've only got the three, but they're nice."

They were. Rachel happily affixed a tag and scribbled her name on it. Meanwhile, Daren had swung the pack off his back. His son had fallen asleep, and the child barely stirred as Daren eased him into a cradle strung between two young birches that had been planted at the edge of the yard. He tucked a hand-pieced quilt around the boy and gave the cradle a gentle push. It rocked slowly and gently in the spring sunshine. "I told Cindy to pull five nice maples for you, but I didn't know how many salal. She has dozens of plants, so I didn't worry about it."

"You are wonderful." Rachel laughed, delighted with this turnabout of bad luck. "Yes, let's do that show next year. It'll be worth it." She handed him the rest of the tags and told him what she'd picked out. "It'll be a week at least before we're ready for them," she told him. "I'll send Julio over."

"I'll put them together for you. And the show's a deal. Let's get together after Iko gets back, and we'll start planning." He waved and headed back across the yard to check on his son.

Pleased at the way the morning had gone, Rachel hurried on to her rendezvous with Jeff. He was waiting for her at the Bread Box, sitting at a small round table in one corner of the deck that jutted over the Columbia. Quite a few early tourists strolled along the boardwalk, buying food, upscale clothing, and bright kites at the small shops that had filled the renovated warehouse along the dock. Some of the shoppers occupied the sleek condominiums that had been built above the retail space. Most of those were vacation homes. More and more well-to-do Portlanders were buying a second home in the Gorge instead of at the coast.

Joylinn Markham, one of the first tenants to sign a lease, enjoyed a prime location on the dock. Her growing reputation among visitors was evident from the crowded tables out on the deck and inside the small bakery, as well. People drove out to Blossom from Hood River to breakfast on her cinnamon rolls on weekend mornings.

Jeff got to his feet as she made her way to the table, took her hand, and kissed her lightly. Rachel smiled as she took her seat, thinking that this was new. Normally Jeff was very reserved in public. To the point that it irritated her, at times. She peered at him. He had taken the bandage off. "I like the haircut." She smiled as he made a face, and turned to the young woman who had appeared at their table.

"I'll have a cappuccino. And a cinnamon roll." To her surprise, she recognized Bob Dougan's teenaged daughter, Melanie. Her cheekbones pressed against the skin of her face, as if she had lost weight. A thick layer of makeup failed to hide the dark circles beneath her eyes and gave her skin the texture and color of a cheap plastic doll. She forced a smile with heavily glossed lips.

"I'll try to be quick with your cappuccino." The girl scribbled on the pad in her hand. "But everyone wants something from the coffee bar this morning, and the other girl's sick. It's awful. You want the roll right away?" She glanced at Jeff's mug, which was nearly empty. "You want something to eat now, too?"

"I'll take one of the cheese and pepper rolls." Jeff gave her a thoughtful look. "One of the hot ones."

"You're braver than me." The teen scribbled on her pad. "She tried these new peppers, this batch. Whew! They need a warning label." Pocketing her pad, she trudged away, squeezing through the forest of occupied chairs that crowded the deck.

"She doesn't look too good this morning." Jeff watched her disappear into the bakery.

"I didn't know she worked here." Rachel looked after her. "Joylinn was talking about hiring more help on the weekends. I guess she did." She looked up and smiled as the girl reappeared with a small tray balanced awkwardly in one hand and a thermal carafe in the other. "Did you just start working for Joylinn?"

"This is my second weekend." Listlessly she set plates, knives, forks, and napkins in front of them, then filled Jeff's cup. "I'm only working weekends until school's out. Mom won't let me have a job during the school year. And Joylinn closes up at four on weekdays anyway, during the winter season." She shrugged. "I didn't know waitressing was such hard work. But the tips are good. Sometimes." She straightened and looked Jeff square in the face. "I took the job so I could pay Roth Glover back for what I stole from him," she said with a trace of defiance. "I don't have to do it—I just am. By the end of next weekend I'll be square with him."

"Good for you," Jeff said gently. "You've got a good attitude."

It would be hard, in a town this small, to walk around knowing that everyone knew what you'd done and had passed judgement on you, Rachel thought. "I bet she's gotten more punishment than if she'd gone to jail," she murmured to Jeff as Melanie moved off among the tables, refilling cups and speaking to the diners.

"She looks as if her dad's death has really hit her hard. Poor kid. It's not going to get any easier, if Dougan really was running that scam." Jeff nodded and bit into his roll. His eyes widened appreciatively, and he grabbed for his water glass. "Nice," he managed to get out in a strangled voice. "Spicy."

"Melanie wasn't kidding about a warning label." Rachel laughed. "I hope nobody has to call 911. Did you get hold of Loper this morning?" Rachel asked as she nibbled at her own roll.

"He's conveniently in Portland. Or so says his answering machine. He's not answering his cell phone." Jeff frowned into his cup. "If I could tie that missing cash to him, I'd go for an arrest warrant. But it may be too late. I have a feeling he's on the run."

"You mean the money my dad paid to that slime, Ransom Loper? I'll tie it to him!"

Both Jeff and Rachel looked up, startled, as Melanie set a short mug of frothy cappuccino down in front of Rachel. The girl's eyes burned in her pale face, and her knuckles gleamed white as she straightened.

"What do you know about the money?" Jeff leaned forward, resting his crossed arms on the tabletop.

"I know Loper was blackmailing my dad." She stared at him, her face pinched. "Dad was doing something crooked. I know that, too. He wasn't the fine, upstanding citizen people thought. Folks would be patting him on the back, telling him how wonderful he was . . . I wanted to laugh." She looked away. "But he didn't . . ." She swallowed. "I think that creep, Loper, found out about what Dad was doing. I think he used it to blackmail Dad. I heard Dad talking to him on the phone that night. They were arguing about money. They were gonna meet later. Dad was really upset." She swallowed again and knotted her fingers together. "He had the money in his briefcase. I know because I looked in it. Ransom Loper killed him." Her eyes blazed. "He took the money and then he killed Dad. I know he did."

"I wish you'd told me this before," Jeff said mildly. He kept his eyes on her face. "But Loper has an alibi for that night."

"No, he doesn't." The girl looked down at her hands, yanked them apart, and snatched up her tray. "He was in bed with me, in his motel room." She met his eyes, her cheeks reddening in spite of her defiant tone. "He left about an hour before . . . before." She drew a shuddering breath, her eyes glittering with unshed tears. "He said he had to deliver some papers to a client. Ha." Her mouth worked. "I turned on the TV while I waited," she said bitterly, "so I know what time it was. He had plenty of time to kill Dad. No matter what he said." Turning on her heel, she threaded her way across the crowded deck, earning more than one annoyed glance from diners as she stumbled past.

"She's barely sixteen," Jeff said in a very soft voice. He got to his feet and laid his napkin down carefully, as if it might explode. "I better go talk to her." He turned to Rachel, his expression colder and grimmer than Rachel had ever seen it. "I'm going to have to get a formal statement from her. Then I'll get a warrant out on Loper. I hope she's sure about the time he left and returned that night." He paused a moment, his eyes hard. "The bastard's married," he said and let out an explosive breath. "I'm sorry, Rachel. This kind of botches our plans for the day."

"Hey, don't worry about it." Rachel touched his hand, thinking that if Loper could see Jeff's face right now, he really would be on the run.

"Finish your food." He glanced down at her cinnamon roll. "I'll call you later. Maybe we can do something then." He made his way into the bakery in the direction Melanie had taken.

Her appetite gone, Rachel left the rest of her cinnamon roll on her plate. Poor girl, she thought as she left a generous tip. Talk about guilt . . . She paused as she started for the bakery door. Her uncle and aunt stood at the foot of the steps that led down to the boardwalk, arm in arm. They saw her as she turned. Aunt Catherine started to wave, then dropped her hand to her side with a guilty glance at her husband. Rachel's lips tightened as she made her way across the deck to meet them.

"Hello, Uncle Jack, Aunt Catherine," she said with determined cheerfulness. "I haven't seen you for a while."

"We've . . ." Aunt Catherine pressed her lips together as Uncle Jack turned away. "We've got to go," she said and rushed after him.

"Just wait a minute." Rachel hurried down the stairs, breaking into a trot to catch up with her uncle's long-legged stride. "Uncle Jack, will you just *stop* for a minute?" She planted herself squarely in front of him, aware of her aunt's breathless anxiety. "Will you stop acting so . . . ridiculous?" She was breathing as hard as her aunt, fists clenched. "Jeff isn't picking on you. He suspects other people—he doesn't really believe that you killed Dougan. But he has to do his job." She heard the note of pleading in her voice and broke off abruptly. "Uncle Jack, can't we just—"

"You made your choice." He stood with his head averted, refusing to meet her eyes. "You're a grown-up," he said in a carrying voice. "You're free to stand up for your family or to side with strangers." He stepped around her and continued on down the boardwalk. Aunt Catherine gave Rachel an apologetic look and a quick squeeze on her arm before hurrying after him.

"And you're free to act like an idiot," she muttered, but she didn't say it loud enough for him to hear. Feeling guilty— and angry at herself for feeling guilty—she went back up the steps to the deck, aware of curious eyes turned in her direction. She straightened her shoulders and drew a slow breath, glad that at least Jeff hadn't overheard any of this.

He was talking to Melanie Dougan in Joylinn's closet-sized office, next to the kitchen. The door was open, and Rachel caught a glimpse of Melanie's hunched shoulders as she went to the register to pay. Joylinn dashed from the kitchen, loaded down with precariously balanced plates of sandwiches. "I hope Jeff finishes with Melanie soon," she murmured as she slipped deftly past in the crowded space. "I can't wait tables and do the kitchen at the same time. Of course Celia had to choose this weekend to get sick! Go ring up that customer, will you?" She nodded at a balding man waiting impatiently at the cash register, then dashed off to whisk the artistically arranged plates down in front of a table full of well-dressed diners.

"I'll take care of you, sir." Rachel hurried to the cash register to take the man's check and ring up his bagel and espresso charges. Jeff and Melanie emerged from the office at that point. Melanie's eyes were puffy and red. Tears had carved mascara-stained rivulets through her caked makeup. She clutched a stained wad of tissues in her hand as she marched through the restaurant and out the front door. Head high, she didn't look around.

"What happened?" Rachel eyed a young couple heading toward the cash register. "She looks awful."

"No kidding." Jeff lowered his voice to a murmur. "Apparently Loper was talking marriage to her—no specific promises—just letting her believe what she wanted to believe. She thought he was single—until she overheard him talking to his wife on his cell phone last night." He sighed, his eyes glinting like ice. "I'm going to have a serious talk with Mr. Loper about his alibi. Melanie is very clear about the time he left and returned." He looked after the girl. "I've got to go get her statement recorded, and get a warrant issued. Let me tell Joylinn the bad news that I've stolen her waitress."

"Go on." Rachel gave him a small push. "I'll fill in for Melanie. Go catch that guy before he gets out of the country." Rachel gave the young couple who were now waiting at the cash register a bright smile. Two more couples dressed like sailboarders had come in and were looking around the crowded bakery. "Be right with you," she called cheerfully.

"Thanks." Jeff kissed her lightly. "Like I said—I'll call you."

She waved him off with a smile and hurried over to take the young couple's money. "I apologize for the wait," she told the impatient sailboarders as she rang up the tab and made change. "We're a bit shorthanded today."

To put it mildly. Oh, well, Rachel thought as she showed the foursome to a table. It beat going home and vacuuming the apartment. Dashing past with another tray of food, Joylinn gave her a grateful smile and a nod.

She would take her pay in fresh cinnamon rolls, Rachel decided as she took the foursome's order for beer and vegetarian sandwiches. She had earned it.

The rush didn't slow down until after three in the afternoon. By the time Joylinn put the CLOSED sign in the front window and locked the door, Rachel's half-eaten cinnamon roll was but a distant memory. She wiped tables and finished busing dishes while the last two couples lingered over their coffee and seemed utterly unaware that the Bread Box was no longer open. Rachel considered mopping rather wetly in the immediate vicinity of their tables but decided that she really shouldn't alienate Joylinn's clients.

But at last they finished and meandered out the door. Rachel locked it behind them and slumped against it. "Melanie wasn't kidding," she announced to the empty room. "This is hard work."

"Better than wheelbarrowing compost," Joylinn called cheerfully from the kitchen. "You can take a break if you want. I'm almost done in here, and there's just the mopping left. I'll take care of it."

"I'm not dead yet. And this is much harder than wheelbarrowing." Rachel straightened, tossed her head, and began to clear the final two tables. Neither of the stragglers had left much of a tip, either. Growling to herself, she wiped the tables down, upended the chair onto them, and fetched the mop from its place in the kitchen. It didn't take long to mop the tiled floor with the disinfectant solution. By the time she dumped the bucket and hung the mop back in its place, Joylinn had the kitchen spotless. The final tray of dishes was in the washer, and she was beckoning from the office.

Rachel entered to find a checked tablecloth spread over the cleared desk, and two plates heaped with salad, cold salmon, and some of Joylinn's coveted dill rolls. "There's mayonnaise and dijon mustard, and I think we deserve a couple of beers. What would you like?" she called over her shoulder as she headed for the cooler.

"An ale," Rachel said. "This looks lovely." Wedges of red-skinned new potatoes, sliced sweet pepper, cooked green beans, and asparagus had been artfully arranged over mixed greens. Slices of hard-boiled egg and tiny cornichon pickles garnished the perfect slabs of pink smoked salmon that held center stage. The mayonnaise had been very gently touched with wasabi horseradish, Rachel discovered. "This is fabulous." She lifted her bottle of beer to clink rims with Joylinn. "You should serve this at lunch."

"I plan to." Joylinn smiled. "I thought I'd test it on you first."

"I'm a bad test subject." Rachel forked up a huge bite of the salmon and greens, crowned with a dab of the spicy mayonnaise. "Right now I'd eat anything that didn't fight back too hard and love it," she said between mouthfuls. "This is a perfect combination."

"I tried pickled ginger in the mayo first." Joylinn began on her own salad. "But it didn't quite go with the salmon, I thought. I'm going to feature it as next Sunday's special."

"I'll be here." Rachel tried not to eat like a starving refugee, and succeeded reasonably well. At least she reached politely for the rolls, instead of snatching one from its basket. The afternoon sun shone on the river beyond the dock and turned the whitecaps on the wind-ruffled water a sparkling white. "I'm happy," Rachel said with a sigh, nibbling on a tender spear of asparagus. "Good pay, lady. I'll take this over money any day."

"Keep your tips, too." Joylinn leaned back in her chair, beer in hand, watching a gull skim along the surface of the river. "Thanks so much for pitching in. I would have had to close up if you hadn't. Celia's got the flu and really is too sick to come in today. I owe you."

"You're paying me, believe me." Rachel scooped up the last of the mayonnaise on her plate with a slender green bean.

"So what happened to Melanie?" Joylinn tilted her head. "One minute she was serving tables, and the next she was leaving with Jeff, in tears." She sat up straight. "She's not in trouble again, is she?"

"No." Rachel hesitated, but Joylinn was one of the few people she'd ever known who simply didn't spill secrets. Ever. So she told Joylinn a brief version of what had passed that afternoon.

Joylinn's face hardened as Rachel explained—more or less—why Melanie hadn't spoken up sooner.

"Poor kid." Joylinn picked pensively at the label on her beer. "She's a hard worker, and I think she really learned a lesson from getting caught by Roth. She doesn't deserve this, too." She sighed and shook her head. "You fall in love, and your brain takes a vacation." She turned toward Rachel, half laughing, half serious. "What is it? Hormones?"

"Good question." Rachel made a face.

"At least you've made pretty sound decisions so far." Joylinn waved the bottle at her. "Although I'd have said yes to Jeff a long time ago."

"He hasn't asked me, dear." Rachel made a face at her friend, blushing at the same time. "And I really don't know what I'd say, so I hope he doesn't any time soon."

"You amaze me," Joylinn murmured, taking another long swallow of beer.

"What about you?" Rachel leaned an elbow on the desk. "You don't even date. Who are you counciling to get married?"

"Well, you know, you get burned good and you don't go grabbing for hot pots quite so fast." Joylinn studied the eroded remains of the label on her beer.

"When did you get burned?" Rachel sat up, surprised, because Joylinn had seemed oblivious to men ever since she'd returned to Blossom.

"Happened while I was San Francisco, studying to be a chef." Joylinn sighed and leaned her chin in her hand. "I learned that I have no common sense where men are concerned, and that until I grow some, I should keep my hormones to myself."

"What happened?"

"I fell madly in love." Joylinn's smile had a soft wistful look to it. "Oh, I was so besotted. Anything he wanted . . . Jules. He was Quebecois." She shook her head, still smiling.

"So what happened?" Rachel asked in a hushed voice. Joylinn had never once hinted about this interlude in her life.

"I got pregnant." She looked up, her eyes clear as the sky. "Jules immediately fell into bed with someone else, and I had some hard realities to face."

"Oh, Joylinn . . ."

"It was tough." Joylinn lifted one shoulder in a pensive shrug. "I . . . put her up for adoption. I had to. I would have ruined both our lives if I hadn't." She raised her head to meet Rachel's shocked stare. "I still think it was the only thing to

do, but sometimes . . ." She shrugged again. "I went through
a private agency. A couple in San Diego adopted her. They
couldn't have children. They were both doctors. They were so
happy to have a baby." The wistfulness in her smile deepened
to a brief sadness. "If she . . . ever wants to find out about her
birth mother, she can get my name from the agency," Joylinn
said softly. "I hope she does one day. But it won't be for a
while." She rose and began to collect their dishes. "She's
only six and a half right now."

"I . . . I'm sorry. I guess." Rachel picked up the rolls and
the empty beer bottles, trying to collect her thoughts. "Or
should I be?"

"Sorry? I don't know." Joylinn preceded her into the
kitchen, her ginger hair tumbling down her back, newly released from the braid she wore during work. "I have a daughter and I believe she has a good life. That's not something to
be sorry for. Anyway . . ." She began to rinse their dishes. "I
feel for Melanie. It's so easy to lose your head when you lose
your heart."

Rachel hugged her briefly and hard, still a little breathless
from Joylinn's revelation. You could be so close to someone,
she thought, and not know something this big.

She checked her machine before they left the Bread Box,
and there was a message from Jeff, saying that he had his
warrant for Loper and had received a tip that he was in Portland. He was on his way there to try to catch up with him.
He'd call her later or tomorrow. Rachel hung up, wondering
about head and heart and which was saying what to her.

"Let's go into Hood River to the brew pub and listen to
music," Joylinn said when Rachel repeated the message.

"On a Sunday evening?"

"Even if there's no live music, we can drink beer and watch
the stars," Joylinn said. "And if we drink too much beer,
we'll just call the Taxi Sisters. It's my treat."

"Sounds like a plan," Rachel said, feeling suddenly lighter
than she had in days. "No conversation about politics or mur-
ders or family misbehaviors allowed."

"Deal," Joylinn said gravely. "We can talk about clothes."

"And food," Rachel said.

They laughed and locked up the Bread Box, and went off to change clothes, feed Peter, and go to Hood River to see if they could find a band playing somewhere.

CHAPTER

18

On Monday morning, Rachel picked up Julio at his sister's trailer on their narrow street above Blossom. She and Joylinn had made a late night of it. After listening to a mediocre garage band in Hood River, they had sat up late on Joylinn's houseboat, talking about Rachel's college years and Joylinn's time in San Francisco. They hadn't mentioned her daughter again.

Rachel yawned and winced, regretting the late bottle of wine they'd opened. On top of their Hood River beer, it had been a little much. She glared at Julio's knowing grin.

"You went to sleep very late?" He spoke with sympathy, but his tone didn't banish the amusement in his eyes. "Very late, yes."

"Yes," Rachel said briskly, wishing she'd taken a couple of aspirin before she'd left home. "Very late." Julio nodded with enormous commiseration, just barely managing not to grin outright.

Well, she'd never been able to hide a hangover. Rachel was relieved when he let the subject lapse. They met Spider downtown, then drove over to Mayor Ventura's house. The mayor had left early, but he had left her a note that he would be in his office all morning if she had any questions.

Rachel, Julio, and Spider started digging out rocks and roots from the areas where she would be laying out the beds. Once they got the debris out of the way, she'd order in the soil amendments. It was the pick-and-shovel stage of the process. Considering the state of her head, she figured this muscle work was a good thing. It was the one sure way she knew to get rid of a hangover, even if it felt awful at the beginning.

"I heard that somebody spray-painted a bunch of stuff on your friend's walls," Spider said as they took a water break in the unseasonably hot mid-morning. "They're tryin' to make it look like one of us, huh?"

"Most likely." Rachel took a long drink from her water jug. "Can you read real gang sign?" She put the cap back on the jug as he nodded cautiously.

"I can read a little." His eyes slid sideways. "I had some friends . . . I never belonged. That was one thing my mom really got crazy about. Gang stuff. She'd have kicked me out." He smiled. "She sure threatened often enough. But she didn't mean it, mostly. I was kind of a jerk. I got a call from her." He sounded suddenly shy. "I guess she's gonna come out to visit again, next Sunday. She said you and Mr. Price came out to see her. She said you were nice." He gave her a brief enigmatic look. "Thanks for bein' nice to her."

"She's a nice woman." Rachel nodded and replaced her water jug in the narrow strip of shade along the sagging board fence. "We'll have to take this fence down, too. I'll see if Harvey can park a truck over here for a couple of days, so we can load all this straight into it." She nodded at the growing pile they'd accumulated in the front corner of the yard. Not only had they unearthed a sizeable mass of blackberry crowns and rocks, but apparently someone had used a burning pile as the main disposal system for all household garbage, once upon a time. Rachel had saved a couple of interesting bottles that had probably held patent medicines once. But mostly they had shoveled up broken bits of dishes and tools and a lot of rusty tin cans.

"You know, you might be able to look at that gang sign." She paused as she reached for her grub-hoe. "I'm sure Lyle took pictures of the place before the cleanup started. As evi-

dence. I'll see if I can get a copy. I've got to go over to the
hardware store anyway.'' She nodded as she hefted her hoe.
''I'll ask Lyle or Jeff for them.''

She went into town when they broke for lunch, deciding
that skipping a meal would be the final atonement for her
indulgences yesterday. Her stomach rumbled sullenly, but she
told it to shut up, and actually found a parking space right in
front of the hardware store—which was across the street from
the bank, next to City Hall. No food in sight.

''Well, hello.'' Roth Glover looked up from the newspaper
he had spread across the counter next to the huge and ancient
cash register. ''What can I get for you today?''

''I just need a box of faucet washers.'' Rachel plucked a
package from a shelf on the plumbing aisle. ''I thought I had
some in my toolbox, but I'm out. All of our mayor's outdoor
faucets drip. It's driving me crazy.'' She plunked the plastic
package of washers down on the counter. ''I'm doing my part
to conserve water. And my sanity.''

''That'll be ninety-nine cents.'' Glover took her dollar bill
and handed back her penny. ''I hear there's another Council
meeting tonight to appoint someone to fill Bob's spot. Bet
that's gonna be another dog-fight.'' He laughed dryly. ''Pete
and Roberta want me in, and the mayor's two buddies don't.
'Cause they know how I'll vote on the annexation.''

''How would you vote on it?'' Rachel leaned on the
counter. ''Or can you say?''

''Like I always said, I think our mayor's full of . . . well,
he's full it it, anyway.'' Glover grunted. ''I've been against
that crazy idea since he first came up with it. Dunno why Hank
West goes for it. Maybe he figures it'll help the bank or something.'' He looked briefly pained. ''I still can't figure out what
made Bob change his mind.''

Especially if he was being blackmailed by Loper. Rachel
wondered if he had suddenly discovered that his daughter
knew about his scam, and if he had told Loper that night that
he wouldn't be blackmailed anymore.

Ransom Loper looked a lot like a murderer.

''Yeah, I think Hank's got a couple o' good bank customers

who were for it," Glover was saying. "But you didn't hear that from me."

"So you're really against the annexation?" Rachel frowned as he nodded. "You wouldn't change your mind at all?"

"Man's land is his to do with as he sees fit." He peered over his reading glasses at her. "I don't hold with government telling folks who they can sell to and who they can't. Me and Ventura had this out more than one time."

"I don't get it. So how come you wanted to talk to the mayor about the annexation the night Bob died?"

"Who said I had an appointment with Ventura?" Glover blinked at her. "Why the hell would I talk to him? What's this? Don't tell me Price is trying to pin this murder now! I was home with my wife." He tore the register tape savagely from his machine and thrust it at her.

"Jeff doesn't suspect you." Rachel sighed and took the register tape. "But Mayor Ventura says that you asked him to meet with you that night."

"Somebody's lying." Glover took off his reading glasses and shoved them into a vinyl case and snapped it closed. "I didn't need to meet with him. I didn't have any reason to meet with him. If you'll excuse me, I'd better get some restocking done." Gathering his newspaper with an irritated rustle, he swept off into the back room.

Rachel sighed again and left the store, frowning as she pocketed her washers. Still frowning, she walked the short block to City Hall and found her way to the mayor's office. His receptionist, secretary, and personal defender, Moira Kellogg, looked up from her computer screen with a motherly smile as Rachel entered the outer office.

"Well, he had a meeting this morning." Her smile was charmingly helpful. "I think he's still with someone. What did you want to see him about?"

Rachel's mother had once told her that Moira Kellogg had the brains of a corporate lawyer disguised beneath a grandmotherly manner. Rachel eyed her bland, rather fuzzy smile. You expected knitting needles and brownies—pictures of the grandkids, and prizewinning county fair pickles. But behind

her unstylish plastic-rimmed glasses, Moira's eyes glinted like
bits of steel.

"I actually stopped in to ask him something about his yard.
I'm landscaping it." She glanced toward the closed office
door. "Do you remember him making an appointment with
Roth Glover to meet him here the evening Bob Dougan was
killed?"

"I know you're landscaping it, dear." Moira smiled
sweetly. "What about Roth Glover?"

"The mayor said he had an appointment with him, the night
Dougan was killed. Roth says that's not true." She shrugged.
"It just struck me as . . . odd."

Moira sat up straight, dropping her fuzzy grandmother act
and tapping her perfectly straight teeth with the end of a pen.
"That's interesting," she said slowly. "I remember that message. It want something like, 'This is Roth. Tell the mayor I'd
like to come by tonight to talk about the annexation.' It came
in while I was at lunch, and Phil was out of the office. The
recording was awful—there was a lot of noise on the line. It
could have been anyone's voice." She looked up at Rachel,
her eyes narrowing in thought. "He forgot about the appointment, he told me." She arched an eyebrow at Rachel. "Phil
wasn't in the office after I left that night. I can always tell. I
told all that to Jeff, by the way."

Rachel didn't ask how she knew, but she believed her. Not
too many people impressed her mother the way Moira Kellogg
did. She glanced up as the inner door opened, and Ventura
ushered Jeff through it.

"Well, hello." Jeff smiled at her, but his eyes were grim.
"I didn't expect to run into you here."

"Trouble?" Ventura raised his eyebrows.

"Nothing but a leaking faucet." Rachel shook her head.
"Actually, I was looking for Jeff." She felt Moira's eyes on
her, didn't glance in the woman's direction. "Do you have
photographs of the graffiti that was painted on your walls?
Spider says he can read some gang sign. He could tell if it
was real or phony."

"Yes, we do. They're in the office." He nodded as he
crossed the office, then glanced back at the mayor. "I'll keep

you posted," he said as they left the office. "I got an arrest warrant against Ransom Loper. He seems to have skipped. When I talked to his wife on the phone, she told me she hadn't heard from him since Friday night and thought he was still at his motel in Hood River. She was pretty upset."

So Loper had killed Dougan? It added up, Rachel thought. He thought he had Dougan in his pocket, and when Dougan decided to set an example for his daughter, he stood to lose a lot of money. Maybe the cash had been a last attempt to end the blackmail. Loper had lost his temper, had hit Dougan. He had found the key she had dropped, and had tried to hide the body so that he'd have time to get back to his motel and Melanie, his willing alibi . . .

It fit.

"I'm looking forward to a long talk with Loper," Jeff growled as they walked down the hall to the small office that constituted Police Headquarters. "Hang on a second, and I'll get you the pictures. Lyle had them out this morning, before he went out on a call." He returned a moment later with a blank white envelope in his hand. "I gave you two good shots. Let me know what Spider thinks. Oh—and don't bother trying my cell phone today. I had to drop it off for repairs."

"I won't." She opened the envelope and took out the two photos. One showed the wall in the main room, red paint dripping like splattered blood from the crude signs. The other had been taken in the kitchen. You could just see the red puddle on the floor that was Jeff's blood. Rachel shivered and thrust the photos back into the envelope, reliving the horror of that moment all over again. Jeff put his arm around her and hugged her.

As she left the building, Moira Kellogg emerged from the mayor's office. "The mayor asked me to give you this." She handed Rachel an envelope. "And he told me to tell you that if anything came up where you needed to contact him, just go ahead and call it a day. He's going fishing with Andy Ferrel this afternoon, and he doesn't want anything to get in the way. He'll be available to talk to you tomorrow."

"Andy?" Rachel blinked in surprise. "What is this? A peace offering? From *Andy*?"

"Apparently." Moira's face gave nothing away.

"That sure doesn't sound like Andy." Rachel shook her head. She had seen him spit on the sidewalk as the mayor passed him on the street. "Maybe his retirement from politics is mellowing him."

"Perhaps." Moira started back into the office, then paused in the doorway to glance back at Rachel. "It surprised me, too," she said, and vanished into the office.

Rachel opened the envelope. Inside she found another photograph. This one was a snapshot of the mayor wearing his leather jacket. A young boy sat on his shoulders, and both of them laughed into the camera. It had been taken in the backyard of the mayor's house. He looked much younger in that picture, Rachel thought as she slipped it back into the envelope, although it had to be recent, since Ventura had bought the house only last year. She guessed that the job of mayor was taking more out of him than he was willing to admit.

Lost in thought, she returned to her truck, and drove back out to the Ventura house. Julio and Spider had made quite a bit of progress in the hour that she'd been absent. At least they hadn't hit solid rock yet. So the drip irrigation should go in easily. The land here was old lava shield, covered with a layer of river silt that was sometimes thick and sometimes thin. You didn't run irrigation lines through solid basalt. And rerouting a planned irrigation system could eat a lot of the profit on a job. But this time, they'd lucked out.

"I got the photos for you, Spider," she called as she climbed out of the truck. "Take a break and come look."

Both teens dropped their shovels with alacrity and hurried over. Spider took the photos and glanced at them. His lip curled. "Not even close," he said scornfully. "Take a look at one Portland bus shelter and you could do a better job of faking it. I bet it was somebody local, who thinks you can do some fancy scribble and call it gang. Well, I guess people around here might believe it." He tossed the photos scornfully onto the hood of the truck.

That might mean Loper wasn't the one who had lain in wait for Jeff. He spent enough time in urban areas to have a little more sophistication. Or maybe not. Rachel picked up the photos and returned them slowly to their envelope. Even if Jeff had seen gang sign before—would he have paid any attention to it? She shook her head and tossed the envelope onto the seat of the truck. "Hold on a minute." She reached through the window to pick up the envelope Moira had given her. "Julio, here's the photo the mayor gave me. The one that shows his missing jacket."

Julio took the photo and glanced at it, his brow furrowed. "I will look for it." He hesitated. "I have seen the jacket . . . somewhere."

"Shit, yes." Spider snatched it from his hand and glanced up at Rachel. "The guy was wearing it. The dead guy."

"What?" Rachel stared at him.

"When we found the body, remember? Oh, yeah . . . you didn't stick around when they were digging him out. It was all covered with bark dust, but it's the same jacket." He shrugged and handed back the picture. "I remember, because it was a cool jacket, and I thought it was a big waste. Funny. The guy sure got his for stealin' it, huh?"

"Yeah," Rachel said faintly. A lot of loose pieces were falling into place, and the picture they were forming frightened her. It was dark when the murder had been committed. The lights that illuminated City Hall left the alley in shadow, and the streetlight on the corner didn't help much. The mayor had an appointment to be at City Hall at a certain hour. A few minutes later, a man appears in the alley, as if he is leaving the building. He is wearing the jacket that the mayor usually wears. He is the right height. The right build. He is in the right place at the right time. . . .

She swallowed, her throat dry. So, maybe this had nothing at all to do with Dougan's vote on the annexation.

Someone had meant to kill Mayor Ventura. She closed her eyes, watching the scene play out in her head. The man bent over his victim, swore and straightened as he realized he'd killed the wrong man. . . . Looked around wildly for a way to hide what he'd done. "Dear God," she said faintly and opened her eyes. Both youths were staring at her.

"You are okay, senorita?" Julio looked worried. "You are sick?"

"No." She bolted for the house. The mayor kept a spare key on a nail hidden beneath one of the insipid junipers that grew along the front of the house. She thrust her hand into the prickly branches, fumbling for the key. Found it after an interminable time. Inside, a clock ticked loudly, and the refrigerator hummed into the quiet. She hurried into the kitchen, her footsteps eerily loud. Dialed Jeff's office number. Got the dispatcher instead. So both Jeff and Lyle were out.

"That's okay," she told the dispatcher. "I have his cell phone number." Dialed it. Counted the rings. Got a recorded message suggesting that the party might have reached their destination and turned off their phone.

Then she remembered his phone was in for repairs. She tried the mayor's number. Again, no answer. Apparently he had turned it off. Because he was out fishing with . . . Andy Ferrel.

Maybe . . . maybe she was wrong. Slamming the receiver down onto its cradle, she dashed outside, nearly colliding with Julio.

"Senorita, something *is* wrong." He blocked her path.

"Yes, it is." She frowned at him. "Can you get a ride for yourself and Spider? He has to go back to the farm. I'll pay whoever can take you."

"You do not have to pay," Julio said with dignity. "I will call my cousin Ernesto. He is not working today and he has a truck."

"Good, good. Spider, if you have any trouble, tell the farm people that it's an emergency, and I'll explain later, okay?" She was already pulling the truck door open, climbing in. She might be right or she might be wrong. Before she went to Lyle, or even Jeff, she had to be sure. And she was pretty certain she knew who could tell her the truth.

"I'll call you tonight!" she yelled to Julio as she gunned the engine. Saying a small prayer that she was wrong, she pulled out of the mayor's driveway, scattering gravel in her wake.

CHAPTER

19

Rachel forced herself to drive at the speed limit as she passed through Blossom. She peered into the lot behind City Hall, but Jeff's Jeep wasn't in its place. So he wasn't there. She bit her lip as she braked for Blossom's one stoplight in the middle of town, her fingers drumming on the wheel.

The light turned green, and she gunned the engine, earning a surprised and disapproving glance from a couple of pedestrians. She increased her speed as she climbed the county road out of town, driving as fast as the twisting road would allow, her tires brushing the center line on every sharp turn. She had to slow again when she reached Beck's long lane. Breaking an axle wouldn't help. She bounced over the ruts, clutching the steering wheel, her teeth rattling. Another truck stood in Beck's small clearing—a brown-and-white Chevy pickup with *Blossom Feed and Seed* emblazoned on the side. Her heart seemed to skip a beat as she parked next to it. Breathless, she followed the sound of voices out to Beck's shop. Two of his cats, sunning themselves on the cabin's rickety porch, gave her narrow green stares.

"Marcy wants room for a hot tub on the new deck," a male voice was saying. "She got bit bad last year at the County Fair. Those salesmen sure can pitch a deal."

Brian, not Andy. Her heart sinking, Rachel halted in the doorway. "Hi, Beck. Brian."

The two men looked around from the pile of cedar lumber they were examining.

"Hi, Rachel." Brian smiled, his eyebrows lifting with surprise. "Didn't expect to run into you here. I'm building Marcy that deck she wants for her birthday." He grinned. "I never did thank you for sending me to Beck, here. That front deck he built sure is a piece of work."

Beck was regarding her with silent intensity. "The Evil One's shadow is on you," he said softly.

"Beck, who was it? Who did you see?" Rachel asked breathlessly. She couldn't bring herself to look at Brian. "The night that the . . . Evil One killed Bob Dougan. Whose face did the Evil One wear?"

Beck looked away. "The face does not matter," he said softly. "Clothes are meaningless. It was Him."

Brian looked from Beck to Rachel as if they had both turned into garden toads right in front of him. Rachel ignored his confusion.

"The clothes matter, Beck." She drew a deep breath. "They matter if the Evil One wears them again . . . to kill again. I *feel* him." It wasn't entirely a lie. "I think . . . I'm afraid . . . he's going to kill again. Wearing that face. I need to *know,* Beck."

He looked away, his skinny throat working, his skin tight over his face. For the first time, Rachel noticed a fine white scar that followed the curve of his jawbone across the pale skin of his neck. As if someone had once tried to cut his throat. She swallowed. "Beck. Please. Someone else may die. Today. This afternoon."

"We all die," he whispered. "Every one of us." But a shiver ran through him, and he dropped his eyes to the stack of new boards in front of him, absently stroking the silky grain of the wood. His shoulder blades jutted against the tanned skin of his back, and he shuffled his feet. "He . . . the man He wore as a skin . . . he is at the feed store." He shot an anxious glance at Brian. "The old one. The bitter one. I saw the Evil shine in his eyes that night. He . . . he struck the man. The man fell against the big truck, then to the ground. I saw his spirit pass and knew he was dead, and I ran away. The Evil One did not see me. So I survived.''

"Wait a goddamn minute." Brian Ferrel stepped between them, fists clenched. "What crap is this?" He turned his glare from Beck to Rachel. "What the hell are you trying to pull here, Rachel? What are you trying to get him to say?''

"Your father thought Dougan was the mayor." Rachel lifted her chin to look him in the face. "He left a message for the mayor to meet Roth Glover at City Hall at that hour, only Roth Glover wouldn't show up, since he didn't know about it. So Andy waited outside and saw a man come out wearing the mayor's leather jacket. Maybe he . . ." She swallowed. "I don't think it was murder," she whispered, aching for the growing horror in Brian's eyes. "I think he punched the man he thought was the mayor, Dougan fell against the truck, hit his head, and died. Then Andy tried to make it look as though someone from the Youth Farm stabbed Dougan." She drew a shuddering breath, wondering why the air was so thin. "Does your father have a key to Harvey's dump truck?''

"What?" Brian started, his expression bleak. "I . . . I don't know. Maybe. The stuff was always in our way, every time we brought in a semi-load of hay. I remember him moving some of the machines around . . ." He shook his head like a horse bothered by flies. "I don't believe this," he said numbly. "Dad wouldn't kill anyone. Punch them, yeah. But not kill."

"I hope not. Your father invited Mayor Ventura on a fishing trip, Brian."

"Fishing?" Brian looked blank. "There's not much fishing right now. River's too high, and it's too early. And anyway, he hates—" He broke off, lips tight.

"Where would he put in?" Rachel grabbed his arm. "Where, Brian?" When he didn't answer, she spun on her heel and raced for her truck. Yanking the door open, she grabbed her cell phone from the seat and dialed the police number at City Hall.

"Blossom City Police." Lyle's voice came over the phone, rough and angry. Rachel wondered for an instant what had wrecked his day.

"Lyle, this is Rachel O'Connor. I'm pretty sure Andy Ferrel killed Dougan, because he mistook Dougan for the mayor. Dougan was wearing the mayor's jacket, and it was dark outside. Now he's invited the mayor out on a fishing trip . . ."

"So good for Andy." Lyle sounded as if he was grinding his teeth. "I sure as hell wish I could go out fishing right now. Lady, you're as crazy as your boyfriend, and I've had just about enough today."

"What?" Rachel looked at the phone in her hand, as if it might have suddenly begun to malfunction. "Lyle, are you listening to me? What if Andy means to kill Ventura? And what do you mean about Jeff being crazy?"

"That head injury got to him, I guess," Lyle snarled into the phone. "He took off out of here as if a swarm of hornets was after him—just about knocked me down when I tried to find out what the hell was goin' on. He's on duty. I'm supposed to be off, and I promised the wife that we'd go into Hood River this afternoon to do some shopping. Ha. You get some evidence that I should worry about Andy, you feel free to come down here and deliver it. If I haven't quit this damn job by then." The phone buzzed in her ear as he hung up.

Slowly Rachel thumbed off the phone, staring at it blankly. Jeff . . . She shook her head, trying to banish memories of her uncle's antics—the one who had received the head injury. Biting her lip, she tossed the phone onto the seat. Where would he go? To his house? She started as Brian came up beside her.

"I . . . I don't want to even think about what you were saying to me," he said in a low voice. "But . . . I think maybe we better go find my dad." The horror had turned his eyes glassy. "I . . . he's been acting . . . strange. Ever since Dougan . . . They were *friends,* damn it!" He swallowed, getting himself visibly under control. "Look, Dad'll take the boat out off the east boat ramp—the one at Heron Point. Maybe we can catch them before they push off."

"We'll have to try," Rachel said grimly. She climbed into her truck and started it. Brian wheeled his own truck in a tight turn in Beck's graveled parking area, scattering gravel and clods of dirt as he gunned the engine. As he roared up the driveway, and Rachel followed, she glanced back. Beck stood in the center of the clearing, arms folded across his bare chest. Black cats were beginning to emerge from the brush, creeping warily on their bellies.

It was impossible to keep up with Brian. Tires screeching, he took curves like a stunt driver in a chase scene, and Rachel said a small prayer that he didn't meet somebody's farm truck on one of the blind curves. The road to Heron Point was gravel, and his dust hung in the air as she turned onto the narrow road. Only locals used the boat ramp. It was a popular place for evening fishing and swimming expeditions with the kids. Today, on a springtime Monday, the graveled ramp, badly eroded by the high winter water, was almost deserted. A single truck-and-trailer rig had been parked in the shade of a grove of old willows at the west edge of the ramp.

Brian's face as he climbed out of his truck told her who the rig belonged to. He hurried over to his father's truck and laid a palm on the hood. "It hasn't been here long." His face looked drawn and gaunt, as if he had aged years in the brief drive. "He's gotten so bitter about the changes going on here. Blames it all on Ventura, but, hey, the world's changing. I don't know." He turned his stricken face to search the river downstream. "I guess I didn't take it all that seriously—what he said. But he kind of quit talking to me when we started feuding about the store." He swallowed, his throat working. "He would have gone upriver, so he could float down." He turned on his heel and started across the dusty lot at a jog.

Rachel followed. Heron Point was a stubby tongue of land that jutted into the Columbia, creating the little inlet that sheltered the boat ramp. A trail led across the brushy point to the upstream side and continued on for a mile or more upriver. The sunlight dimmed as they reached the trail. A clammy chill and the smell of rotting leaves lurked beneath the dense growth of willow and scrubby alders that clawed at them with lush spring twigs. The western horizon had filled with a tumbling mass of gray clouds that promised rain soon.

They emerged from the trees onto the far bank. Spring grass and lush young thistle plants bent before a sudden gust of wind. The Columbia River had turned a sullen gray beneath the thickening clouds, and the rising wind raised a white chop on the water. There, well out into the main channel of the river, a silver-and-white boat bobbed on the chop, fighting its anchor. A couple of nesting mallards quacked from a marshy slough farther along the bank, protesting the disturbance. You couldn't hear the interstate traffic down here. The only foreign sound was the distant buzz of a boat motor somewhere downstream, beyond the point.

Rachel ran the few yards down to the bank, her hair whipping into her eyes. A part of her brain was noting that the trees and the bank screened this stretch of river from the highway, and that no houses overlooked the bank. You could see the boat from the far shore, but the Columbia was a wide river. Without binoculars, what would you see?

What was there to see?

Andy Ferrel stood with his back to them, legs spread against the rock of the boat, holding an oar in his hands, as if he was pushing the boat free from a snag.

He was alone.

At Rachel's shout, he looked over his shoulder. "Well, hello!" he yelled. He didn't straighten. "Didn't expect to meet you out here."

"Where's the mayor?" Rachel cupped her hands around her mouth. "Andy, where is he? Let go of the oar!"

"Boat's hung up." He turned his back on her, jabbing suddenly with the oar, leaning his weight into it. The boat tilted and sidled beneath him, and water splashed on the far side. Like a hooked fish thrashing.

"Dad!" Brian's anguished shout echoed from the thick willow. "Don't do it."

Andy Ferrel's head rocked back, as if someone had punched him in the face, as if he hadn't noticed his son charging down the bank behind Rachel. On the far side of the river, tiny cars and trucks rolled along Washington Highway 14, unaffected by the drama unfolding in their sight. He made as if to stand up, then hunched his shoulders and drove the oar deeper into the water.

The splashing stopped. Brian tore off his boots and began to wade into the cold gray current.

The boat motor roared suddenly louder. Rachel looked

downriver, saw a small boat rounding the point, coming in fast, its bow pointed directly at Andy, a white wake churning behind. Jeff crouched in the boat's stern, his face grim.

Brian halted, waist-deep, legs spread against the thick tug of the current. "Dad!" he yelled. "Let him up!"

"Phil's there!" Rachel yelled, waving and pointing, her voice lost in the chain saw–roar of the overtaxed motor. "In the water!"

Jeff cut the motor and yanked the tiller hard over, slewing the small boat around so that it slid broadside into Andy's craft. He stood, balanced for a moment on the rocking boat, then, an instant before the craft collided, he dove over the edge in a long, shallow arc that took him into the water almost beneath the bow of Andy's boat.

The boat hit Andy's with a dull *thunk,* and the shock nearly jolted Andy off his feet. He staggered, the oar flailing wildly as he fought for balance. He nearly went over, but then he caught himself, steadied, and swung the oar upward. With the oar poised above his head, drawn back like a long bat, he watched the surface of the water intently. His shoulders bulged, thickly muscled from the thousands of hay bales and feed sacks he'd tossed into pickups and trailers over the years.

"No!" Rachel screamed. "Andy, *no!*"

"Dad!" Brian waded deeper, barely able to keep his feet in the current.

Jeff's head broke the surface, and the oar quivered in Andy's hands. Rachel wanted to close her eyes, but all her muscles had frozen, and she could only watch.

"Dad!" Brian's voice cracked with anguish. "Please! Don't! I love you."

The oar jerked downward . . . then faltered. Slowly Andy lowered it and stared at it a moment, as if its presence in his hands surprised him. Then he flung it away with a violent gesture. The wooden oar skittered across the water like a skipped stone and began to float downriver with the current. Rachel looked back at the boat, dizzy with relief, just in time to see Andy throw himself into a long, flat dive. He began swimming strongly toward the far shore of the Columbia.

"Dad!" Brian waded deeper. "Stop! You can't make it!"

"Help me!" Jeff gasped from the water. He was struggling in the swollen river, his arm locked in a lifesaving hold beneath the chin of Phil Ventura. The mayor's limp body floated deeply in the river's strong slow current, dragging Jeff downstream and away from shore.

Brian gave his father one last agonized look, then swore and waded deeper, holding one hand out to Rachel, reaching for Jeff with the other. They made a chain, the two of them, linked Jeff into it, and slowly, step by step, pulled their limp burden from the river's sullen clutch. Rachel fell as she stumbled backward onto the dry ground. Knee-deep in the water, Brian was helping Jeff, who could barely stand, haul the unconscious mayor onto the bank. Rachel staggered to her feet and ran, wet jeans clinging to her legs, stumbling on the clumps of new grass. Sobbing for breath, she raced back along the path to her truck and the cell phone she cursed herself for not bringing with her to the riverbank.

She could barely hear her own words to Lyle over the roaring in her ears. When he had hung up, she scrabbled her first aid kit from the cab and grabbed the emergency blanket that she always carried with her. As she started back, she paused for a moment. Far out in the middle of the river, a small dark object might be the head of a swimmer. Or it might be driftwood. She lost sight of it and couldn't find it again. Shivering in her wet clothes, stung by the first drops of falling rain, she ran along the road to where she could cut directly down the bank to where Jeff was giving the mayor mouth-to-mouth resuscitation.

Brian stood over him, staring out at the river, rainwater running down his face like tears. For a moment, his eyes met Rachel's, and the naked pain there made her turn her face away. Then Ventura coughed and choked weakly, and she dropped to her knees beside Jeff, offering the blanket. The mayor choked again, and Jeff rolled him onto his side as he vomited water onto the muddy ground.

In the distance, an ambulance siren wailed with the sound of catastrophe.

2 0

Rachel straightened up from connecting the last section of the mayor's new drip watering system, and stretched, wincing at the ache in her thighs. After a few days of rain and wind, the weather had turned warm again. Squatting in the unseasonably hot midday sun, Beck lovingly assembled the short planter bench that edged the deck on one side. Steps led down to a newly laid stone path that in turn guided the eye to the far end of the yard where Rachel was finishing the water system. Beck had shyly offered to build an arbor and bench for the space—an offer that had surprised and delighted her. Beck didn't do "furniture pieces"—as he called anything but basic construction—for hire.

His "furniture pieces" were genuine works of art.

She stretched her arms over her head, caught Beck's gray-blue gaze on her, and smiled at him. He blushed, gave her a brief smile in return, and quickly bent his head over the joint he was working on. Shy man, she thought. She had gone back to the clearing two days ago—to see if the face in the tree trunk had emerged any further. You could see a little more of the eye, another inch or two of cheek. The eye was narrowed a bit. In joy, or anger, or grimace of pain—you couldn't tell. Not yet.

•   •   •

"This is the last of the compost," Julio announced with satisfaction, as he scraped the last dark crumbly grains from the
wheelbarrow. "Plant later, Senorita Boss Lady?" He glanced
hopefully at the sun. "Time to eat?"

"Yeah, I think it's lunchtime." Rachel smiled, although it
was only eleven-thirty. "You've earned it." Spider hadn't
showed this morning, so Julio had been stuck wheeling gravel
for the paths and compost for the planting holes by himself.
She hoped Spider wasn't in trouble at the farm. But she had
to admit that she was a bit annoyed that he hadn't called her
to say he wasn't coming.

Leaving Julio to retrieve his lunch cooler from the truck,
Rachel went over to sit on the edge of the deck where she
could watch Beck work. She ran her fingers across the smooth,
satiny grain of the clear cedar planks that made up the deck's
floor. Even one of his decks was a work of art, she thought
as she watched him mitering a corner so that the edges came
perfectly together. Every plank had been considered and
placed so that the pattern of grain in each board merged into
a subtle unity. Sawdust clung to his hair and clothes, and his
bare shoulders gleamed with sweat in the early heat.

Beck turned off the saw and looked up, then down. "The
wood is happy here." He stroked the boards the way you
might stroke the thigh of a lover. "The Evil One has left this
place." His clear eyes clouded, and he looked away. "He is
hiding," he said softly. "For now."

"Maybe he went away for good this time. Beck, this deck
is lovely." She sighed. "I want to own a house one day. So
that I could hire you to build me a deck."

Beck's smile lighted his face. "Anytime you want something," he murmured, "I'll build it. Just ask."

"What an offer!" Rachel laughed. "Beck, be careful. I
could think of a lot of things I'd like to have you build." She
looked up at the sound of the patio door opening.

"How goes it? Wow." Jeff whistled as he surveyed the
deck and the nearly completed yard. "That's a big change in
a short time."

"Small space." Rachel laughed, pleased. "It'll look a lot

better with the plants in place. Kind of a war zone now.''

''Nice layout, though.'' He hopped down off the deck and took her arm. ''Can you take an early lunch? I'll buy.''

''I'll take it. Back shortly,'' she called to Julio as she tossed her gloves onto the deck. ''You can start bringing the plants in from the trailer when you're finished.''

''I will do it:'' He managed a credibly martyred expression as he scooped beans, peppers, and chicken from a plastic container. ''I will do that. Alone.'' He heaved a heavy sigh.

''Spider didn't show.'' Rachel made an effort not to smile at Julio's theatrics. ''Julio has been stuck with all the hard work.'' She and Jeff exited the yard through the gate in the board fence beside the house. ''I hope Spider hasn't gotten into any new trouble. I like that kid. He's actually working almost as hard as Julio.'' Which was pretty darn hard. ''So how are you doing?'' She searched Jeff's face and caught her breath. ''You found Andy,'' she said softly.

''Two kids did, yeah. Finally.'' Jeff rubbed his face, looking suddenly tired. ''They were playing hooky with their dog this morning. It . . . he caught in a snag a couple of miles downstream. Brian came down to identify the body.''

''That must have been rough. I'm sorry.'' Rachel looked down the slope to the broad sheet of the Columbia, shimmering in the sun. A couple of bright sailboards skittered across the surface like colorful water bugs. ''How's Phil doing?''

''It really shook him, that someone tried to kill him for what he was doing.'' Jeff put his arm around her as they walked out to the street where he had parked a police car. ''I went to see him in the hospital last night. He did a lot of talking.'' He shook his head. ''I hope he stays on here and runs for another term. I think he's what we need.''

''Isn't he going to stay?'' Rachel looked up, alarmed. ''Was he talking about leaving?''

''Yeah. But I don't think he will.'' Jeff opened the door to the car. ''He's got a lot of guts, after all, he's a city guy. He's stubborn.'' He smiled briefly, then sobered. ''I told him the town needs him.''

''No matter what my uncle says.'' Rachel made a face at the heavy grill that separated front and back seats as she slid into the car. "I always feel as if I'm on my way to jail when I ride in this thing."

"I could take you there." Jeff gave her a sideways look. "For failing to notify an officer about the commission of a crime. Accessory after the fact . . ."

"Ha. You couldn't and you know it." She made a face at him. "And I wasn't sure what had happened until Spider told me about the jacket. And I did try to call you, but you didn't have your phone, and then you took off like a crazy man. According to Lyle."

"I remembered who hit me. And the mayor had told me about the fishing trip." Jeff started the car and pulled away from the curb. "We found Loper, by the way. He's in jail, in Los Angeles. Turns out he has an outstanding warrant down there—for unpaid traffic tickets. I guess he was on his way south to Mexico with the money he got from Dougan when he got pulled over for speeding by the Highway Patrol. They checked, found the warrant, and took him in."

"What a nice bit of irony." Rachel sighed, thinking of Melanie Dougan's wounded eyes on that afternoon at the Bread Box. "I hope he spends a lot of time behind bars."

"He admitted to meeting with Dougan." Jeff turned left on Main, then took a right, heading for the riverbank. "Although he claims that he wasn't blackmailing him, that he merely wanted to convince Dougan to oppose the annexation after all."

"Yeah, right."

"I agree." Jeff slowed. "The Bread Box all right for lunch?"

"Always!" Rachel frowned. "Did Loper and Dougan meet at City Hall?"

"Behind it. Near the Dumpster. It's pretty easy to come in from the back alley without being seen. We need a light out there. He said he went out the way he came, while Dougan went up the driveway toward Main."

"The way the mayor would have gone, if he'd left by the side door." Rachel frowned as Jeff turned into the parking lot between the dock and the street, and found a space next to a brand-new Suzuki with two sailboards on the roof. "How did he come to be wearing the mayor's jacket?"

"I don't think we'll ever know for sure." Jeff frowned as they walked down the ramp that led to the dock. "He had a leather jacket that didn't look all that much like the mayor's, but it's at least brown. Don't forget—he was pretty upset, between the blackmail, the reaction to his change of heart on the annexation, and his daughter's shoplifting. Maybe he picked up the wrong jacket after the meeting that afternoon. That's when Ventura missed his jacket, remember? Maybe he wore it that evening because it was cool out, and the jacket was right there in the car. Maybe he wore it as a disguise. Who knows?" Jeff shrugged.

So much can turn on so little. Rachel paused at the entry to the Bread Box, her eyes on a distant tug guiding barges downriver. Cherry harvest would be on in a few weeks. Then wheat, then apples. She shook her head. One week of rain at a bad time—you lost a lot of the year's income. One wrong jacket on a chilly night, and you lost your life.

Her mother had once told her how she had met Rachel's father—when they had both been assigned the same study desk in the student library at college. What if the mix-up hadn't happened? Rachel wondered. It was a big school. Maybe they would have passed each other and never . . .

"Thinking?" Jeff touched her arm.

"Sort of." She gave him a crooked smile. "Thinking about chance. Luck, I guess. Good or bad."

"Scary, sometimes."

Yes. A couple exited, in their twenties, perhaps, dressed in expensive sportswear that looked brand-new. The Suzuki's owners? Rachel wondered. She wondered, too, how they came to have so much money so young, what the price was, and if they minded paying it. Inside, the Bread Box was about half full—not bad for a weekday and the early hour. They took a table at one of the big windows and got a hurried wave from Joylinn, who was on her way into the kitchen.

"I'm not even sure Andy meant to kill Ventura." Jeff studied the menu briefly, then lowered it. "I wonder if he didn't just mean to beat the daylights out of him. I guess I just don't see him going there to kill him. Dougan had one bruise on his jaw that probably came from a fist, the pathologist says. So I figure Andy swung without speaking, caught Dougan by surprise, and knocked him down before Andy even realized that this wasn't the mayor. Dougan hit his head on the corner of the truck's tailgate on the way down. Died.'' He shrugged. ''Andy panicked then.''

''It fits. I can see Andy taking a swing at Phil—even beating the daylights out of him. I can't see him meaning to kill someone.'' Like Uncle Jack, she thought with a bit of a chill. He could have been there instead of Andy. It could have played out the same way. Rachel shivered as she watched Celia, Joylinn's longtime kitchen assistant and waitress, making her way toward their table.

''He had a key to the truck, by the way.'' Jeff had been perusing the menu again and hadn't noticed her moment of chill. He laid the menu down. ''Andy had a ring in his pocket with nearly sixty keys on it—I don't think the man ever threw a key away in his life or stopped carrying it around. He had keys to all the equipment Harvey used to park on his lot. Came as a surprise to Harvey. I'll have the soup and sandwich special,'' he said to Celia as she reached the table.

''Sure thing, Chief.'' She winked at Rachel as she turned Jeff's coffee cup right-side up and filled it. ''You want the salad special, Ms. O'Connor? It's kind of a twist on the Greek salad today. You know—salty cheese and those yummy olives? Only she mixed in this pasta stuff, sort of like big rice. And the dressing is real lemony.''

''Orzo,'' Jeff said.

''Whassat?'' Celia looked blank.

''The pasta stuff. I think I'll change to the salad,'' he said. ''It sounds good.''

''Me, too.'' Rachel handed her the menus.

''Be right back with the cream.'' Celia whisked away with the menus and their order.

''I guess we're regulars.'' Jeff winked at her.

''I would hope so.''

''How are you doing?'' Joylinn appeared at their table, wiping floury hands on her apron. ''I'm making an extra batch of

cinnamon rolls,'' she explained. ''This couple stopped in and
bought everything I had for some kind of outing this morning.''

''Drat.'' Rachel pouted. ''There goes dessert. And you have
flour on your nose.''

''They'll be ready at three.'' Joylinn swiped vainly at her
face with the back of her hand. ''Good time for a coffee break.
On me. I heard about . . . about Andy.'' She sighed and looked
out the window, to where the tug churned along with its train
of barges. ''Hard to believe,'' she said softly. ''Well . . .
maybe not so hard. Andy had a lot of anger inside.''

''Especially since his wife died,'' Rachel said slowly.
''Mom told me that he was pretty mellow, back when Brian
was a kid.''

''Poor Brian.'' Joylinn shook her head, glanced back at the
kitchen. ''I hope he doesn't sell out and leave. He's a good
person. I got to get back.'' She gave them a distracted wave
and hurried off toward the kitchen, greeting customers as she
went.

''The price of fame,'' Jeff murmured. ''I had a talk with
Beck.'' Jeff tilted his head and regarded Rachel with a curious
expression. ''Talk about a strange guy . . . He thinks a lot of
you.''

''He's a genuinely good person, I think. And, yes, strange.''
Rachel made a wry face. ''Did he tell you about . . . what he
saw?''

''More or less.'' Jeff sighed. ''I don't think I'd want to see
him end up on a witness stand. But he did admit that he saw
the Evil One—who happened to look exactly like Andy Ferrel—punch Dougan. It took me an hour to get that much out
of him.'' He shook his head. ''Was he that bad when we were
kids? I don't remember much about him at all. He was older—
at least a grade. And just . . . there.''

''That's about what I remember.'' Rachel sat back as Celia
swooped down with a laden tray. ''Wow, that looks good.''
She eyed the mound of orzo on her plate, lushly studded with
black calamata olives, tomato, parsley, and chunks of feta
cheese. A twisted lemon slice garnished the generous portion.
''I'd better work this afternoon!'' She reached for the basket

of crisp bread sticks Celia had set down in the center of the table. "Those are good! Cheese," she said as she took a crunchy bite.

"So what have we missed?" Celia clasped her empty tray to her chest, her eyes wide with avid curiosity beneath her cap of tightly permed and utterly red hair. "Did Andy really mean to kill everybody on the City Council?"

"Oh, come on, Celia." Jeff gave her a stern look as he unfolded his napkin. "Give me a break."

"Well, I mean, he killed two men—well, almost killed the mayor."

"Read the paper." Jeff gave her a bland smile. "It's all there on page one of today's issue. We only made the B section in the Hood River paper." He picked up his fork.

"Oh, I can take a hint." Celia let out her breath in an explosive sigh that seemed to be intended to represent resignation but sounded more like a horse snorting. Well, maybe a pony, Rachel thought.

"I'm too busy to chat anyway," Celia said, and flounced off, waving her tray in a manner that menaced several unsuspecting diners.

"I don't know why we need a paper," Jeff murmured into his coffee cup. "Not when we've got Celia. Think of all the trees we'd save. . . ."

Rachel giggled, then sobered. "I think Joylinn might be right to worry about Brian moving. I hope he doesn't."

"He seems to be holding up okay. Nobody's blaming him for Andy."

But their mood had been dimmed, and they both finished their meals quickly and without a lot of further conversation.

"I'd better get right back," Rachel said as they rose. "I want to get that irrigation closed up before the mayor gets home. He called last night to say they're letting him out of the hospital today." The onset of pneumonia had kept him in the hospital in Hood River for several days following his near drowning. "We've really made some changes while he's been gone."

"His sister stopped by." Jeff picked up the check that Celia had left on the table. "She's bringing him home. She was pretty worried about him.'' He shook his head as she reached for her wallet. "I said I was buying. You can cook dinner some night to repay me.''

"Tonight is free.'' She gave him an arch look as she replaced her wallet. "Meet you outside.'' She made her way toward the door that led to the dockside seating as he headed toward the cashier's desk.

Outside, her uncle and aunt sat at a waterside table eating sandwiches and drinking iced coffee. Rachel hesitated, overcome by a weary sense of déjà vu. She was not up to another cold encounter with her uncle. Slipping along in the shade of the eaves, she reached the ramp that led to the parking lot at the end. They hadn't seen her. But as she started up the ramp, she looked back to see Jeff emerge from the restaurant.

He hesitated in the doorway, then straightened his shoulders and strode across the plank deck. Rachel wanted to cringe as her uncle looked up, his smile hardening as he recognized Jeff. He looked away, his jaw set, eyes locked on the passing barge train. Aunt Catherine looked quickly at her plate, her distress almost palpable as she twisted her napkin into a shapeless knot. With a jerk of her thin shoulders, she got suddenly to her feet, snatched up her handbag, and hurried off in the direction of the rest room. Rachel wondered briefly if she should stay out of sight or blunder into the middle of this. In the end, she stood still, her eyes on the stiff tableau at the table.

Jeff—now standing beside her uncle—said something in a low voice. For a moment, Uncle Jack continued to stare at the barge, as if Jeff didn't exist. Then, almost reluctantly, he spoke. Like Jeff's, his voice was too low for Rachel to hear anything, but Jeff pulled over an empty chair and sat down. He began to speak, one elbow on the metal tabletop.

Uncle Jack continued to stare out at the river, but after a while, he nodded. It was a stiff gesture—like that of a mechanical doll whose joints hadn't been oiled in a long time. Then, to Rachel's utter surprise, he turned to face Jeff. Said a few words. Both men rose to their feet, and it was Uncle Jack who offered his hand first. Then Jeff turned and threaded his way among the tables to where Rachel waited.

"Ready to get back to work?'' He smiled, his expression

betraying nothing. "Sorry if I put you behind schedule."

"I'll live." She walked with him to his car, climbed in, and fastened her seat belt as they pulled out of the parking space. Jeff drove in silence through the noontime streets and turned onto the mayor's street. As they approached the house, Rachel could stand it no longer. "Are you going to tell me or not?" She crossed her arms and raised her eyebrows. "You realize you probably pulled off a minor miracle back there. Uncle Jack does not kiss and make up. Not ever."

"We didn't kiss." Jeff raised an eyebrow as he pulled over to the curb behind her parked truck. "He's not my type."

"Jeff!"

"I just told him the truth." Jeff gave her an innocent look. "That I didn't particularly like him, and I knew he didn't like me, but I have a lot of respect for him. I was really glad he hadn't lost his damn temper and knocked Dougan into a dump truck bumper."

"Wow!" Rachel let her breath out in a rush. "I mean . . ." She made a face. "You're still in one piece! I can just imagine what would have happened if I'd said something like that."

"Maybe you should try it," Jeff said in a tranquil tone.

"I did." Rachel pressed her lips together. "Not too long ago. My stock is not high with my uncle right now." She laughed and blew out a gusty breath. "Well, maybe he's finally mellowing in his old age."

"Maybe." Jeff was maintaining his innocent expression. It made Rachel want to shatter it.

She got out of the car and came around to his side, bending down to kiss him hard on the lips. "Shall I cook up at your place or at mine?"

"Let's eat out on the deck. I've got a table out there now." His voice sounded slightly husky, which made her grin.

"Seven?" she suggested.

"I'll provide the wine." He caught her hand and lifted it to his lips. "See you then."

"See you." She gave him an arch wave and started to walk away, then halted as he called her name.

"Just one thing." He leaned through the car window. "I

don't know if your uncle has mellowed or not, but don't ever underestimate how much he loves you."

Rachel stared after him as he pulled away, trying to make sense of that last remark.

"Hey, Ms. O'Connor. Boss Lady!" Spider's shout jolted her from her reverie.

"Finally made it, did you?" she drawled as she followed the new stone walk they'd laid around to the backyard gate. "I was afraid you weren't going to show today."

"Yeah, well, I told Julio I was sorry he got stuck with all the work. I'm gonna do extra this afternoon. He can go lay in the shade."

"Lie," Rachel corrected automatically.

"Lie in the shade, then." Spider dug his toe into the newly raked soil around a freshly planted shrub, but his eyes danced. "My mom showed up this morning, is why I didn't come. I called your machine. Go check." He skipped ahead of her.

Skipped. Like a kid. Gone was the careful tough-guy walk and wary squint. He could be a kid just released from school for the summer. Hope, she thought with a jolt. That was what she was seeing in his face. It transformed this youth with a man's face—as if someone had turned back the clock. "She must have brought good news," Rachel murmured. In the yard, Julio perched on the corner of the gleaming deck, looking pleased.

"Yeah, she brought news. Bard . . . Mr. Bard . . . was in on it, too." Spider grinned at her. "I guess some guy from this foundation called Mr. Bard. I guess somebody from town or something had tipped them off about my mom getting scammed, and how I wasn't going to get much of a chance to ever go to college because of it. I guess they do this kind of thing all the time—give money to kids who don't have any. For college." He paused to suck in a gasping breath, still grinning, still glowing. "Anyway, this guy said the foundation had checked into me, and they're awarding me a scholarship when I finish high school. I have to take the SAT and get accepted into college, just like any kid. If I make it in, they pay for tuition, books, board—everything. But I have to keep my grades up and not get into trouble. I'm gonna meet with the

councelor every week—let them know if I need help, or a
tutor, or whatever. Can you believe it?'' He did a little dance
on the newly raked border along the deck—an act that elicited
rolled eyes and a heartfelt sigh from Julio, who had done the
raking.

"Sorry, man." Spider beamed down at the churned-up border. "I'll fix it. Sorry." He was grinning again instantly. "Can
you believe it? Just like that!" He flung out his arms and went
bounding around the yard. "My mom is so happy. I thought
she was gonna pass out. I guess Mr. Bard didn't tell her the
whole story—just said she needed to come out here to get
some good news about me. Hoooeeey."

"That's great." Rachel laughed. "I think your foundation
has restored my faith in humanity." A bit of good to balance
the darkness of the past week, she thought. "What are they
called, anyway? I'll sure give them a charitable donation. Any
day."

"Weird name." Spider collapsed onto the deck where Beck
was squatting on his heels, watching the scene and smiling
shyly. "It's called the Deborah Foundation. I figure it's some
kind of Christian thing, although the guy who showed up—
some kind of lawyer, I think—didn't sound like one of those
religious nuts. And they didn't want me to promise to go to
church or anything."

Deborah Foundation. How interesting. "Did the man from
the foundation drive a sports car?" she asked innocently.

"Nah. He came out from Portland in a Beamer. Fancy
suit." Spider shrugged. "Nice guy."

"Older?"

"Old, I guess. He had black hair, but it was starting to get
gray at the sides. One of those fancy blow-dry cuts the suits
get."

Rachel hid a smile. Her mother would not care for Spider's
definition of "old," thank you. It hadn't been Joshua, then.
She had thought . . . The Deborah Foundation.

Maybe. Maybe not. She smiled to herself. She'd ask Joshua
outright, one day.

"Mom was just . . . She cried." Spider looked away, his
expression suddenly as shy as Beck's. "I didn't . . . I guess

you don't really think about how what you do might . . . make your folks feel bad. I never really worried much about how she felt. I mean, she just went to work. Came home.'' He laughed, cleared his throat. ''I guess I was too busy bein' mad at my dad to think about her.'' He cleared his throat and rubbed his face on his sleeve.

Beck leaned over and put a hand briefly, firmly, on his shoulder, then removed it.

Spider raised his head, and for a moment, their eyes met.

''I guess I'd better get busy.'' Spider jumped down from the deck, brushing his hands on his jeans. ''I owe you a lot o' work this afternoon, Julio.''

''*Sí,*'' Julio said gravely, although his eyes danced. ''You do. A lot and a lot of work.''

''Lots and lots, man,'' Spider corrected. ''So, okay, let's get me to it, huh?''

''Sure, man.'' Julio snapped his fingers. ''You can bring me out to get the plants . . .''

Rachel smiled as Spider trundled Julio through the gate in the wheelbarrow. Julio whooped and urged him on, and Spider laughed.

The Deborah Foundation was going to get its money's worth, Rachel predicted as she went to get her gloves from the truck. Something glinted in the crevice between the back and seat on the driver's side. Rachel shifted her gloves to the other hand and dug after the metallic gleam. A quarter, she thought. From her pocket. She touched cold metal and pulled it out.

She stared at the small silver key.

All this time.

She shook her head at herself, because she had *looked* there. Twice. Now she tucked the key carefully into her pocket. She would have to give it back to Harvey, she thought. Jeff was going to laugh at her.

She smiled and went back to the yard to start planting the mayor's shrubs.

LANDSCAPING TIP

When planning your new landscape, remember that a judicious planting of trees and shrubs can significantly reduce your heating and cooling bills. Deciduous trees planted near your house will shade it in the summer but let that precious winter sunlight through, once the leaves have fallen. Deciduous vines such as grapes or kiwi can shield the south and west walls of your house from the hot summer sun. Evergreen shrubs can provide a wall of insulation between your exterior walls and the cold winter winds.

< A FELICITY GROVE MYSTERY > **THE**

DEAD PAST

Tom Piccirilli

Welcome to Felicity Grove...

This upstate New York village is as small as it is peaceful. But some-how Jonathan Kendrick's eccentric grandma, Anna, always manages to find trouble. Crime, scandal, you name it...this wheelchair-bound senior citizen is involved. So when the phone rings at 4 A.M. in Jonathan's New York City apartment, he knows to expect some kind of dilemma. But Anna's outdone herself this time. She's stumbled across a dead body...in her trash can.

BERKLEY PRIME CRIME

❏ 0-425-16696-1/$5.99

Prices slightly higher in Canada

PENGUIN PUTNAM INC.
Online

Your Internet gateway to a virtual environment with
hundreds of entertaining and enlightening books from
Penguin Putnam Inc.

*While you're there, get the latest buzz on
the best authors and books around—*

Tom Clancy, Patricia Cornwell, W.E.B. Griffin,
Nora Roberts, William Gibson, Robin Cook,
Brian Jacques, Catherine Coulter, Stephen King,
Jacquelyn Mitchard, and many more!

Penguin Putnam Online is located at
http://www.penguinputnam.com

PENGUIN PUTNAM NEWS

Every month you'll get an inside look at our upcoming
books and new features on our site. This is an ongoing
effort to provide you with the most up-to-date
information about our books and authors.

Subscribe to Penguin Putnam News at
http://www.penguinputnam.com/ClubPPI